"May I help you?" Her voice cracked.

"I'm not sure." He swiveled his head, scanning the entire room. Scrubbing a hand over his face, he stuffed his hands in his jeans pockets and shrugged. "I must have wandered into the wrong building."

"Oh, of course." She stopped tapping and lifted the corner of her mouth in an approximation of a friendly smile and relaxed her shoulders. With her lifetime experience of constantly meeting new people at auditions and on sets, she should be used to the basic conventions of polite introduction. Six months of interacting with the same faces, however, she'd grown rusty. "I'd be glad to guide you to the right building but…" She pursed her lips. Why was he so familiar? His eyes glinted like chrome and triggered some recognition past her memory's reach. Did she know him? "Since you're here, do you mind helping me?"

He stood taller and puffed out his chest. "Do you need me to move something?"

She scanned the muscles straining under the basic T-shirt. He probably purchased a multi-pack on a grocery run, yet the cotton hugged like a custom fit highlighting a trim figure. As she met his gaze, she spotted the fine lines around his eyes. He was definitely a few years older than her, but not by much.

Her chin trembled. "No, no, heavy lifting." She smoothed a stray tendril behind her ear, brushing her fingers against her warm cheeks.

Praise for Rachelle Paige Campbell

"With interesting and complicated characters, a strong off-ship presence of both plot and characters and plenty of conflict with the third-wheel-ex-fiancé I found [*LOVE OVERBOARD*] to be a well written, interesting and lovely full-length story."

~*Long and Short Reviews*

~*~

"It is character development at its finest, and a nice change in a familiar genre. The read [*LOVE OVERBOARD*] is light and fun, full of warmth and humor, a wonderful sweet romance."

~*InD'tale Magazine*

~*~

"Great read! [*HOLIDAYS, INC.*] I liked the characters and couldn't wait to see what happened with them! A sweet read to make you look forward to any holiday!"

~Marie F.

~*~

"Rachelle Paige has again created a small town you'd want to live in and characters you'd want to be friends with. [*HOLIDAYS, INC.*] A modern small town love story at its best."

~Jackie V.

~*~

"A sweet story [*HOLIDAYS, INC.*] about two people at a turning point in their lives. Combining romance with values that support individual growth and how caring for one another can change a community made me like this book even more."

~Hilary D.

Holidays, Inc.

by

Rachelle Paige Campbell

Finding New Hope, Book 1

Holidays, Inc.

Cover Art by *Tina Lynn Stout*

The Wild Rose Press, Inc.
PO Box 708
Adams Basin, NY 14410-0708
Visit us at www.thewildrosepress.com

Publishing History
First Sweetheart Rose Edition, 2020
Trade Paperback ISBN 978-1-5092-3401-1
Digital ISBN 978-1-5092-3402-8

Finding New Hope, Book 1
Published in the United States of America

Dedication

For my mom.
I'm blessed to be your daughter
and lucky to call you my best friend.
Thank you for never accepting less than my best work
and encouraging me to keep trying.

Chapter One

Danielle Winter brushed the stray hair off her face with the back of her paint-splattered left hand. She tightened her right-handed grip on the roller and painted a blue streak across the plywood backdrop. If she wanted her brand-new dinner theater to open on time, she couldn't waste a second fixing a ponytail. She shook her head. Wanted was too weak a verb. Obligated better fit her circumstance.

In her adopted, one stoplight town, New Hope, Wisconsin, she sold her show business dream to a desperate community. With less than seventy-two hours until opening night, she couldn't second-guess herself, or she'd lose the last hope for her future. In the empty auditorium, nothing silenced her internal ticking clock, not even the approaching footsteps on the wooden stage. Twisting her neck, she met the gaze of the new arrival but continued painting. "Jill, I'm almost done."

Jill Howell frowned, her brow knitting together. "Dani, come on. You need a lunch break, too. You can't survive on paint fumes."

Underneath her heavy bangs and thick glasses, Jill's blue eyes darkened to the color of a stormy sea. A knot of tension formed between Dani's shoulder blades. If she dropped her chin to her chest and rolled her neck, she would momentarily ease the physical discomfort. But Jill would catch the fatigued gesture, and she'd ignore Dani's protest to leave the building for a much-needed break. Everyone in town depended on Dani's business idea sparking a financial resurgence. With her savings emptied into the business, she was fully invested, too. Delivering on her promise was her only option. "I swear I only need another five minutes to finish painting the backdrop. I'll meet you at the diner."

"Okay." Jill sighed. "I already sent the high school crew on break. Don't be too long, or I'll return and drag you to lunch."

The corner of Dani's mouth lifted. She liked her friend's slightly exasperated tone. Before arriving in New Hope, Wisconsin, she never experienced unprompted kindness. Of course, Jill wasn't entirely selfless. No one was. Dani sucked in a sharp breath and glanced over her shoulder. "Sounds like a plan." She forced a smile.

With a nod, Jill turned toward the door.

On the floor, Dani knelt and dipped her roller into the tray, painting the bottom two feet of backdrop. If she focused on one task at a time, she had control and could manage her never-ending to-do list. With a final stroke, she leaned back on her heels and scanned her handiwork. She tilted her head from one side to the other and dangled the still-wet paint roller in her hand. The chemical smell of fresh paint tickled her nose, and she scrunched her face. Something wasn't quite right. She dropped the roller in the pan, stood, and dusted her hands on her old jeans.

She needed an opinion from someone without a vested interest in her success. Neither her enthusiastic crew of teenagers from the township's high school nor Jill would critique her work. If she called in everyone from lunch, she'd lose a rare moment of silence. She'd have to solve this problem on her own.

Stuffing her hands in her pockets, she walked off the stage. At a table near the center of the room, she sank into a chair. Folding her arms over her chest, she leaned back and narrowed her gaze. The sky blue of the backdrop's Atlantic Ocean didn't match the turquoise of the shining sea across her hastily painted United States of America.

Propping an arm on the table, she rested her chin in a palm and studied the scenery from another angle. Would anyone else notice? Filling her lungs to capacity, she inhaled the sharp scent of paint and rubbed a hand over her itchy eyes. If she skipped lunch, she had time for a trip to the hardware store to color match and repaint the backdrop before the final day of rehearsals. She hadn't stopped working for months.

With any luck, she'd open her business to rave reviews and be rewarded with a packed schedule of long days stretching into the distant future. She sighed and dropped an arm flat on the table, pillowing her head. From her perspective, she couldn't see past the edge of the stage. Drawing in a deep breath through her nose, she slowly exhaled and shuttered her eyelids.

A crash echoed through the room.

She twisted toward the door and lost her balance, crashing to the ground. On the carpet, she untangled her limbs from the chair, her shallow breaths rattling her ribs. Had the intruder heard her? She peeked over the table and scanned the empty interior toward the double doors under the exit sign. At her sides, she tightened her hands into fists. In her ears, her heartbeat drowned out all other sounds. Had she imagined the noise? On the floor, she positioned herself like a victim. Grabbing the chair, she stood and righted the seat. Straightening to her full five feet two inches, she spotted the large shadow near the darkened entryway. "Hello?" Her voice was a high-pitched squeak. Swallowing the lump in her throat, she pulled back her shoulders, instilling herself with strength and bravado.

The shadowy figure stepped closer.

She gulped. In the faint rays of stage light, she spotted a man of the well-sculpted-jaw-and-broad-shoulders variety.

He neared.

Closer inspection of his dark hair, gray eyes, and lanky figure triggered something hazy in her mind. In her twenty-eight years of living, she'd never seen him, but he looked oddly familiar. Exhaling a shaky breath, she remained tense and ready to flee. Long ago, she learned a good-looking man was equally capable of nefarious deeds as any other.

The man stopped on the opposite side of the table.

With five feet of separation, she relaxed her hands but remained alert. If threatened, she trusted her ability to bolt. He was slender but not overly muscular like a body builder or trained killer. His T-shirt hugged his body, clinging too tight for concealing a weapon. He wrinkled his brow, deep lines slashing across smooth skin and marring his chiseled features. *He looks lost*.

She transferred her weight to her left and shuffled her right foot, unable to stop her stress-related tap dancing. Her ten-second nap ended way too soon. "May I help you?" Her voice cracked.

"I'm not sure." He swiveled his head, scanning the entire room. Scrubbing a hand over his face, he stuffed his hands in his jeans pockets and shrugged. "I must have wandered into the wrong building."

"Oh, of course." She stopped tapping and lifted the corner of her mouth in an approximation of a friendly smile and relaxed her shoulders. With her lifetime experience of constantly meeting new people at auditions and on sets, she should be used to the basic conventions of polite introduction. Six months of interacting with the same faces, however, she'd grown rusty. "I'd be glad to guide you to the right building but…" She pursed her lips. Why was he so familiar? His eyes glinted like chrome and triggered some recognition past her memory's reach. Did she know him? "Since you're here, do you mind helping me?"

He stood taller and puffed out his chest. "Do you need me to move something?"

She scanned the muscles straining under the basic T-shirt. He probably purchased a multi-pack on a grocery run, yet the cotton hugged like a custom fit highlighting a trim figure. As she met his gaze, she spotted the fine lines around his eyes. He was definitely a few years older than her, but not much more.

Her chin trembled. "No, no heavy lifting." She smoothed a stray tendril behind her ear, brushing her fingers against her warm cheeks. With her years of repeated exposure to attractive people on TV sitcom sets, she hadn't been susceptible to another person's good looks in years. Taking in a steadying breath, she crossed her arms. "Getting an honest opinion in New Hope can be a little difficult."

He ran a hand through his dark hair.

His fingers nearly disappeared in thick locks overdue for a trim. The slightly unkempt hair suited him. With his even features, he'd look too perfect with a short haircut. She gave her head a shake. She wasn't casting him for one of her productions. The stranger would answer her question. She'd steer him to his destination and would never see him again.

"Really? You can't get someone's unwanted opinion in this town?" He arched an eyebrow.

Pursing her lips, she cocked her head to one side. His incredulous tone raised her hackles. "Since I moved here, I've heard nothing but yes, ma'am. Not that I mind." She uncrossed her arms and held up both hands, palms to the sky. "I'm not used to the consideration."

"Interesting. I've had the opposite experience. I'm told no before I finish asking the question." He folded both arms over his chest.

"Maybe somewhere between us is one person who has the benefit of constructive criticism with positive feedback."

"Perhaps." He lifted the corner of his mouth. "What's on your mind?"

Too much. She swallowed the lump lodged in her throat. His half-smile invited her to drop her guard and speak freely. He sparked an instant connection, like running into an old friend. Was he someone she'd forgotten? If she told anyone her fears—even a helpful stranger—she empowered her insecurities. She refused to ever give anything—or anyone—agency over her life again. Everyone was counting on her plan, and she wouldn't disappoint. "I'm wondering if you think the backdrop looks okay." Spinning on her heel, she faced the backdrop. "I painted the Atlantic a different color from the Pacific."

"Rob couldn't color match for you?"

"You know Rob?" She twitched and turned toward the stranger. He knew the owner of the hardware store on a first-name basis. What if he wasn't passing through town? Dragging her gaze over his face, she pursed her lips. She'd swear she never saw him, but doubt tickled her mind.

He shrugged. "Of course, I know Rob. Everyone does." He narrowed his gaze and stared once more past her toward the stage. "The background looks like blue and blue. The left side is a little darker, but nothing significant. If you hadn't prompted me, I wouldn't have noticed a difference."

"Oh, good. Thanks." She sagged her shoulders. "I can tweak the lighting. My staff wouldn't have been so forthcoming."

With a nod, he lifted the corner of his mouth.

A smile of commiseration? She shook her head. Why was she sharing anything with this mystery man? "They're wonderful. My employees are a little green but very determined. Converting a movie theater into a real stage for live performances has tested everyone." She clamped her mouth shut. Would he spread her comments through the local gossip mill? She shuddered. Some lessons—like be careful who to trust—never took, despite learning the hard way.

Frowning, he drew back his chin. "Movie theater?"

"Sure." She rocked back on her heels, grinning broadly. "Welcome to the former Howell Cinemas, now home to my musical theater company."

Twisting his neck, he scanned the room from top to bottom. He wrinkled his brow, spinning clockwise then counterclockwise. "What's going on here?"

She nibbled the inside of her cheek. His choppy

movements and scowl were disproportionate responses to the conversation. Their talk switched gears so rapidly from surprise to friendly banter to anxiety, she couldn't keep track. Why should the stranger radiate such shock? He walked into *her* building. When she met his gaze, she recognized the low fire of disappointment burning in his gray-blue eyes. Pulling back her shoulders, she extended her arms. "Welcome to my dinner theater. We open this weekend."

"Dinner? Theater?" The lines in his forehead deepened. He stared ahead.

"Yes, you know, put on a show and serve people an evening meal?" She lifted her arms shoulder height and circled her wrists. The gesture was meant to be lighthearted and encompass her domain in a nonchalant manner, but the air pulsed with tension. She dropped clammy hands to her sides.

He ran a hand through his hair again, dropped his shaking head to his chest, and sighed. "Does my sister know about this plan?"

She tilted her head and tapped her chin with a finger. *Who's your sister?* The retort tickled Dani's tongue. How was she supposed to know the details of the stranger's family life? Nothing about the impromptu introduction followed any conventional conversational standard. After calling in every remaining favor to build what little online buzz she could, she definitely hoped his sister and the entire tri-county area knew her plans. She sold tickets to forty-percent capacity. While she wouldn't classify the advanced sales as exceptional, she earned enough to keep the business open for the Fourth of July weekend. Of course, she no longer had any outstanding IOUs with bloggers and social media influencers for spreading the word about the next show.

She shook her shoulder-length hair behind her back. She could have a crisis of confidence later, without a distractingly arresting man questioning her plan. "I'm sure she does." Dani tipped up her chin, but her false bravado couldn't stop the icy feeling slipping down her spine. She invested her entire savings into the business. Her residual checks stopped a year ago, and she had no back-up plan. "*Home for the Holidays* will be a huge hit." Her cheery voice cracked. She clasped her hands behind her back and pressed together her lips.

"Excuse me? *Home for the Holidays*?" He lifted his chin, crossed his arms, and planted his feet shoulder width apart. "You're opening a dinner theater with a dubious name in New Hope, Wisconsin?"

Arching his eyebrow into his hairline, he ruined his handsome face with wrinkles and an unwelcome opinion. Stiffening, she drew back her shoulders. "I am, and my business does not have a dubious name. The name is perfect. We're only open on holidays with an original musical each time."

The mystery man drew back his chin. "You think people will abandon their extended families and travel here for a stage show? Your plan involves monopolizing precious days off work and starting new traditions? I wouldn't call this place home."

He shot her a hard, unrelenting look. The run-down movie theater was more welcoming than any other residence she'd ever had. She opened her mouth, and her chin trembled. His question squeezed something tight inside her. The honest answer earned her nothing with a stranger. "I imagine we'll become a destination for the whole family."

He narrowed his gaze.

"Some of us don't have anyone who'd miss our company." She caught her bottom lip. Disclosing her lack of family wasn't exactly polite small talk, but she couldn't stifle the words. Since coming to town, no one pushed her for details on why she was opening a holidays-only business. The community supported her without diving into her personal business. A stranger asked a basic question, and she crumbled. The business was bigger than one person staying occupied during the days of the year set aside for spending time with loved ones, but the reason factored into her initial plan.

"You're starting a business so you won't spend holidays alone?" He sniggered. "I don't think others will agree with your plan."

Sucking in a sharp breath, she filled her five-foot-two frame with every ounce of oxygen in the room. Her dinner theater meant control and stability. Six months ago, she received worse side-eye glares, disbelieving nods, and hurried whispers from her inner circle. She left Los Angeles to work around the clock in a deserted small town and hadn't let anyone else's opinion carry any weight.

Why did his words sting? His pinched features shouldn't impact her. The unspoken contempt hit her like a slap across her face. Faced with a fight-or-flight decision, she'd stand her ground. "What's so difficult to understand? A woman is taking charge of her future? Or that a small town is getting another shot after its factories closed? I am supported by the community."

He raised his hands and stepped back. "Look, I'm sorry. I didn't mean to offend you. I…"

Her nostrils flared. Verbal altercation wasn't a line

item on her long, pre-opening checklist. He wandered onto her turf with less than three days until the curtains rose. She wouldn't capitulate to his galling questions.

"But you did, so I'll ask you to indulge me. What is so offensive? My dream? This town? Me?" She crossed her arms and held her biceps to keep from poking him in the chest with an index finger, hammering home each point. She gulped and tightened her grip, fighting the fluttery sensation in her limbs. A physical confrontation would place her too near the handsome stranger.

He shrugged and stuffed his hands into his jeans pockets. "Do you really think you'll get an audience? New Hope isn't even mapped for the Internet."

She straightened, stiffening every muscle in her spine. He honed in on the oversight that plagued her over the past few weeks. How could she share information with travel blogs and tourism boards without a central online landing page? She couldn't show him her worry. With every word, she feared he wasn't passing through town. After months of work, she didn't want any complication tearing down her business and couldn't afford him sharing his concerns with the community. "Within four months, New Hope will be on everyone's radar."

He studied the floor. "Okay."

His muttered tone had the irritating edge of *if you say so*. "Look, guy." She dropped her hands to her hips. "I don't know who you think you are, but let me tell you about me. I grew up in show business. Stage productions are in my blood, and I know this dinner theater." She waved her arms to encompass the whole room, her entire safety net at risk. "I will be a success."

"I'm just a guy who spent his childhood in this

town, ran after a big, scary dream, and got knocked down to earth. I'd hate for someone else to ruin their life. Sorry to disturb you." With a half bow, the man backed away.

Following each step of his retreat, she seethed. Who waltzed into someone else's property and picked a fight? Every pulse point on her body vibrated with adrenaline. His words ripped the scabs off the slowly healing wounds Mom and her best friend left on her heart. When she lost track of him in the shadows, she dropped her shoulders and her chin.

The double doors shut. After a few seconds' pause, the heavy lobby front door opened with a whoosh and slammed. The clang resounded throughout the building.

She rolled her neck but couldn't ignore the burn coiled low in her stomach. The stranger's words were more a reflection of his insecurities and fears than of her business acumen. He didn't know her. Perhaps he shared a sentiment from his past experiences. She rubbed a hand over her heart. His careless comments hit too close to avoid injury. Moving here required all the gumption and moxie she'd been told her whole life she had. She couldn't let an anonymous person impact her.

Rationalization didn't shake his parting words. *I'd hate to see someone else ruin her life.* Who met someone and completely annihilated the stranger's day? Why had he strolled inside in the first place? Why did she care who he was or if she'd see him again?

Chapter Two

With every last ounce of self-control, Paul walked up the aisle of the theater and opened the door. Striding across the tiled lobby, he pushed through the glass door and raised a hand, shading his gaze against the bright glare of midday sun. Behind him, the door slammed shut. He jumped. The harsh metal-on-metal sound was as abrupt and unwelcome as entering his family's former business and meeting her. *I could have handled both situations better.*

If he shut his eyes, he replaced Main Street's shuttered storefronts with open signs and familiar faces. He breathed deep and filled his lungs with the scent of home. A whiff of sweet grass lingered in the fresh air. Retreating into his memory, he wasn't a stranger.

He scanned the street. Returning home—no matter how short the visit—meant resuming his role as the Howell twin with too much promise and not enough drive. His late father's vocal opinions echoed in his mind. Dad declared him a bad investment who couldn't stop throwing away good money. In the end, Paul proved the old man right.

Dipping his head, he tucked his chin against his chest to avoid detection. His family's movie theater sat in the center of town. Since the silent film era, their cinema was the heart of New Hope. At the end of the block, he relaxed, dropping his high alert. He had no cause for concern. He wasn't likely to be spotted. The shops on either side of the street were vacant.

Jill informed him of the town's goings-on during their weekly calls. He shouldn't be surprised witnessing the dire situation firsthand. New Hope was an hour north of Milwaukee, but their manufacturing core never fit the typical image of a bedroom community, and commuters settled elsewhere. Unlike other towns dotted throughout the state, New Hope didn't have a lake or river to lure vacationers. Their town didn't quite fit with people besides long-time locals. One woman vowed to achieve the impossible, and his neighbors believed her?

The faint sound of a bell jingled.

He raised his chin and scanned the street.

A few blocks ahead, at the corner of Main and Washington, a man entered the Come Again Diner.

With a sigh, Paul dropped his shoulders. At least he could still get a good meal at the beloved local establishment. *Maybe Jill wandered there for lunch and can explain what is going on.* He bent his head to study the broken pavement for cracks. Rubbing a hand against his ribs, he breathed through the tightness in his chest. The small town never offered him a chance. He shouldn't have begrudged the mystery woman hers. Striding across the intersection, he checked for traffic in the deserted streets and came up empty. He half expected tumbleweeds to roll past.

Pushing through the diner's front door, he stepped over the threshold, and the bell chimed. He swept his gaze through the restaurant from the counter on one side to the booths along the windows on the other. A few heads turned and glanced in his direction. He recognized none of the faces. An excited chirp caught his attention. He again scanned the room and settled on the woman standing near the back booth.

Nearly six feet tall, the slim brunette with gray-blue eyes was striking, especially standing straight and beaming with a broad smile. She waved and fiddled with her glasses.

With a nod, he approached, ignoring the curious looks he passed. He closed the distance and wrapped her in his embrace, pressing his cheek against hers. He missed her. "Hey, Jill."

She stepped out of his hug. "Hey, yourself." Tucking a strand of hair behind her ear, she hunched forward, rounding her back.

He swallowed the sigh building in his throat. The town changed, but not his twin. For most of their lives, his sister slumped and slouched in her never-ending quest to avoid attention. As fraternal twins, they shared a remarkable number of physical similarities, including height, dark brown hair, and gray-blue eyes. In the light, her eyes looked blue and his gray. By choice, Jill faded into the background. He'd utilized those exact attributes to stand out in a crowd.

Her smile lit her whole face brighter than the old marquee outside the theater. He slid across the smooth bench seat and interlaced his fingers on the Formica tabletop. With a deep breath, he counted to ten but couldn't calm the throbbing in his temples.

"I'm so glad you're here." She dropped her menu.

"Are you?" He set his jaw, gritting his molars.

A ponytailed, blonde server filled two water glasses and handed him a menu.

Jill pushed up her glasses on her nose and squinted. "Do you want to order?"

Her careful perusal yielded the wrong result. She couldn't assign his current mood to hunger. "I'm not hungry." His stomach grumbled. Jill shot him the *I'm-your-twin-you-can't-lie-to-me* smirk.

"Can Ted make him a BLT with a fried egg?" Jill rolled her eyes and turned toward the teenage server.

Crossing his arms over his tight chest, he arched a brow. Once again, someone made a decision on his behalf without consulting him. What else did he expect? He'd returned home.

"I'll ask." The young server jotted the order on a pad and retreated.

Paul guessed the server to be no more than fifteen, old enough to memorize the menu Shirley refused to change. His sandwich order was the only exception. He followed the teen's progress through the swinging doors to the kitchen, her blonde ponytail bouncing the entire way. He was hungry, but he had other concerns. Folding his arms over his chest, he leaned against the back of the booth and studied his sister. How could she look so happy? "I stopped by the theater."

"I told you we sold."

The color drained from Jill's face. "You didn't mention any specifics." He forced the words from his tight throat. Dropping his arms, he flattened his palms on the table and focused on the veins on the back of his hands. He hadn't spent more than a night in New Hope in twelve years, but he always considered the town his home. When had everything changed? Had he stayed away too long? Returning was supposed to be a temporary respite from his chaotic life. He wasn't sure of his welcome. Without his safety net, where would he go? He cleared his throat. "I figured some big movie chain bought the property. I walked into a shell of our family business. The seats are gone, the screen vanished, concessions disappeared, and some woman owns the building."

"A big chain?" She widened her gaze and snorted. "Because New Hope is fielding a ton of interest from major corporations?"

The sarcastic edge in her tone reflected his bitterness and not his sweet twin. He flinched and shifted on the bench seat, hating the role reversal.

"Or maybe I didn't realize you wanted details. You'll have to forgive me. I got the impression you'd rather not know what was going on here." She pressed her lips into a flat line and averted her gaze.

Her rebuke was tense. Hugging his sister always neutralized her annoyance. With a table between them, he inched his hand across the surface.

Batting away his touch, she grabbed a water.

"Fine." He pulled back his hand and ran it through his hair. "I deserve the jab. But a dinner theater?"

Cradling her glass, she rested her elbows on the table and held his gaze. "Dani has a marvelous idea. She's got big plans to bring in a lot of business. If anyone can carry off a miracle, she can."

"I'll say." He reached for his water and sipped, washing the dull metallic taste from his mouth.

"Wait, you met her?" Squinting, Jill pushed the thick glasses to the bridge of her nose and leaned close.

Scrubbing a hand over his face, he broke away from her unblinking gaze. "I did."

"And?"

Tracing the water rings left by his glass, he considered the best response. On the surface, he should be intrigued by the new venture. He left town for show business and returned home to discover a musical theater company in his family's former cinema. His timing was perfect. Or so his sister and the rest of the world would believe. He boarded the red-eye flight and relinquished his dream. During the ride-share trip from the airport to Dad's house, he doubled down. By the time he started the old pickup, arrived at the theater, and discovered Dani, he accepted the end of his dream only for his goals to slap him across the face. Someone else was taking a chance and doing so with full-fledged support. Raising his chin, he met Jill's gaze. If he voiced his inner dialogue, he'd cause unnecessary worry. He made his choice. Instead, he feigned ignorance. "And what?"

With a sigh, she rested her chin in a palm.

His twin was the unchallenged champion of the staring contest. Did he really want to spend all day here? His left eye twitched. He rubbed his lashes. "OK, fine, I'll cave. I don't like her."

"What?" Jill scrunched her nose. "What's not to like? She's smart and capable. She's nice, she's funny, and she's breathed new life into this town."

He studied the old coffee stains on the table. Their hometown needed more than CPR to be saved. The community required nothing less than a full transplant. He sipped the water and swallowed his retort. His sister wasn't a blind optimist, and he wouldn't underestimate her knowledge of how far the town tumbled from the manufacturing days of their early childhood. Jill was a dogged worker and a loyal soul. She never quit believing in him, even when she should have. She wouldn't stop fighting for New Hope either.

The facts and figures didn't add to a positive total. How could one attractive woman with a stubborn streak achieve a miracle? He groaned. Even his subconscious betrayed him, reminding him the petite blonde showstopper matched his exact type. She was also a powerhouse with a lashing tongue. After suffering verbal battery, he'd have no problem with distance.

"Whether you like her plan or not, we need Dani."

Her words teetered on an edge of warning like the piercing beep of the theater's smoke alarm when someone forgot the popcorn in the long-since-vanished kettle. More often than not, he'd been the one at fault, too busy dreaming about escape to stay in the present. "Why? Why stay?" Reaching across the table, he grabbed her clammy hands. "Nothing is left. He's gone. The theater's sold."

She dropped her chin to her chest. Her shoulders rose and fell. "Where would I go?"

"Anywhere."

"No. This town is home. I'm not leaving." She squeezed his hands. "Besides, you're back. Maybe fate dragged you here."

With a wince, he released her hands. Sure, the siren call of his childhood lured him here and not after missing the big chance he'd been working toward for his entire career. Using most of his savings as a last-ditch effort in the process, he was disillusioned and broke enough for the unthinkable act of returning home. He preferred her narrative.

"Speaking of, I have a great idea."

She realigned her features into her usual cheek-to-cheek smile. She had resting nice face, a phenomenon that inspired contagious grinning in close proximity.

His mood generally lightened around Jill. If he was the moody twin, he met his foil in his even-tempered sister. *The undisputed favorite.* "What is it?" He teased each syllable, cautious with the question.

She fluffed her bangs and pushed her glasses into place. "Let's talk to Dani about getting you a job."

He pinched the bridge of his nose. If he worked for her, he forced his creativity into her parameters. Restrictions never aligned with his rule-breaking nature. For Jill's information, he'd already offered help. A flash of Dani's bright red cheeks as she raked her gaze over his biceps popped into his mind's eye clear as a film reel. For a few minutes, he enjoyed her company. Would offering his skills as a manual laborer reestablish the initial impression? He couldn't offer Jill a full confession. "What would I do?"

"Write some musicals. You could easily draft a few scripts. I've seen you do more with less."

A hundred retorts swirled in his mind. He frowned. Top of the list, he wasn't a sell-out. Without a creative vision, he couldn't produce original work for someone else on demand, especially at his family's former business. Shifting on the bench seat, he leaned forward and opened his mouth.

She arched an eyebrow.

Dani's too easy to talk to. He shut his mouth. If he confessed about the connection sparked between him and the new owner, he wouldn't have a reason to avoid her. Initially, he found her conversation refreshing. In his younger years, he didn't relate to many people in New Hope. Along his journey from New York to Los Angeles, he never fit with the other transplants he met. For the first time in years, he relaxed. Unfortunately, the moment was short-lived. Once he understood the reality of the situation, he spoke without thinking and was treated in kind. He didn't want her unflinching honesty directed at his work.

The silence, along with his sister's smile, stretched.

He cleared his throat. Nothing good could come of spending time around Dani. "Why would I?"

"What else will you do here?"

"Not that." With his hands outstretched, he pushed against the air. "I'm not working for *her*." The pronoun soured his mouth, and he swallowed. "I'll find something else. I'm here for a little while. Not forever."

"I guess we'll see." She shrugged. "For my sake, please talk to her."

The server returned and dropped off their orders.

Her appearance saved him from delivering a snappy comeback. Pithy replies weren't popular here. He reached for a napkin from the holder and stared at the sandwich, his mouth watering. The scent of crisp, pan-fried bacon tickled his nose. His favorite meal couldn't solve his problems. He hadn't come home in pursuit of a career as a rip-off playwright. He might not have specifics about what he could do or for how long. Working for that woman, with her iridescent blue eyes and dazzling teeth, was definitely not what he needed. He'd returned for a break from complications. Everything about her, from her pushy personality to her sharp perception, screamed one giant problem.

****

Dani rubbed the grit from her eyes and stared into her mug. Only a few coffee grounds remained in the bottom. Frowning, she raised the rim to her nose and sniffed a trace amount of nutty brew. For survival over the next forty-eight hours, she needed more than fumes. She set the mug on the stage and drummed fingers against her thighs. To start her day—and refill her cup—she had business to settle.

Turning her head toward the woman at her side, Dani dragged in a deep breath. "I'm only meeting him because you're the kindest person I know. If he's your twin brother, he must share some of your sweetness." *Somewhere.*

"Thank you." Jill pushed her glasses into place and dropped her gaze. With her chin against her chest, she focused on the ground.

Dani spotted the upward tilt at the corners of Jill's mouth and exhaled, releasing the vice-like grip squeezing Dani's ribcage. If she could do right by Jill, she would. When Dani had discovered the online real estate listing for the old movie theater, she never imagined employing the seller. After the sale closed, Dani expected to embark on her project alone.

Instead, Jill stayed. Once the papers were signed and the lawyers departed, Jill welcomed Dani with a fruit basket and listened.

In the months since, Jill encouraged every idea and worked tirelessly at Dani's side. During the renovation, Dani often found Jill ripping up stained carpet and swinging a sledgehammer alongside the crew. Whenever Dani's determination flagged, she was renewed by Jill's dedication.

"I'm sorry he barged in unannounced yesterday." Jill shook her head.

Her shoulder-length hair swung shut like a curtain, covering most of her face. Dani uncrossed her legs and swung them over the edge of the stage, circling her ankles. She hated Jill's position in the middle of an unnecessary situation, especially with so much remaining on the to-do list. In the remaining two days, they had to sell more tickets, scrub the theater, train the staff, and finish rehearsals. Dani couldn't waste another precious second on tall, moody, and handsome Paul. His quick dismissal still burned her the next day. Why should she let his unwanted opinion upset her? She didn't know him. He didn't matter. She'd devoted too much energy yesterday replaying his curt words and earned a sleepless night in the process. He didn't deserve any consideration.

"I wish I could change your first impression."

Me, too. Exhaling a heavy sigh, Dani dropped her chin and rolled her neck. She didn't have time for distractions. Involving a man in her life, in any capacity, was trouble she didn't need. A sideways glance at Jill's tight smile, however, disavowed Dani of her determination to avoid Paul.

If Jill wanted her brother close, she should have him. Dani wouldn't stand in the way. She owed her friend more than one favor. With any luck, the cantankerous Paul would leave town of his own accord sooner rather than later. "You'd better call him and tell him to get over here before I change my mind."

"He's outside. I'll go get him." Jill leaped from the stage and scurried away.

As long as he plays nice…

Dani curled her upper lip. Meeting with Jill's worse half was inevitable, but she could control her behavior. If he wanted to provoke her, he'd leave disappointed. Unclenching her jaw, she relaxed her face and reset her expression.

Heavy footsteps thudded against the carpet.

A subtle shift in the air made her squirm like someone stared through her. She lifted her gaze and spotted the pair.

They navigated around the maze of round tables leading to the stage. Jill moved her mouth. Paul didn't respond. He clasped his hands behind his back and bent his head toward his sister.

Perhaps the benefit of a night's sleep cooled some of his ire. She refused to take a chance. Today, she wasn't playing defense. Hopping off the stage, she landed easily on the ground. She dusted her hands on her jeans and strolled toward the pair, her throat tightening.

She met them at the first row of round tables. Standing side by side, she studied the siblings up close. The twins shared the same gray-blue eye color. Their expressions changed Dani's interpretation of the shade from one to the other. She always equated Jill's smiling eyes as sparkling like a tropical sea. Yesterday, Dani stiffened at the metallic gleam in Paul's gaze.

A whiff of clean soap and hot-from-the-dryer cotton wafted past her nostrils. She scrunched her nose and studied him. Dressed in another basic T-shirt hugging his broad chest, Paul fit the universal casting call directive for hometown hunk. Growing up in LA, she developed immunity to movie star good looks from repeated exposure. In a city full of aspiring stars, however, he'd warrant a double take. Lifting a hand toward him, Dani forced her mouth into a welcoming smile.

He stared at her hand before extending his.

Her rough calluses from round-the-clock manual

labor scratched his smooth skin. "I'm Danielle Winter. We didn't get a chance to properly meet yesterday." She instilled her voice with a jovial tone honed during acting classes.

Tilting his chin, he met her gaze and tightened his clasp.

His unflinching stare pinned her in place like a steel-barred prison cell. She trembled.

"I know who you are." He dropped her hand.

Dani stilled, her breath catching. Great, he'd searched her name on the Internet and formed an opinion based on her years of a celebrity-adjacent life. She crossed her arms, tucking clammy hands against her ribs. Her story was the sad footnote in her former best friend's impending memoir. She wanted recognition for her merits. With her resume so readily accessible on the Web, would she ever have a chance at avoiding snap judgments?

"I told him all about the dinner theater, Dani." Stepping around her brother, Jill crossed to Dani's side.

"Oh, good." Anyone could search online and learn more. *If they learned my stage name.* Dani exhaled a heavy sigh and smoothed damp palms on her jeans. She'd forgotten the slim protection her real identity provided from the ghosts of her past.

"I think he could be a big help," Jill said.

Frozen in place, Dani glanced between Jill's beaming smile and Paul's stoic expression.

He narrowed his gaze and clenched his jaw.

The muscle twitched in his cheek, like he had more to say and only just stopped himself. "Really?" She dragged the word. Tilting her head to the side, Dani tapped a finger against her chin. "We've hired enough stage crew."

"No, not manual labor. For the shows." Jill pitched her voice. "Paul is a writer. He's been in Hollywood for the past few years."

Sucking in a sharp breath, Dani frowned. Had she somehow come across him in her previous life? Despite the tourists and countless starstruck new arrivals, tinsel town was an interconnected web. "Interesting. What's on your resume?"

"Nothing you've seen." Paul flicked a wrist.

Was he waving off a proud sister's hyperbolic words or displaying false modesty? Dani swallowed a sigh. She didn't have time for either. "But you're a writer? Like screenplays?"

"Mostly stage plays. After college in New York, I moved to Los Angeles. I tried off-Broadway first, but a friend had some connections in Hollywood." He glanced away and shifted his weight from foot to foot.

That didn't deliver. No wonder he'd vacated the theater so quickly yesterday. Returning home and finding everything changed must be terrible. She shuddered. For a woman raised without a stable home, she understood the isolating terror of not having control over her life. Mom climbed the social strata and dragged Dani along. She found the security she craved from another family. After losing that bond, she chased after her big, scary dream. Settling in the Midwest wasn't terrifying because the life-changing move was her choice. "I'm sure Jill explained we are putting on a new original tribute musical for every major holiday, four performances each on ten weekends of the year."

He arched an eyebrow, and a dimple peeked in the side of his jaw.

Catching her bottom lip with her teeth, she ignored the fluttery sensation in her stomach. She would rather not share secrets. He should be a stranger. If she hadn't shared so much in the first fifteen minutes of their meeting, she'd be better positioned to continue an aloof association. "I've been adapting lyrics to popular songs. I scripted the first three shows but don't have anything beyond the summer. I could use the help. The fall and winter will be here soon. The break between those holidays shrinks to only a handful of weeks."

Stuffing his hands in his pockets, he rocked back on his heels. "No, thanks."

"No, thanks? That's it?" Dani raised both eyebrows, her forehead wrinkling into her hairline. Reaching up, she smoothed a hand over the tight skin. As far as she knew, New Hope didn't have any doctors certified in administering facial injections. He wasn't worth the stress lines.

He shrugged. "I didn't come home to get wrapped up in a failed project. My reputation can't take the hit."

With a gasp, Jill scrunched her face and covered her mouth with both hands.

So much for best behavior. Ignoring the burn in her gut, Dani drew back her shoulders. She refused to double over in pain from his low blow. Giving him a second chance and dropping her guard, she arrived at the same insolent outcome. "Suit yourself." Raising an arm, she extended a hand and studied her chipped manicure finger by finger. After a thirty second delay, she lowered the arm to her side, met his gaze, and shrugged. "If you're too scared to take a chance, you'll probably never book a job or build a decent career."

He pressed together his lips, forming a flat line and

flaring his nostrils.

"I trust you remember the exit? I have a lot of work and no time to waste." She spun on her heel and stalked across the carpeted room to the steps at the side of the stage. Climbing the stairs two at a time, she didn't stop moving until the heavy curtains swung behind her.

Bracing her hands on either side of her waist, she bent and dragged in a long breath, returning her shallow pants to normal breathing. Why did he set her nerves on fire within ten seconds of a greeting? Why did she care about the opinion of a cynic? She came to New Hope to build something real. No one, not even a too perceptive stranger, had the authority to ruin her big plans unless she granted the permission. *Not in this lifetime.*

****

Paul shuffled into the kitchen, glanced at the ancient microwave clock on the counter of his childhood home, and slumped. Five in the morning. *Finally.* After he abandoned his old twin bed at two a.m., he spent hours at the dining room table, staring at a blank legal pad.

Rubbing the crust from the corner of his bleary eyes, he leaned forward and glanced through the doorway to the empty page flashing like a warning light on the table. In the past, he discovered his best ideas after eleven and found success from all-night-all-he-could-write sessions. Nothing about his homecoming fit his typical behavior. Instead of losing himself to a bout of creativity, he'd spent hours replaying his bad behavior. Why had he provoked her? What response did he expect?

Her jibe about building a sustainable, long-term career pulled the scab off his barely healing emotional wounds. She didn't know him or his situation at all but hit the bullseye. He rubbed a hand over the dull ache in his gut. He needed a break. Retreating to his room, he pulled on a pair of jeans and faded sweatshirt. In his hometown, folks were early to bed and to rise. Despite growing up here, he'd never fit either attribute. Today, he could take advantage of the latter for a hot meal.

Strolling to the kitchen, he fished the keys to Dad's rusted truck from the chipped, crystal bowl on the corner of the counter. He toed into a worn pair of boots in the hall and walked through the unlocked front door, carefully avoiding heel drops in the silence. He shut the door and paused on the porch. Breathing deep, he filled his lungs. Damp hung in the air from a nighttime rain shower. The morning dawned crisp and clean. He sniggered. He couldn't remember his last fresh start.

Under the thin shoe soles, he crunched the gravel from the unpaved drive in front of the three-bedroom ranch house and navigated around Jill's sedan parked next to Dad's vehicle. Why had she kept it? One person didn't need two cars. He rounded the front of the truck, slid behind the wheel, and turned over the engine. Maybe he should be grateful Jill hadn't sold the house or the truck when she'd sold their livelihood. Without the property, he'd have been truly stuck on the coast.

Unless she expected my return. He shook his head, dislodging the dangerous thoughts. Unloading the movie theater was a stroke of luck on par with discovering a pot of gold. Their failing family business in a faded town wasn't worthy of the grand term of livelihood. He had no reason to blame Jill for selling what she could, but hadn't he beaten up himself enough? Couldn't she share some of the burden of their diminished prospects?

The three-decades-old pickup rumbled along the two-lane road a few miles from town. If he had any neighbors left, he'd be worried about waking them. He parallel parked in front of the Come Again Diner across the street from the hardware store. Climbing from the cab, he studied the unofficial entrance to downtown. The two businesses were part of only a handful still operational. He strolled around the corner of the diner and stared down Main Street. At the end of the block, past the old movie theater, the library/city hall sat on a small hill overlooking town. His earliest memories centered on the few blocks of downtown including Fourth of July parades, Christmas carol sing-alongs, and Halloween costume contests. Each holiday filled their town with smiles and laughter. The empty streets were a punch to the gut.

With a shake of his head, he retraced his steps to the diner and pushed through the front door.

The overhead bell jingled.

Stepping over the threshold, he inhaled the scent of melting butter and sizzling bacon. He licked his lips and scanned the restaurant. Only a half dozen customers filled the booths. No one met his gaze. He might not be sure of his welcome, but he could still depend on home-style cooking. Turning toward the counter, he spotted a familiar profile.

A man seated near the door swiveled on his stool, a broad grin spreading across his features.

Paul dipped his head.

Rob slid off the bar stool, crossed the tile, and pulled Paul into a one-arm embrace. "Paulie, hey, man. Never dreamt I'd see you again."

The cheerful words slapped Paul's cheek. He held his breath and battled the sharp pain. Not every inconsequential greeting was an insult. Breaking free, he claimed a free stool and leaned against the counter. "Hey, Rob, how are you?"

"Me?" Rob poked a finger into the center of his chest and sat. Reaching for his mug with both hands, he drank deep and drained the coffee.

Under the fluorescent lighting, Rob's pale skin contrasted with the dark under-eye circles. If Paul didn't know any better, he'd assume Rob sported two black eyes from a barroom brawl. Through their years of teenage angst, Rob remained a bright spot and a friend to all. Was everyone in town worn out and exhausted, except for the beautiful newcomer?

"I'm managing." Rob scrubbed a hand over his face and bald head.

The server approached, topped off Rob's coffee, and poured a fresh mug for Paul.

Paul drank deep and returned the steaming cup to the counter. The heat scorched his tongue, scalding his taste buds. Swallowing, he tasted a delayed bitter flavor and a few errant grounds stuck in his molars. He forgot the particularly earthy richness of the diner's strong brew. "You still running the hardware store?"

Rob nodded.

For a hundred years, following parents' footsteps into the family business was a proud New Hope tradition. Such exclusivity had—inevitably—cut off newcomers from belonging in the tight-knit community. *Until recently.*

Rob rested his chin in a hand and tilted his head. "What are you doing back, man?"

Rachelle Paige Campbell

Paul shifted on the bar stool. The question efficiently summed up his precarious situation. Without a family legacy, why was he here? When he'd snuck into town for his father's funeral a year earlier, he avoided the theater and slipped out of the state before anyone realized he returned. Over the years, he ignored wedding invitations and class reunions. Desperation wasn't an envy-inducing state. He was better off keeping his situation under wraps, or he became toxic. He set his mug in the saucer on the counter. "I needed a break."

"You picked a good time. The new theater's grand opening tomorrow is the biggest event to happen in a decade. Maybe longer."

"Yeah, the theater." Paul's words were flat. Gritting his teeth, he loosened the coffee grounds stuck in his teeth and studied his mug.

"You don't like it?"

Paul shrugged.

Twisting his head, Rob pulled his chin into his neck. "I'm surprised. With you breaking into movies and stuff, shouldn't you be excited?"

"Why are you so…" Paul exhaled a heavy sigh. Calling the town tired wasn't fair. Maybe he was projecting himself onto the community. Chasing after a dream, he hadn't cared about his Dad's loud objections. If Paul listened years ago, he wouldn't be broken now. He returned home empty. He couldn't help at the theater because he didn't have anything left. Before he even started, he was finished.

"So what?" Rob nudged him in the ribs with an elbow. "Hey, buddy, why am I so…? What?"

"Exuberant. Everyone in town acts like the woman

spins gold from thread."

Rob chuckled.

Paul sipped his coffee. The bitter brew didn't wash away the foul taste in his mouth or his petulant tone. Hunching his shoulders, he transformed into an old grump hovering over his mug. In their blissfully ignorant youth, Rob and Paul mocked those men and vowed never to fill their roles. If Homecoming King Paul had a crystal ball, he wouldn't have been so flippant.

"Look, man, I get your point of view." Rob leaned an inch closer. "Coming home and learning your family's business has been completely transformed can't be easy. I can't imagine if my hardware store vanished." He shook his head. "To be honest, we're desperate. Most folks would welcome a highway going through downtown, if we'd see some benefit."

Over phone calls from a thousand miles, Paul listened to news of shuttered businesses from Jill. Each sad update about the rough situation in New Hope reverberated against his heart. He loved his hometown. The community was family. Rob was right. Dani had enthusiasm and drive. Her infectious spirit didn't falter, even when he fought his sister's job opportunity. But was Dani too late?

"Give her a chance." Rob rubbed a hand over his head and rested his elbows on the counter. "Maybe you should help. They could probably use you, with the big plans and all."

If I had anything to give, I wouldn't be here. He stared into the mug, his chest tightening. When he looked in the mirror, he saw a man without purpose. What did his sister and friend see that he missed?

Someone talented? "Yeah. Maybe I will."

"I hope so. I hope she succeeds. We all do." Rob leaned closer and tilted away from the server, bustling by to refill mugs. "I've got enough to keep going for a year, and then I might…" Twisting his neck from side to side, he met Paul's gaze and motioned his hand in a slice across his throat.

"You would close? Your family settled this town." Paul scrubbed a hand over his face. The New Hope Hardware Store traced its roots to the pioneer days, starting as a general store for travelers on the railway. Through the decades, the business evolved into a one-stop shop, carrying everything from nails to school supplies. How much longer could the town operate without Rob's store? The community would be in irrecoverable trouble. *We'd vanish.*

"Go, help them. Test some new material before you leave again." Rob clamped a hand on Paul's shoulder and slid a few bills under his empty coffee mug. With a nod, he left.

The hard edge in Rob's words chilled him. Paul took another sip of the coffee to warm up. With first-hand knowledge, he couldn't shake the truth. New Hope needed a savior. If Dani wanted the role, what was the harm in helping her? She assumed the liability.

Without a miraculous intervention, the community would crumble. Where would he go? He had no place but home. If he could overcome the pain of chasing his failed dream, he had a chance to be part of a real solution. He drained his coffee and left some cash under his mug.

The bell jingled.

Paul turned toward the door.

Jill walked through the entrance. "Thought I'd find you here."

"Did I wake you with the truck? Sorry if I did."

"No, I was awake." She batted the air. "Come on, let's talk and eat breakfast." She pointed at his mug and frowned. "Unless you already did?"

"No, just a coffee."

With a nod, she led the way to their booth.

If he wanted another shot, he needed Jill's help before he approached Dani for a third first impression. He slid across the seat opposite and opened his mouth.

Jill held up a palm. "You've had a lot to say over the past few days. Now, it's my turn."

He rested his chin in a hand and covered his mouth.

"We both deserve honesty. I'm sorry you are upset about the theater, but I'm not sorry I sold to Dani. She has the passion and the drive to start a resurgence. You're back. I know you don't have any plans for what you're doing here or where you're going next. You might not get a choice. We need a big idea to revitalize this town, or we'll all be out. I'm backing Dani and the theater because it's our best option."

He nodded. Jill was right. Swallowing his pride, he'd returned but his bad attitude, combined with past patterns of behavior, trapped him in the same rut.

"For the first time, in a long time. I have hope." Her chin quivered. "When Dad was sick and you were gone, everything started piling up. I couldn't make decisions because Dad wouldn't let me. Venting my frustrations over the phone wasn't fair and wouldn't resolve anything. The past few years were awful. After the market crashed and the factories closed, our neighbors started losing homes. I barely held on for as long as I did. I hated selling the theater. Dad fought to keep a family business for our future, but I had to start making choices for my present."

Immobilized, he devoted his complete attention to her words. Her tone didn't censure or lecture. She spoke plainly, employing an upfront frankness she hadn't for years. Telephone calls and text messages couldn't hold the subtleties in her body language or the pleading in her eyes to listen.

"Every day, I'm grateful Dani bought the theater." She averted her gaze and studied the table. "She's brought hope. I'm excited to be part of restoring our town. I want your help because I believe in your talent. You've been hurt badly enough to return home. Don't let failure be your story. Find inspiration and help us."

Clapping filled the air.

Swiveling in his seat, Paul turned and spotted Shirley, patting her brown helmet-like hair into place, standing nearby.

"Well said, Miss Jilly." Grinning, she retrieved her coffee pot from the counter and filled their mugs.

Jill blushed and brushed her bangs with her fingers, lowering her chin to her chest. "Thanks, Shirley."

"You're right." Paul lifted his gaze, connecting first with his sister and then with Shirley. He wouldn't hide from the truth. "I'm not here because I want to be. But I am, and I can help."

Shirley rested a hand on her cocked hip, the elbow jutting at a right angle. "'N so?"

"Yes." His voice cracked. He cleared his throat. Turning from Shirley, he inched his fingers across the smooth table and rested his palm over his sister's.

Slowly, Jill raised her chin.

"Can you help me?" Paul dropped his voice.

Jill held his gaze.

He squeezed her hand.

Pulling back her hand, she fluffed her bangs. "Give me a couple days. We have to get through this show, and then I'll revisit the conversation."

Inhaling, he held the deep breath in his lungs. After making a decision, he hated prolonged delay. On his exhale, he relaxed his tight chest and nodded. She was right, and he trusted her judgment.

"Good, I'll get you both the breakfast special." Shirley stalked to the kitchen.

Paul sipped his coffee and let his sister's words sink into his brain. She finally voiced what he'd long suspected. He told himself he shouldn't prod into her personal business. In truth, he avoided town and the inevitable confrontation with their father. Since his teenage years, they had been oil and water. Once Paul understood his career path, he refused any other discussion of alternative plans. The fights began in his junior year of high school.

Dad swore he wouldn't waste any of his money on a bullish kid with no direction.

Paul earned the full-ride scholarship to East Coast University and left town. He never looked back, not even to gloat. As a teen, he'd been headstrong and stubborn. The adolescent traits weren't atypical, but he feared returning to the people who knew him at his worst. Dad often voiced his opinion. The words reckless and headstrong from his father's condemnations echoed off every inch of the town. In his mind, the community sided with the senior Howell. Staying away, he sought to protect Jill from the family power struggle. He was wrong.

Despite his best intentions, he complicated Jill's life. Since his lackluster homecoming, he hadn't done much to prove he changed since his reckless youth. *Home for the Holidays* might save the town and him. Would helping Dani compromise his convictions or establish his future?

Chapter Three

Sliding her fingers over the smooth, tufted velvet, Dani peeked through the thin break in the maroon curtains. The grand opening arrived, and, in less than sixty minutes, her dream materialized into reality. Her grip slipped, and she dropped her hand. She didn't have time to fix a fallen curtain. She'd have to find another way to anchor herself so she didn't float away. From her position on stage, she experienced the excitement both behind the scenes and front of house. She needed to remember the moment forever.

The audience's collective conversations buzzed, and the cast warmed up their vocal cords with scales. The occasional, high-pitched titter pierced the steady drone on each side of the curtain. Sawdust from the sets mingled with the light floral notes of expensive perfume, creating a new eau de opening night. Light bounced off the polished silverware on the tables and the casts' sequined costumes.

Inside her black heels, she curled her toes. The theater filled to half capacity. For an out-of-the-way town and untested venue, the feat was remarkable. She blinked her watery eyes. With a sniff, she pulled back her shoulders and rested hands on her hips. After she waved farewell to a smiling crowd, raving about her first musical, she could cry alone.

A hand grazed her shoulder.

She turned, stumbling back a few paces. Smoothing her hands over her trim black pants and top, she pressed a hand to her rapidly rising chest and met Jill's gaze.

Jill frowned and fluffed her bangs. "I didn't mean to startle you."

With her downcast expression and hunched posture, Jill was better suited to a funeral than opening night. Dani crossed her goose bump-covered arms over her rolling stomach. Was her business DOA? An awful metallic taste filled her mouth. "What is it? What's wrong?"

"We have a problem in the kitchen." Jill darted her gaze. "You'd better come."

Dani pursed her lips. The hushed words were closer to a hiss than a whisper. Spinning in a slow circle, she studied each detail, willing the images to stick to her memory.

Crewmembers hoisted props into position. In the wings, the cast studied scripts and warmed up.

On her next breath, she turned and nodded at Jill. Tiptoeing over set pieces, ropes, and wires, she led the way through backstage on tiptoes. At the side door, she propped the exit with her back and waved Jill ahead. Crossing the threshold after Jill, Dani set her jaw. Whatever challenge lay in her path, she'd meet it with determination. Muffling the closing door with both hands, she power walked down the hall.

At the end of the long passageway, Jill jogged ahead and held the door leading to the alley.

Stepping outside, Dani was hit with a wave of warm air between her theater and the restaurant next door. Oil and roasting meat filtered from the exhaust, blowing hot smelly air at passersby. She never imagined owning a restaurant, but the purchase had been fortuitous. The bank was delighted to sell the foreclosure. The fully-operational kitchen simplified her initial renovation of the theater. Eventually, she would connect the two buildings and eliminate the brown brick alley. *If I'm a success…*

With her hand on the door, she scrunched her face. When she mentally simulated her worst-case scenarios, she never factored in the kitchen staff. After hiring the chef, she'd been relieved to unload an entire department into someone else's care. What had she overlooked? Twisting the knob, she opened the door.

Sound erupted from all directions.

Swiveling her head in a loop, she scanned her surroundings. If backstage had been a dreamland of sparkly costumes and hushed voices, the kitchen was cold reality.

Pots clanged, knives chopped, water rushed, and cooks shouted directions.

Dani narrowed her gaze, sweeping past the rows of plates, servers, line cooks, and settling on the chef.

With his arms crossed over his chest and a fierce expression darkening his features, Mr. Ralph was the only person not moving. Wearing the chef's hat, he stood over six feet tall and nearly as wide. The broad man could have doubled as a body builder.

Rubbing together her clammy hands, she ignored her twisted stomach. She'd never done well with confrontation. If she had, she wouldn't be miles from her problems, geographically speaking. Smile and ignore the slight, the fight, or the indignity was her life's mantra. In the current situation, however, she couldn't relent, no matter how uncomfortable the conversation. She intended to start her career as a business owner with unquestionable authority.

"Mr. Ralph," Dani called over the commotion. "What seems to be the problem? What's going on here?" She stopped two feet away from the burly man.

He turned toward her, his Adam's apple bulging.

Under his glassy-eyed stare, she gulped. Had she shouted? She hadn't meant to reprimand him in front of his staff, but she could hardly hear herself think. She opened her mouth to apologize.

He held up a hand.

Was he blocking her? She raised her fingers and massaged her aching jaw, hovering near her racing pulse point under her ear. *Calm down, you need him.*

"What's going on here…" he said.

His exaggerated tone mocked, teasing each syllable of every word. She swallowed the white-hot burn in her throat.

The chef outstretched his arms. "I can't cook without help."

"They are here. Your staff is willing and eager to learn from your guidance. I don't understand the problem." Dani brushed her right toe and dropped her right heel. Repeating the move on her left, she kept the rhythm steady.

"The problem is, I can't be expected to produce sixty perfect soufflés by myself. I can't perfectly cook and slice enough beef to serve an entire theater without help." Mr. Ralph unbuttoned the top of his chef coat. "I can't do my best here. Under these circumstances, I'm teaching every second, not creating." He raised his voice and waved his arms over his head.

The ambient noises stopped, like someone abruptly pulled the plug on the sound system.

Gesturing like a man who fell overboard, he held the rapt attention of the entire kitchen. With her heartbeat pounding in her eardrums, Dani stopped moving. Whatever she said next determined her management style. Either she declared herself the boss with word and action, or she caved to a threat. Lifting her chin, she met the man's gaze. "We've already discussed the menu limitations for the budget." Her words were slow and deliberate. "We aren't running a Michelin-rated kitchen. All I want is to serve delicious, home-style, meat-and-potatoes fare to an audience eager for a Broadway-caliber show."

"See, right there." He shook a finger. "You admit. You don't care about the food! I can't work under these circumstances. I need professionals. I quit." Unbuttoning the rest of his coat, he shrugged it off, flung the fabric at Dani, and strutted away.

Murmurs filled the room, slowly increasing from a low rumble to rasps of discontent. Shaking the apron, she folded the fabric and dropped the neat bundle on a free inch of stainless steel counter. If Mr. Ralph's performance meant to extort more money, the man acted in vain. Dani sniggered. She didn't have any extra cash. But if she did, she wouldn't fund his theatrics.

Jill leaned close. "What will we do?"

Her hot breath burned Dani's neck. Straightening her shoulders, she stepped away and addressed the silent staff. "Keep plating the salads. Let's serve the first course. A new chef will arrive momentarily." She gestured toward Jill and tipped her head toward the exit. The soundtrack of a busy kitchen resumed. With her head high, Dani didn't turn and survey the scene. Every complication had a resolution. The rest of the evening would run without issue. She had no other choice but blind optimism.

The door shut softly. In the alley, Dani faced Jill, her heart sinking. Under her right-hand's too-long bangs, Jill wrinkled her brow, concern etching her face into a colorless mask. Dani nibbled the inside of her cheek. She didn't want to change Jill or give her a makeover, but she needed her friend to project confidence. "Run to the diner. Beg for their help. Buy all their pies."

Jill widened her gaze. "What if Shirley says no?"

In the fading light, Jill's eyes were almost gray, like her brother's. With a shake of her head, Dani crossed her arms and tapped her fingers against her biceps. Would she be stretched so thin in a crisis if he accepted her job offer? She needed workers, not doubters. *I need everyone.* If approached with an apology, she'd hire him on the spot.

"Hey? You okay? What if Shirley can't help?"

If she couldn't secure Shirley's help, Dani would cook. For a person incapable of boiling water, she didn't love the back-up plan. "Just…be convincing. Plead. Tell her the truth, I should have consulted her from the beginning. We need her."

"Okay." Jill lifted the corner of her mouth.

Dani smiled back at the lopsided grin. If Jill believed in Dani, maybe she had a chance at success.

"Excuse me, ma'am?" a quiet voice asked.

Turning, Dani spotted the head of the box office, a frowning high school girl. A sigh bubbled in Dani's throat. Fearing any display of emotion might send the poor girl running in the other direction, she forced air deep into her lungs and exhaled. "Yes, Emma? What do you need?"

"We're having a… ugh… few issues with the tickets." Emma twisted her fingers in her black bob. "Do you mind coming up front?"

"Really? Issues now? The show's about to start." Dani dried damp palms against her pants.

Emma shrugged.

Until Dani could hire separate managers to oversee the kitchen, the box office, and the backstage, she'd fill those roles. With a glance over her shoulder, Dani watched Jill disappear down the block. *Every problem has an answer.* Dani stepped to the door, twisted the knob, and walked through the carpeted hallway. She crossed the empty, tiled lobby toward the small box office tucked into the corner of the building. She peered through the box office window, her frustration evaporating.

Ten people queued in front of the building.

Approaching the microphone set in front of the glass, Dani pressed the talk button. "What seems to be the issue?"

The man in the front of the line approached the window. "We didn't print our tickets. We downloaded them to our phones. None of us can access your network, and cell service isn't working."

Do we even have Wi-Fi? The town was hardly a technological hotspot. Dani wasn't sure she'd seen a cell tower within city limits. "I'm so sorry, sir. Please give me one moment." Backing away from the window, she exited the booth, holding the door with her back as Emma followed. "We have plenty of seats available tonight. We'll start a backup system for tickets tomorrow." She strolled across the lobby, her heels clicking against the tile like the celebratory church bells after a wedding. She opened her business, and customers came. At the main entrance, she pushed open one of the heavy glass and metal doors and waved the line inside. "Emma will be glad to lead you to your tables. The show's about to start."

The high school student led the crowd through the lobby to the auditorium doors.

The cool evening breeze snaked past Dani's nose, a hint of blooming lilacs wafting through the air. Stepping away from the door, she exited the building, strolled to the center of the sidewalk, and closed her eyes. New Hope was almost perfect. If she could resolve her missing link—family—she'd feel like she was home. *If I can serve my guests dinner, maybe I can stay and send Mom another email.*

"You need some help?" a female voice called.

Dani snapped open her eyes and turned.

The owners of the Come Again Diner, Shirley and Ted, strolled down the sidewalk with Jill in their wake.

Dani sagged her shoulders. Rescue arrived. The power of community impressed Dani from her arrival in late December. The people of New Hope eagerly welcomed her and wanted her to succeed. *They showed up.* "Only if it's from the best in town." Her voice carried, crisp and clear, without betraying the flutters in her heart. Hiring the Milwaukee-based chef was a justifiable expense to deliver the best for her guests. Her wrong decision, trusting an outsider, carried almost catastrophic consequences. Had the sentiment been the same motivation behind Paul's words of warning? *What makes me different?*

Shirley chuckled.

The deep rumble shook the loose cement in the broken sidewalk.

"Flattery will get you everywhere," Shirley said. "Miss Jilly, show me and Old Ted where to go. We'll get your dinner problems solved."

With a cheek-to-cheek smile, Jill led the couple around the building to the alley.

Alone on the sidewalk, Dani crossed her arms and filled her lungs completely with crisp, late spring air. She had a lot of work ahead. Possibilities replaced the scary blank void of her former life. Hope surged through her.

"Penny for your thoughts?"

The familiar voice stroked down her spine like slipping on a plush robe after a warm shower. She hated to break the spell of her solitude, but she owed his friendly question a response. Slowly, she turned her head and met his gaze. She blinked several times. If he was handsome with a scowl, he glowed with a grin. Rare miracles—or more accurately, holiday-adjacent magic—abounded in New Hope.

"How about I tell you mine for free?" Stopping at the nearest sidewalk square, he stuffed his hands into his pockets and rocked back on his heels. "Can we start over? I've been a jerk." On a sigh, he hung his head.

His exhausted tone tugged her heart. She'd been desperate and devastated a few times in her life. Recognizing someone else in a low state was easy. She hated to rake him over the coals. On first impression, she liked him. Could they return to easy camaraderie? "Are you admitting guilt and apologizing?" She arched an eyebrow. "I'll take both. I'm surprised you came."

"Everyone in town is talking about you and this place. Figured I better come and lend my support. Is it too late to buy a ticket?" He shrugged.

Raising her chin, she tapped the cleft in her jaw with a finger. "Yes. It's too late."

He frowned.

His scrunched expression burst the floating feeling inside her chest. "Help me." Her words were breathless, and she covered her mouth with both hands. She couldn't afford another miscommunication. Dropping her hands, she shrugged. "Come on board for one show. Find out if you like the job, and if I like your work."

"I don't know." He ran a hand through his hair and darted his gaze toward the old theater.

Turning, she stared at the building. She'd kept the original façade, box office, and sign. The forties-style marquee suited her. Inadvertently, she'd tricked him into expecting a warm greeting on arrival. For someone who grew up here, he was oddly out of place. On every encounter, he vibrated with nervous energy. He was a stranger in his hometown.

Her breath hitched. She understood the sensation better than anyone should. She hated to witness someone else experiencing the lonely phenomenon. She broke away from his gaze and brushed her right toe rapidly against the sidewalk. "I'll give you complete creative control. If I like your show, I'll give you a fair contract. If I don't, I pay you for your time. I promise no hard feelings."

"Aren't you in show business? Didn't you come here to stage musicals? You really won't have any opinions on what I'm doing?" He narrowed his gaze.

Maintaining a steady expression, she submitted to his up-close inspection but didn't stand still. He made a fair point. She had come here to put on shows. Unfortunately, she'd underestimated how much other work the business required. She needed him. "I can't." Her voice cracked. Exhaling a heavy sigh, she stopped tapping and slumped her torso. Without the rush of adrenaline, she could barely hold up her head and definitely couldn't fight the truth. "I don't have the luxury of running everything on my own. Until I have a full managerial staff, I'll be extinguishing fires and lighting other ones."

"What happens when you do?" He lowered his brow and fixed his stare. "Don't you want to score and direct your shows?"

She caught her bottom lip. He had a point. Growing up, she was slotted into various roles assigned by others. Starting her business, she seized control of her choices. Agreeing to share the responsibilities and consult with a partner had never been part of her plan. Could she share her dream? "To be honest, I don't know. At some point, I'd like to return to the productions. When the time comes, maybe we collaborate, or we have another conversation about roles. We're talking a long way off."

He crossed his arms and nodded. "I'll consider your offer on one condition."

When he spoke, his gray-blue eyes lightened, matching the turquoise she'd painted the backdrop Atlantic Ocean. Her heartbeat quickened, and her mouth went dry. *Anything.* She swallowed, snapping to attention. "What's your requirement?"

"Change the name. It's confusing. You aren't

operating a hotel. People aren't staying overnight."

"Fair point." She nodded. "Do you have any suggestions?"

"I do." He stuffed both hands in his pockets and shrugged. "What about *Holidays, Inc.*?"

Her jaw slackened. The name was perfect. Why hadn't she thought of it? Unless he was meant to run into her path. Drawing in a deep breath, she sighed. She needed a solid eight hours of sleep to recalibrate and stop her waking daydreams. "*Holidays, Inc.* I like it." She extended a hand.

He grasped her fingers in a big palm.

She stared at their clasped hands. His touch was warm and secure. On her next breath, she inhaled the scent of lilacs mixed with his typical warm cotton. For another second, she remained still. In her life, she'd had so few perfect moments. Maybe they could form a team like so many great duos in musical theater history. Pumping her arm, she shook his hand. She dropped the heavy limb to her side, ignoring the sensation of her heart sinking to her stomach. They'd either shaken on an alliance… or a ceasefire.

Chapter Four

Paul blinked several times, clearing his blurry vision. After a restless night's sleep and a change in mediums, from pen to keyboard, he still hadn't unlocked his creativity. Shifting forward on the threadbare tapestry seat at the head of the dining room table, he propped an elbow on the shiny surface. Lemon polish ticked his nostrils. Dad had insisted the furniture in this room maintain an impeccable standard of cleanliness. If the man's ghost glimpsed the computer on the buffed veneer top, he'd lose his temper. Judging by the neat mail stacks piled on one end, however, Jill relaxed the rules. Somewhat.

He wiped a hand over his nose and refocused on the computer screen. The cursor blinked on a digital blank page like the end of a film reel at the movie theater. If he shut his eyes against the laptop's warning glare, he was still assaulted by bird calls outside the front window. With each passing second, he ran out of time.

Leaning back, he rubbed a palm over his heart. In the week since he'd signed on to write the Fourth of July show, he wrote nothing. Dani offered him a deadline and a check. He needed more to tap into his fickle muse. He pressed fingers against his temples. Back in town indefinitely, everyone he encountered repeated the same sad story. The town teetered on the brink of collapse. Without Holidays, Inc., they'd be sunk. In his world, exile wasn't anything new. If he could save his friends and neighbors the experience, he should and prove his worth.

Since his teens, every choice he had made hurt someone. Dani's offer promised too much for his future to be possible. Salvation *and* a second chance? He pinched the bridge of his nose, searching for the catch. How much did anyone know about Dani? She'd referenced a vague background in entertainment but offered no specifics. He needed more. Who was she? With his wounds barely healed from his former partner's betrayal, Paul didn't intend to repeat the painful mistake. Without trust, he couldn't revive his stalled writing career.

"You awake and decent?" Jill called.

"Yeah." He straightened and shut his laptop.

She appeared—already dressed—in the doorway between the kitchen and dining room. Leaning against the side of the archway, she wrinkled her brow. "How long have you been awake?"

Scrubbing a hand over his face, he touched the puffy bags under his eyes. "I don't know, couple hours maybe?" He shrugged. "I'm avoiding clocks."

With a nod, she clenched her jaw and pointed to a mug next to his computer. "Did you put on the coffee?"

The lines between her eyebrows deepened into a fierce scowl. He gulped. "Oh, right, sorry."

She mumbled something unintelligible and pushed off the wall, shuffling into the kitchen.

Every night, his sister set the coffeemaker to brew a fresh pot before her alarm. Since his return, he pushed the Start button and drained the entire pot before sunrise. Standing, he grabbed his mug and studied the cold remains. The caffeine had been wasted. After staring at a blank screen for hours, he hadn't produced anything. Following her into the kitchen, he stopped inside the tight room at the ancient refrigerator. Hardly anything changed in the house. Jill lived inside a time capsule. He drank the rest of his coffee and swallowed, clearing the sour taste from his mouth.

With her back to him, she emptied the old grounds, washed the carafe, and refilled the reservoir. Her shoulders bunched.

Before her first cup of coffee, she was a fire-breathing monster able to destroy a person with a single scorching glance. He'd already committed the capital sin of delaying her immediate caffeine gratification. What was the harm in committing one more unforgivable act? "What do you know about her?"

Jill jumped. Shooting him a glare over her shoulder, she pressed a hand against her chest and, with the other, hit the button to start brewing. "This conversation again?" She turned, leaning back against the counter and crossing her arms.

He stopped at her side, leaving the mug on the counter next to the sink. "Until I get answers, I'll repeat my questions."

"Aren't you supposed to be writing the next show?" She nudged him with her shoulder, grabbed his cup, rinsed it, and loaded it in the top rack of the dishwasher. Shutting the machine, she glanced over her shoulder. "Do you have time to start an investigation?"

"Maybe time is all I have."

Turning, she grabbed his shoulders.

Lifting his chin, he met her steady gaze. When he

left for college at East Coast University in New York City, he was one of New Hope's biggest success stories. Without his sister boosting his confidence, however, his doubts eroded the thin layer of bravado.

"Losing the TV pilot wasn't your fault." She emphasized each word with a shake of her hands. "You've got to keep going."

"You weren't there." Raising his shoulders, he shrugged free from her grip and ran a hand through his hair. "I devoted twenty-hour days, seven days a week, for six months to the pilot. I wrote and rewrote the first six scripts at least a dozen times. I collaborated and listened to feedback. I did everything right. In ten seconds, I was pushed aside. My partner took my family drama and morphed the story into a futuristic survival fantasy. How can I trust anyone again? How can I be free to be creative without knowing Dani?" Dropping his hands to his sides, he clenched his fingers into tight fists, squeezing until the veins popped on the backs of his hands. Without answers, he couldn't work. His trust had been shattered by someone he'd known for years. What made Dani different?

"No, I wasn't there." She raised her chin. "I stayed in our hometown, like always."

With her direct words, she doused the flames stirring inside his tight chest. Exhaling a heavy sigh, he flattened his palms against his thighs, his arms too heavy to lift and hug his sister. "I'm sorry."

"Don't be." She held up a hand. "We both made choices. I stayed. I never wanted to leave. I'm not you." With a shake, she dropped the hand and shrugged. "I don't harbor any ill will toward being the one to take care of Dad and the movie theater. But I need you to understand. I want to be here. I want to save this town. Until Dani bought our movie theater, I don't think our community had a chance at a viable future. No one did. I know what she's told me. I don't need any more."

Understanding her stance didn't mean he agreed, he nodded. For his part, he needed answers. Learning who he could trust wasn't Jill's problem. His gut instinct drew him close to Dani. For that exact reason, he should run the opposite way.

The coffeemaker beeped.

Jill dropped her hands, retrieved a mug, and poured a cup.

Her words eased something buried deep inside, guilt over not giving her the choice to leave. He reached into the upper cabinet over the sink, grabbed a mug, and filled it to the brim. Through the ceramic, the drink warmed his hands. He blew across the steaming top and sipped. When Dad got sick, Paul packed for his move from New York to Hollywood. Everyone assured him the relocation was the best shot for his big break. He could have come home and eased her burden. She never asked, and neither had Dad. Relief mixed with guilt. The heady combination spurred him to work non-stop in his quest to *make it* and prove to everyone his potential wasn't wasted. After three years in LA, he finally had a shot with a major producer, only to be sidelined by his writing partner. At thirty, he lost the energy and money to chase an impossible dream.

"What's the play?" Jill sipped from her cup.

A relaxed smile softened her blue eyes. "I'm hitting a wall." He crossed his arms. "Do I write something grand about America? Do I focus on New Hope? Maybe a big, splashy, cheesy tribute to the decades? I have no clue. What would she like?"

"I think she'd like any of those options." Jill lowered the mug to the counter. "For what it's worth, I understand your hesitation. I only know what she's told me. I don't need to hire a PI. Why don't you talk to her today? Ask her directly."

"Come on." He scoffed. "If she ended up here, can she really have a celebrity network? No offense."

"Some offense taken." She sighed. "I can list any number of reasons why someone might choose a town like New Hope."

"Like she's on the run from the law? Or she's conning the town and planning to bolt?" His instincts about people swerved way off base with his last partner. If he'd been cheated by a friend of ten years, how could he believe Dani—a stranger—and her too-good-to-be-true job offer? *She doesn't judge me.* He drank the rest of the coffee, quenching his dry mouth. Being a good listener didn't absolve Dani of nefarious motives.

"You are so annoyingly stubborn. Ever think maybe this town is cheap enough she could buy half a block of downtown without feeling a pinch? Or maybe growing up in a city, she wanted a small-town life, like the reverse of you?" She drained her mug, set it in the sink, and grabbed a muffin from the breadbasket on the counter. "What do you need?"

"Answers." He stared into his empty mug and frowned. If he possessed any coffee-ground reading clairvoyance, he wouldn't have hit rock bottom.

"I can't help you with Dani." She peeled the wrapper off the muffin and took a large bite.

"I'll settle for a different question. Why you haven't changed this house?"

She swallowed and shrugged. "I'm not the sole owner. I can't make choices without your input. We share the deed. Do you want me to buy your portion of the house? I haven't spent my share of the inheritance."

He set his mug on the counter behind him, turned, and rested his back against the edge. Taking her offer would simplify his life. With an infusion of cash, he could return to LA and try again. Dropping his hands to the counter, he gripped until the sharp Formica edge dug into the meaty flesh of his palms. He needed more than money to rebuild his life. Pulling off his hands, he brushed his palms against his jeans. "You don't have plans for what you want to do with the money?"

"Nothing definitive. The offer stands. If you want to be clear of the house, I will buy your share." She stuffed another bite of muffin into her mouth.

"I can't imagine why you would." He angled his body toward the doorway and folded his arms over his chest. "If more of Dad's money goes to the worthless twin, he'll roll in his grave or start haunting you."

She swallowed and rubbed the back of her hand over her mouth, wiping away crumbs. "No one thinks you're worthless. He didn't. If you stuck around town for long enough, you could've seen you were valued. You still are. As kids, we weren't really part of the community. We were dependents."

He grabbed the paper towels off the stand by the sink and handed her a torn-off piece.

She smiled and accepted the offering.

Her words tugged at the broken-down part he hid under the façade of boredom. He never fit here. Dani swooped in and received the sort of instant acceptance he wanted. If he stayed, could he really have a shot at becoming part of the fabric of their community? Did he want to belong?

"I'm off to the theater. I hope you get something accomplished today." She kissed his cheek and exited through the entry toward the front hall.

The deadbolt unlatched. The door opened and shut.

He stared through the archway into the dining room. He didn't want to explain himself to Dani. Unfortunately, he didn't have any better way to clear his mental obstruction.

****

Sitting on a park bench with her lunch bag on her lap, Dani shivered. Earlier in the morning, she glimpsed outside her bedroom window. The bright blue sky and green leaves on the trees fooled her. After a long winter and eventual thaw, Wisconsin couldn't shake the chilly breeze in early June. She should have dug in the box in the back of her closet and pulled out her tattered, too-big sweatshirt. *I'm out in public.*

She shifted, uncrossing and recrossing her legs. Tucking the floral print skirt of her tea-length summer dress under her legs, she constructed a thin barrier between her skin and the cold metal slats. She dressed with intention and not practicality. With tailored outfits and heavier-than-normal cosmetics, she projected the glamor of her business. As long as no one studied her false eyelashes closely, the rest of the world wouldn't see the glue holding her in place.

In her lap, the paper bag crinkled. Reaching inside, she grabbed the tinfoil wrapped sandwich from the diner, peeled open one corner, and took a bite. A dark shadow fell across her lap. Swallowing the mouthful, she raised her head and squinted.

Paul towered over her, blocking the sun.

With the light at his back, he was outlined by a hazy aura. *He's almost heaven-sent.* She nibbled the inside of her cheek, rewrapped her sandwich, and returned it to the sack at her side.

He crossed his arms and stroked his chin. "Hi. Sorry to interrupt."

Dragging up her gaze, she admired the strength his wide-legged stance and crossed arms highlighted in his biceps. *Keep thinking of him as Jill's brother.* If she remembered her friend's connection, she stood a chance against the surge of lightheadedness. She shaded her eyes with a hand. His gray-blue eyes softened, mirroring the bright sky instead of a stormy sea. Maybe her reluctant employee would play nice? "You've caught me on my lunch break."

"Sorry." He ran a hand through his hair. "Jill told me where to find you."

"Of course. It's no problem. Please take a seat." She gestured to the bench and stiffened, spotting her sack lunch. Covering her mouth with a hand, she shielded her breath. "Your sister banned me from eating tuna salad at the theater. Are you sensitive to smells like your sister?"

"No." He chuckled and joined her on the bench.

Sliding down the cold iron slats until the armrest prodded into her side, she turned toward him. Should she use cool professionalism or friendly banter? She longed for the easy camaraderie of their initial hello. With the forced proximity, however, she struggled. Her arm tingled from his body heat only inches away. His laundry-fresh scent wafted past, and she breathed deep.

He leaned forward and rested his forearms on his

thighs. After a few seconds, he readjusted, reclining on the bench and draping an arm over the back.

The metal seat squealed.

With a frown, she glanced at the armrest digging into her side. She didn't notice any rusty or loose bolts threatening her physical safety. Raking her gaze to his fingertips only centimeters from her shoulder, she ignored the static electricity surge along her skin.

He crossed one ankle over his knee, interlacing his fingers in his lap. Then he reversed the posture.

She gulped. The energy radiating off him weighed down her arms. *Not another problem.* "How's progress on the new show coming?"

He flinched, the veins in his neck throbbing.

"Wrong question?" Her breath hitched. Dealing with the rest of the business demanded more than twenty-four hours a day. Without a chef, she shouldered more of the kitchen responsibilities, not wanting to stress Shirley and Ted and potentially lose their help. In the wake of the positive reviews for the Memorial Day show, she'd already sold over sixty percent of the tickets. If no other option existed, she'd take charge of the show. She couldn't assume responsibility for the productions without relinquishing something else, like meal breaks or sleep.

"I'm hitting a wall." He studied his hands.

"How can I help?" She bit her tongue and shut her mouth. With an opening to abandon the project, would he leave? For too long, she'd been a pushover for everyone she needed. When she required help, she was abandoned. Her mom established the pattern, and everyone else in her life followed along. She tapped her toes on the sidewalk. Coming to New Hope, she'd vowed to do better, act smarter, work harder, and yet, she fell into the same nice-girl trap she always set.

He gazed at the ground. "I don't know what I can give you, when I know nothing about you."

She frowned. He wanted her tragic backstory? Long ago on set, she learned everyone was more interesting with an air of mystery. The lesson rivaled another, how empty and meaningless words often were, for most, life defining. She preferred action to platitudes and promises. "Come on, what does my history have to do with your show?" She chuckled and stretched her lips into a tight contortion she hoped resembled a smile.

"I need to trust you. I can't write if I don't..."

"Feel safe?"

He nodded and pressed his lips into a thin line.

Filling her lungs, she held her breath for a second before exhaling. "I am a former child actress turned dinner theater proprietor. In my previous life, I used a stage name."

"Wait, you're what?" He narrowed his gaze.

Could she flee without stoking more curiosity? She smoothed wispy tendrils behind her ears, pressing cold fingers to the hot skin. Until her late teens, she considered her life normal. Working on soundstages since childhood, she proudly supported herself and her mom. She'd come to learn her experience was atypical in America as a whole. Highlighting her former life made her squirm. "I was advised against using my real name for acting credits." Explaining her past and justifying the decisions made first for her and then by her was an exercise in vulnerability. From under her lashes, she studied him.

"You really grew up in show business?" His eyebrows drew together in the middle of his forehead.

Even with a unibrow, he's still good looking. Crossing her arms, she studied him. His tone was incredulous and disbelieving, but she didn't hear censure. She suffered prejudgment enough in her life to err on the side of giving everyone the benefit of the doubt until lied to her face. Short of declaring herself an alien, she couldn't imagine he'd be more shocked. "I don't know why you don't believe me. When would I have had the time or energy to fabricate a cover story and Internet resume?"

He cringed.

Leaning her back against the bench, she chuckled and shook her head. "You searched my name on the Internet."

Dropping his gaze to the ground, he shrugged. "I didn't find anything beyond mention of your dinner theater. You really left a successful life for a ghost town? Why?"

He's digging. Good thing she hadn't shared her stage name, or he would have been very successful uncovering her secrets. She shuddered. If she relived the rawest and most painful moments of her life, she'd do so with the people directly involved, not with Paul. If Dani wanted his trust, she had to offer something honest. "If you've only known sets and soundstages, my past work isn't so interesting."

Crossing his arms, he leaned back and tilted his head. "Anything is more exciting than New Hope."

"I don't need exciting. I need a community, people I can trust, I need a…" Her throat constricted. She swallowed, pushing past the sudden lump of emotion.

"A community I can count on like family."

"Don't you have parents? Siblings?"

She shook her head. "I have a mom-ager. The woman who gave me life and immediately put me to work, all legal, thanks to lawyers." She kept her tone light. Accepting Mom and the limitations inherent in their relationship, however, didn't stop Dani from yearning for approval. If she could, she wouldn't have emailed Mom once before she left and again after she arrived. Six months later, she still didn't have a reply.

"I'm… I'm…" He ran a hand through his hair. "Wow. I don't know what to say."

"Don't say anything. Please." She folded her arms over her chest. "After a lot of years of searching, I found what I needed here. This town is a balm soothing my weary soul."

"You're a remarkable person. The community adores you."

His flat delivery scraped her tender heart. Fighting the off-balance sinking sensation in her stomach, she sat straighter. "You don't like the town welcoming me?"

He blew a sigh. "No. I didn't come home to mope around town. I'm back because I have nowhere else."

She shut her mouth half a second before gaping. "What happened?"

"For half a year, my writing partner and I worked on a big pitch. We went into a meeting. He read the mood in the room and switched gears." He snapped his fingers. "I was tongue-tied. In a matter of seconds, he sold an entirely different project, and my role was eliminated."

"I'm sorry, b—" She bit her tongue, adding her

commiseration wasn't helpful. Growing up in the business, she couldn't remember her first betrayal, but the final deception cut the deepest. "You are adamant against change because of your history?"

"I'm not used to *frenemies*." He raised his hands, curling both index and middle fingers. "People being nice to your face and then immediately turning on you isn't something I understand. New Hope has problems, but fakery isn't one."

Her shoulders crept to her ears. His concerns touched too close to her heart for denial. She curled her upper lip. "People are terrible everywhere."

"You're a cynic." He drew back his chin.

She scrunched her nose. "Are you asking a question or stating a fact?"

"I'm not sure." He scrubbed a hand over his face. Dropping the hand to the back of the bench, he smiled.

The corners of his eyes crinkled, but his gaze hardened to cold, impenetrable steel. She gulped. "I don't have any ulterior motives. I'm here permanently. I have no intention of ever returning to the west coast."

He nodded and dropped a hand to his lap.

With the tip of his fingers, he brushed her arm in a whisper of a touch. She jerked forward. Biting her lip, she half rose, deliberately shifting on the seat. He didn't respond to the accidental touch. Her nerves were on edge from discussing and defending her not-so-past life, and nothing else.

She'd done the Hollywood thing. Celebrity had never been her focus. Far away from LA, she could be herself without disappointing anyone. Did she really want to involve herself with someone who couldn't appreciate New Hope? As soon as he could, he'd leave.

For the time being, she needed his help and vice versa. He was hungry for a taste of the spotlight. As a writer, his words would be twisted and teased into something other than his original intention. His eventuality wasn't her problem. She'd offer him creative control and a fair wage. He'd make his own choices. "I have contacts." Leaning forward, she tucked her legs under the bench and crossed her ankles. "I'd appreciate your help at my theater. I'll pay, and maybe—if you're any good—I'll help you get a big break."

"If? If I'm good?" He poked his chest with a hand and flashed his dimple.

She held up her hands in surrender. "I hired you without an audition. I'm giving you complete creative control for the Fourth of July show. If I've successfully plucked talent from obscurity, I'll see you on your way back up the show business ladder."

"Deal." He extended a hand.

She grasped his fingers, and an electric tingle sizzled from her palm to her arm. She stared at the connection, expecting flames to engulf their hands. When she didn't smell smoke, she pumped their clasped grip in an exaggerated motion. Finally, she dropped his hand. If she found their interactions confusing, she was clear about their potential. She couldn't add more trouble, and a movie-star-handsome guy with dreams to leave promised plenty of complication.

"It's a deal. I'll see you around." She stood and clutched her paper sack to her chest, crossing her arms. Spinning on her heel, she stalked from the park and power walked across the street. She wasn't escaping him, but she couldn't waste time outdoors all day.

When she pushed open the front door of her theater, she brushed hot cheeks with cool fingers. She hadn't flushed in decades. Since meeting Paul, she needed more than her icy hands to chill the simmer. She dropped her hands to her stomach, breathing through the sinking sensation. What else was she wrong about?

Chapter Five

Seated behind the upright piano on stage at Holidays, Inc., Paul rested his elbows on the music rack and stared at the keys. For the past week, he'd spent eight hours every day in the same spot. Positioned in the center of the boards, he was in the middle of the action.

Rob stopped by with supplies for the ongoing renovations, using the auditorium as a holding zone.

Jill flitted in and out of the space, constantly completing a list of tasks.

Crewmembers hired for the Memorial Day show tore down the sets.

Paul provided the occasional quip to the bystanders or played a flitting tune on the keyboard. Most of the time, however, he dropped his chin to his chest and interlaced fingers behind his neck. *If you're any good.*

Her tease echoed in his mind, drowning out his new melodies after a few decent bars. Had she intended the verbal jab, delivered with a playful smile, as a taunt? He finished the sentence without her help. If he was any good, he wouldn't have needed the job. Talent should have kept him working on his choice of projects on either coast. Instead, he returned to the town he escaped and couldn't recall the multitude of reasons for vanishing. Reunited with family, he rebuilt abandoned relationships with friends and neighbors. If he could rediscover his creativity, he had a chance at something like happiness.

"Still? Nothing?"

Snapping up his head, he turned toward the source of the incredulous questions.

Jill approached from the wings, tiptoeing over the minefield of tools, cables, and cords left in piles on the boards.

Her loud steps on the stairs gave him a few seconds of warning she intended a full-scale confrontation. "I'm waiting on inspiration to strike." He straightened.

She rolled her eyes.

He slid down the smooth bench. With crossed arms, pursed lips, and an unflinching stare, she epitomized immovable annoyance. He patted the free space at his side.

Childhood piano lessons ended with a yearly spring recital. The duets were the most overt display of their twin-ness. In a small town, neighbors marveled at the pair. He'd absorbed the positive attention. She hated every performance.

"Fine." She uncrossed her arms and sat. "Just start." Arching fingers over the keys, she played scales. "Don't be immobilized by perfectionism. You can't fix a blank score."

With the tip of his elbow, he poked her in the ribs. "You're right. Of course."

"Of course." She pulled her hands off the keyboard, pushing her glasses up her nose.

He liked the smile in her voice. He'd been voted most likely to succeed, but he relied on his sister's commonsense advice for guidance. "Where is she? By the way." He lowered hands to the keys and played a simple melody. Spending his days in Dani's theater, he willed her to appear and challenge him on the show's lack of progress. Dani never stepped foot in the auditorium.

"At the Come Again Diner, menu planning with Shirley and Ted. Then she's meeting with…"

"Me," a deep voice boomed.

Leaning back, Paul spotted Rob.

Jill shifted and raised a hand to her throat.

Paul dodged a pointy elbow in the split second before it would have connected with his cheek. Why was she so jumpy? She hadn't squirmed so much since the summer before junior year. He swallowed a groan. His sister was still in love with his buddy?

Rob, the quick-to-laugh charmer, had cut through the ranks of their class until falling for his high school sweetheart. Paul explained in clear terms his sister was off limits and encouraged Rob to pursue Ellie. During the course of locker room talk, Paul high-fived Rob and laughed. If he caught the guy smirking in Jill's general direction, Paul would beat him to a pulp. In ten plus years, the rules hadn't changed.

"She'll return in twenty minutes." Jill fluffed her bangs.

"Great, I have more time to convince you of my proposal's positives. I come with a lot of benefits." Rob focused on Jill.

Paul clenched his jaw and leaned forward, pressing his cheek against the music stand. Jill's face was redder than the time she fell asleep while suntanning on the theater roof in high school. Rob stood within a foot of Jill, far closer than necessary for a professional conversation. Neither glanced at Paul. While he'd been gone, he hadn't erased the boundary lines between his sister and friend. He cleared his throat. "Or you could let Jill work and listen to what I've scored so far."

"Sorry, Paul, I prefer the better looking twin's company." Rob winked.

Jill slid off the bench. "You know, I actually had some numbers to crunch before our meeting." She walked backwards. "I'll see you in twenty."

"Bye," Rob said.

With a nod, she spun and crossed the stage.

Turning his neck, Rob followed the departure.

Pushing off the bench, Paul stood with hands fisted at his sides and gnashed his molars. No way could Rob think his behavior was okay.

At the stairs, she raced down the steps to the carpeted ground, jogging through the room.

Her heavy footfalls echoed through the cavernous space like sonar.

The doors at the back of the room shut.

Rob turned and met Paul's gaze. "Hey, man, how's it going?"

Paul raised a fist and smashed the opposite palm against the knuckles. The smack reverberated through the auditorium.

Taking a step back, Rob lifted a shoulder. "What? You forget what playful banter sounds like."

"That was not playful banter. You were…fl-flir— Y-you were talking to her like…" Drawing in a shaky breath, he opened and shut his jaw but couldn't release the words stuck in his mind. He reached a hand to his burning throat. "Don't speak to my sister again."

"What?" Rob crossed his arms. "We interact on a daily basis for our jobs."

"You weren't treating her like a colleague." Paul massaged his neck. "You were talking to her like she's…she's…"

"A woman?"

Blood pounded through Paul's veins, throbbing at his temples and flaring his nostrils. At his side, he clenched a hand into a tight fist. "Come on, man. She's not Ellie."

"Is that what you think?" Rob rubbed a hand over his smooth scalp and retracted his chin. "You've been gone a long time man. Jill isn't a kid."

Paul curled his upper lip. "I know she's not. She's still my sister."

"Hey." Rob held up his hands. "I didn't come here for a fight. How are you coming along?"

Rob's words were ice-cold water poured over a roaring campfire. Paul ran a hand through his hair and sank onto the piano bench. Resting his elbows on the music stand, Paul rubbed the corners of his eyes. He couldn't clear away what he didn't want to acknowledge. If he failed, he disappointed more than just himself. The stakes had never been higher. He hated the mounting pressure. "Barely."

"Today's meeting is about contacting the crew to build sets next week. Without a show, we can't start."

"You'll have a musical." His cheek twitched. Pride forced the statement. After weeks with no success, he threw an empty promise into the air like candy at a parade. He had to deliver. Dropping hands to his lap, he straightened. "I'll be ready."

"I hope so. Did you know we're the only town in Wisconsin without a major chain of any kind in city limits? New Hope's commerce is entirely mom-and-pop shops. The postal service was even threatening to close our branch. Can you imagine? Losing civic jobs will be the final nail in the town's coffin."

After witnessing the changes in town firsthand, Paul didn't need the lecture. He dropped his chin to his chest. "I get it."

"Be sure you do. We're counting on everyone to make this business a success and save the town."

A door crashed against the wall.

Paul slid off the bench and jumped to his feet. Squinting through the darkness, he spotted his sister at the back of the auditorium.

Striding through the darkness, she stopped at the first row of tables. "Sorry," Jill called. "She's back early, Rob, if you want to chat."

"Sure, thanks." Rob turned. Standing with arms crossed, he set his jaw and narrowed his gaze.

No longer the charming kid, Rob wasn't messing around. He was playing for keeps. The flicker of determination set the spark of an idea from sputtering flame into roaring fire. Paul could do his part, too.

"I'll see you around, man. If you want to hang, you let me know."

"Yeah, I will." Paul studied Jill at the back doors and her deepening blush at Rob's approach. She was an adult. He had enough work without involving himself in his sister's personal life.

If you're any good... With a groan, he dropped to the piano bench and dashed fingers over the keys. He'd prove he was better than good and kickstart his career. With nothing to lose, he couldn't fall any harder unless he was stupid enough to mix professional obligations with personal desires. He wouldn't fall for his boss. If he had any pride left, he'd steer away from a romantic entanglement and leave as soon as possible.

****

Dani rubbed her eyes and squinted at the computer screen. Her meeting with Rob concluded quickly. Until she had more information about the next musical, she could only offer educated guesses about what supplies and how large a crew the Fourth of July show required. Rob left with promises to do his best based on past experience, and she committed to a marginally larger budget than the previous show.

Leaning back in her desk chair, she cocked her head to one side and then the other. After an hour spent staring at the numbers on the spreadsheet, she couldn't focus. When she dreamt of her Wisconsin project, she left the practical elements, like balancing the books, out of her fantasy. Until she turned a profit, however, she remained at her post in the tiny office. She tackled the clerical and managerial work, relying on Paul for the theater's showmanship.

Paul. Her hands shook. She folded arms over her chest, tucking trembling fingers against her ribcage. What was he doing? Did she have time to find out? Every day of the past week, she snuck to the auditorium, cracked open one of the doors, and listened for a maximum of twenty minutes. If she lingered, she'd be discovered and was too tongue-tied for an easy explanation. She wasn't in close proximity to micromanage but gained nothing with the truth. He intrigued her, and she wanted to know him better. With her future dependent on his skills, she couldn't afford any distractions, including pursuing a friendship.

With a sigh, she returned her hands to the computer

keyboard and focused on her work. A trilling tune played in her mind, like one of the songs he played yesterday. During her eavesdropping, she never heard the same chords twice. She was both elated and concerned at his seemingly boundless creativity. Shouldn't he have scored the show and started rehearsals already? If he needed a suggestion, he only had to ask. From her post in the hall, she had pressed together her lips. She yearned for collaboration. Instead, she gave him space. Intruding on his time with a joke or another accidental confidence wasn't the best use of his working hours. Of course, trapped in a cramped room with her inner dialogue stuck on a continuous loop, she didn't model efficiency.

A knock shook the closed door.

"Come in." Her voice cracked, and she cleared her throat.

With her gaze on the screen, she moved the cursor to hit Save on her document. Before she glanced up at the visitor, she sniffed a pleasant, sun-warmed cotton scent. *Paul.* Breathing deep, she lifted her arms off the desk and lost her grip. The rolling chair shot backward and tipped. With a loud smack, she crashed to the ground and stared at the water rings discoloring her ceiling. Paul appeared, blocking everything else from view.

"Dani? Are you hurt?" Wrinkling his brow, he frowned. "Is anything broken?"

Heat engulfed her, flaming every inch of skin. She shut her eyes. If she was perfectly still, maybe she could pretend to be asleep? Could she invent a reason for her clumsiness that didn't involve him? She tensed her muscles limb by limb, testing for any physical injury. Wounded pride wasn't worthy of attention. "Yeah, I'm okay." She flicked a wrist and rolled to her knees, focusing on the ground.

He extended a hand.

She stared at the offered palm and remembered how her rough skin scrapped against his smooth hold. If she accepted his chivalry, she was setting a trap for disappointment. *We can't be friends or anything else.* Tugging her maxi dress free from the wheels of the desk chair, she dropped her head under the guise of studying her actions. If she continued projecting emotions onto him, she'd scare him. The spreadsheet told her, in black and red numbers, she couldn't lose him. His departure would ripple through her entire business. With a shake of her head, she extended her fingers. Accepting his help wasn't saying yes to a bended knee proposal.

Straightening, he tugged her to her feet.

The gesture meant nothing. He barely clasped her fingers. Warmth slid up her arms and down her back. Lifting her chin, she met his gaze and stifled a shiver at his darkening look. He lowered his eyelids a fraction over his silver eyes and raised the corner of his mouth. Dragging his thumb over the back of her hand, he traced her knuckles with a whisper of a touch and dropped her hand. Her skin tingled.

Covering his mouth with a fist, he coughed.

When he removed the hand, he resumed the bored expression she knew so well. With a perpetually wrinkled brow, the man standing before her wasn't impressed by her credentials or interested in her dream. Whatever she imagined glimpsing moments ago, she was mistaken. They stood on opposite sides of the desk appropriate to their roles. She was in charge. Her employees and neighbors needed her focused. Unreliable feelings wouldn't divert her from her purpose. Success wasn't a given. "Take a seat." Bending, she lifted the chair and sat, anchoring her arms flat on the desk.

"Are you sure you want to sit there?" He arched a brow and pointed to the chair.

"I'm fine. What can I do for you? How can I help?" She clasped her hands.

"I'm ready for the dress rehearsal. If you have any last-minute suggestions about the show or staging, now is your moment to tell me."

"I wish I could. I trust you'll do your best work. We're counting on a great show." In the two weeks since Memorial Day, she hired a few more employees for the kitchen. As her stake in the town grew, so did her pressure to succeed. A muscle in her cheek twitched.

"The focus of the show is on the town's history. Glossing over our current state of affairs." He dropped his voice.

"Of course." She nodded and drummed her fingers on the desk, ignoring the dull ache in her jaw from a forced smile. Why was he here? She'd been avoiding him specifically to prevent such a moment. In close quarters, he overwhelmed her, filling the tiny room with broad shoulders and his clean scent soaking into every surface. Staring at his mouth, she waited for him to explain some unforeseen terrible complication. She was under his spell with every twitch of his lips. She coughed. "I'm sure the library has been a big help."

"Not particularly. My family's lived here since the

town's founding."

"Really?" She tilted her head to the side. "Jill didn't mention that fact." *Unless she didn't want to discourage the renovation.*

Nodding, he ran a hand through his hair. "When the town was settled in the nineteenth century, my many times great-grandparents stayed during the winter."

"Your family chose to spend the coldest months of the year here?" She clapped a hand over her mouth.

He chuckled.

The easy laugh loosened the knot between her shoulder blades, and she rolled her neck.

"My family worked as traveling actors."

"Like vaudeville?" She rested her chin in a hand and leaned forward.

"No, actors."

His gray eyes darkened, hardening into an impenetrable stonewall. Wincing, she opened her mouth. Her careless words struck a nerve.

"They had a theater troupe and would perform throughout the summer, traveling from town to town." He shrugged one shoulder. "When they settled here full-time, they were in high demand."

"Why here? Why not New York City?"

"They had plenty of Broadway offers, but they wanted peace. For half the year, they traveled with the children. For the other six months, they stayed in one place. This"—he extended both arms toward the ceiling and dropped the limbs to his side—"movie theater was originally a stage theater purchased so the family could perform during their time here."

Right place, right time. She raised a hand to the

skin tingling on the back of her neck. Was her discovery of the cinema for sale circumstantial or something bigger? Had her destiny always been to find the town? If she wanted a home here forever, she couldn't rely on fickle fate. "Jill never told me."

He nodded. "You unknowingly restored the theater to its original iteration."

Straightening, she lifted higher in the chair, a sudden lightness releasing the tension weighing her down. She studied his blank expression. He didn't smile. She tapped a forefinger against her chin. "But you don't like my renovation?"

He folded his arms over his chest. "Have you ever lacked the authority to control your choices?"

She shivered. Until her twenties, she hadn't understood how few decisions were hers. Trusting others to guide her, she overestimated her former friends and colleagues. For her entire life, she longed for a community that supported each other and didn't act in the self-interests of its individuals. Until she moved to New Hope, she imagined her desire far-fetched. She couldn't hold his opinions against him, but she could control how she let his words impact her. "I'm sorry you don't approve." Clenching her jaw, she massaged the pressure points under her ears and studied the computer monitor. The screen showed a spreadsheet filled with data. The hard facts listed the theater's vital operational requirements. She bit the inside of her cheek. His words didn't reroute her path toward success.

"No, Dani, I—" He hovered a hand over the desk.

Only a few inches separated them. Wrinkling her brow, she dragged up her gaze.

"What you're doing here is great, and I appreciate the job. I just meant to say…" He pulled away, running a hand through his hair. "After the family settled, the three oldest left for New York City. My great-great-grandmother stayed, cared for her parents, and assumed control of the theater. Several generations later, my grandfather repurposed the building into a movie theater. Thanks to manufacturing jobs during World War Two, our town experienced a boom. My grandfather wanted to pass on a family business, and he did for one more generation. New Hope is part of a sad history of working class towns being left behind in the digital age. Small-town America disintegrated before our parents' eyes, and our generation has limited options to save our piece of the country. What you're doing is good. The whole town is behind you."

She frowned and studied the desk. Fighting against outside forces was overwhelming. She hated the hurt in his words. Her limbs were too heavy to lift. Defending herself was exhausting. No matter what she told herself, she cared about his opinion. "You're not?"

"I am, but…" He sighed. "I'm not here to stay. This opportunity is my catapult to chasing after my dreams. I want to make sure we both understand."

He was right. She nodded. Boundaries existed for a reason. "I respect your honesty. You know the grass really isn't greener in Hollywood. With years of drought, barely any green remains."

"True." The corners of his mouth lifted. "But the grass grows year-round."

Her arms shook. She wanted to rattle sense into him. He grew up in a place she couldn't have imagined in her wildest fantasies. The supportive community rallied around him for no reason other than he was theirs. Belonging to people so intrinsically was her deepest wish. He didn't appreciate his good fortune. "I didn't have a tight-knit town in my youth. No one cared enough to ask questions. I'm not bothered by interest in my life now."

"You're from LA, right?" He arched an eyebrow and crossed his arms, leaning back. "Any tips for me?"

"I spent my first twenty-eight years there. I don't think location had any impact on my childhood, besides how easy it was for my mom to use me as her conduit." Her voice cracked. She sniffed and rubbed her itchy nose. At their first meeting, she over-shared part of her complicated relationship with Mom. She regretted confessing so much with a person who wouldn't stay. "Mom would have molded and pushed me no matter where we lived. If I'd been raised here, I'm sure she would have made me the quintessential high school cheerleader, prom queen, and popular girl. Our proximity to Hollywood meant I worked, and she spent the money."

"I'm sorry."

She shrugged. Her mother's past antics didn't upset her anymore. In her way, Mom was a straight shooter. She didn't act in the best interest of her daughter, but she never lied about her self-centered motivations. No longer a dependent, Dani proposed a different relationship. Sending another email, however, would expose her too much. *No one likes eager.* Mom's words trained Dani to avoid any show of weakness. Composing another heart-felt missive definitely fit into the category Mom schooled her to avoid. After the betrayal by the family she found, she avoided any situation demanding her vulnerability or trust. She swallowed the sour taste in her mouth. "Just be careful. Spotting good people from bad isn't easy. You have to be your own advocate."

"Thanks. Well, you better get back to…" He gestured toward the screen.

"Yeah, thanks." She rolled her eyes. "And you keep furthering my dream of a great new show for every holiday of the year."

With a nod, he backed from the room.

The door shut, and the lock clicked in place.

Hunching forward, she exhaled a pent-up sigh and fluttered the neat paper stacks on her desk. Sharing her closely guarded secrets, she lightened her emotional baggage…but at what cost? He was nice, sometimes charming, and a surprisingly good listener. Those three qualities were reason enough to rescind her offer and run as far as she could.

Chapter Six

Whistling with the songbirds, Paul strolled down Main Street. After working through the night, he finished scripting the show and composing the score. He should be exhausted. When he glanced in the bathroom mirror while brushing his teeth, he spotted under-eye bags as dark as bruises. Adrenaline and desperation surged through his nervous system, propelling him forward.

He hadn't earned the community's forgiveness or the second chance at a career. He appreciated both and vowed to reward everyone's faith in him as he stepped into directing his show. *It's not like anyone else needs me.* He paused mid step and stopped his song. In the weeks since returning home, he was no closer to planning his future. No moment of fevered inspiration for his next big break struck, and he hadn't fielded any calls from the coast. His LA friends already forgot him. Tipping back his head, he shut his eyes and absorbed the sunshine on the cloudless day. A hint of sweet grass wafted past. Focusing on one task at a time, he'd prove his worth.

Exhaling a heavy breath, he opened his gaze and strode forward. After a handful of steps, he froze. Something caught in his peripheral vision. Turning in a slow circle, he avoided the deep cracks in the pavement and gazed at the buildings he'd passed. A month ago, the short distance from the diner to the movie theater looked like a ghost town. Walking down the faded thoroughfare, past broken panes of glass from long deserted shops, filled him with dread. Today, something changed. He retraced his steps to the building he'd just passed.

The windows were repaired and covered with brown paper from the inside. At the edge of one section of glass, the paper didn't line up with the frame.

He peeked through the exposed corner and glimpsed a bucket and a rag.

"Hey, are you coming to the theater today?"

A cheerful voice called. Over his shoulder, he spotted his boss. Wearing a flowing dress and heels, the petite powerhouse barreled down the sidewalk toward him. He lifted the corner of his mouth. If determination alone could save the town, she would prove victorious.

Stopping a few feet away, she clutched a stack of spiral bound notebooks and binders to her chest and a big purse hung on her shoulder.

The light scent of citrus shampoo tickled his nose. If he shut his eyes, he'd swear he sniffed sunshine at the beach. He pictured her lounging on a chair in the sand with a fruity drink in one hand. He'd like to join her there. He coughed. "I was considering my options. Look here." He stepped to the side and ran a hand through his hair.

"What's happening here?"

"Maybe a defibrillator to the heart of the town?" He shrugged.

"Har har, please leave out the comedy in your show." She stepped closer, studying the window.

Her forced laughter tugged the corner of his mouth

higher. With only a few feet between them, he counted his inhalations and timed his exhaling breaths. In his life, he'd never been more aware of another person's every twitch. The timing had never been worse. He rubbed his palms against his jeans. "Where are you headed? Do you need help?" He extended both hands.

Her mouth gaped, and she stood rooted to the pavement.

Still not accepting help? He arched an eyebrow. If he had to learn to lean on others, he could tutor her.

"Yes, I'd like your assistance." With a sigh, she handed over two binders and a spiral-bound notebook.

He frowned at the slight bundle in his arms. He could take on more, but he'd earn her confidence first. "See? Not so hard."

"No." She dropped her shoulders. "Thank you. I need to accept assistance every so often I suppose."

"Aren't you already? Didn't you reach out to Ted and Shirley?"

She shook her head. "I had no other choice."

Is that why you hired me? His mouth filled with a sour taste. He accepted her offer because he had no other option. Was the same true in reverse? Were they bound together only by necessity? She gave him a job and a purpose. He refused to analyze her intentions deeper. "My high school cast won't stop singing your praises. Everyone I run into shares how glad they are you came."

"I'm lucky to be here." She tilted her head to one side. "You've been burned by people you trusted. You understand." She dropped her gaze to the broken sidewalk.

He nodded and rolled his neck. They'd both been

used, and maybe they were too world weary for the blind optimism of the generous community they shared. From his firsthand experience, he understood being dubious about accepting compliments after a betrayal. He didn't like seeing her anything less than bright and bubbly. "How can I help you this morning? Where are you headed?"

"I'm dropping off show tickets at the diner and the hardware store." She tapped her back foot. "Shirley is my top salesperson by far."

"She knows everything going on in town." He inclined his head the way he'd come. "Shall we?"

After strolling a few steps, he matched her pace and scanned the street. Main Street was devoid of cars. If anyone ventured into town, they stopped at Shirley and Ted's diner or Rob's hardware store without assessing the sad state of the rest of the street. Ambling past the boarded storefronts of his neighbors' former businesses, he breathed through the persistent, dull ache in his ribs. He had to do his part. From the corner of his gaze, he studied her serene expression. He hated to break the companionable silence but couldn't waste an opportunity to pick her brain. If nothing else, she was his boss. The upcoming show was an audition, and he had a lot to prove to everyone, including himself. "I was wondering…"

She nudged with an elbow. "Yes?"

"Would you consider holding open auditions for the whole town? A lot of people would like to participate."

She scrunched her nose and pursed her lips.

He chuckled. "What's that look?"

"I know the high school kids are…green. But they

have some raw and unstudied talent."

Pressing his tongue against the roof of his mouth, he considered how best to spare her feelings. The success of her Memorial Day show owed everything to novelty and not the cast. The teens' understanding of the script bordered on satirical. He needed more than accidental comedy for the shows to spark his resurgence. "You might be surprised by our town. In high school, I volunteered at the retirement center. The seniors loved group sing-along."

"We're talking about something a little bigger than gathering around a piano."

"True, and I helped at the center over a decade ago. I don't know the current level of talent. It's an idea." He shrugged. "You don't have to hire anyone you don't like. I'm the director. I'll be the bad guy."

"I don't want to disenchant anyone. I like the enthusiasm."

"Lucky for you, I have a long history of disappointing everyone." He winked. "I can handle the town's collective ire." *Why did I say that?* He needed his boss's confidence. Highlighting his past wasn't likely to help his future.

She frowned.

"I'm kidding." He tightened his grip on the bundle, the notebook's spiral coils digging into flesh.

"If holding auditions helps, I'll support you." She stopped walking and turned, pressing together her lips in a straight line.

"What?"

"If you think they praise me, you should hear the compliments I get on a daily basis for employing the golden boy. The town stands behind you."

Believing her would ease a lot of the disquiet in his soul. He studied the ground and let her words wash over him. Coming home had never been his end goal, but he was glad for the safe haven to rest his ego. "I left town to escape a dogmatically practical man who never understood my dream. I moved zip codes, but I never really left New Hope. This place is always with me."

"You sound like Jill." She lifted one corner of her mouth.

He shifted the binders and notebook, running a free hand over his face. "I don't deserve your praise. She loves this town in a way I've never understood. I appreciate her commitment, but I struggle with her unwavering loyalty."

"She's dedicated to people, too. Like you."

"Even when she shouldn't be," he murmured. "Dad got sick, and she told me not to come home. I knew better. She needed help, but I stayed away."

Dani stepped forward, the separation narrowing from feet to inches.

His skin tingled, the hairs standing on end. She grazed his forearm with her fingertips as light as a landing butterfly. Staring at the point of contact, he frowned. Why should such an inconsequential gesture stir such a response? She was his boss, and he wasn't sticking around town. Nothing could happen.

"I've learned you can't hurt yourself over other people's choices." She leaned close. "Especially when the decisions are made on your behalf."

Her warm breath tickled his cheeks. He jerked his arm. "Is that why you're here? Did someone make a choice for you?"

Stepping back, she wrinkled her forehead. With

crossed arms, she raised her bundle to her chest. "I'm lucky to know your sister and live in New Hope."

He clenched his jaw, the defensive words scraped like a rake over his nerve endings. Once again, he lashed at her for his issues. "I'm sorry. I didn't mean to say any—"

"Don't worry about it." She shrugged and smiled. "Without Jill, I wouldn't have opened by Memorial Day or at all. My project's success depends on her support. I don't want to use her."

"I understand the feeling." He muttered under his breath. Shaking his head, he dropped his gaze from her too-bright grin to the ground and spied a toe rapidly brushing against the rough pavement. With her constant toe tapping, she shouldn't have any shoes left. His perpetual second-guessing should have destroyed his stomach lining weeks ago. Together, they were quite a pair. She agreed to his request and shared more personal information than an employer should. He trusted her. No one had a clear vision of the future. Why did he expect her to answer questions he hadn't asked? He cleared his throat. "Do we have time for some coffee at the diner?"

"Only if Shirley has pie." She darted her tongue over her lips and strolled past.

Overdressed for New Hope, she strode off. She really wanted to stay? He frowned. If she was dressed for where she was going, she charted a course to a destination as far away as possible. *Trust actions, not looks or words.*

She spun and cocked her head to one side. "You coming?"

He forced a tight smile and jogged the half block to

join her. Sharing a piece of pie was an innocuous invitation. For the time being, he chose to follow her. His every action and decision remained his alone.

****

Open mouth, insert coffee.

In the last booth in the Come Again Diner the next morning, Dani nearly levitated off the seat. After months of practice, she hadn't mastered brewing a decent cup of basic black coffee at home or in the tiny kitchenette backstage at the theater. Of course, her poor kitchen skills provided a good excuse for avoiding both the piles of laundry at her rental cottage and the guy she'd nearly kissed in her office.

On her next sip, she jerked, the jolt of caffeine electrifying her nervous system. She needed food. Until she sorted through her latest dilemma, however, her swirling stomach refused cooperation. When she'd said the words aloud to Paul yesterday, she finally linked her thoughts. Her deep-rooted fear—using Jill for her own advancement—gripped her tight.

Without Jill's guidance, Dani didn't know where she would be. She didn't want her friend running in circles and working long hours. Jill's stubborn dedication to abandon an unfinished task, however, opposed Dani's intentions. Short of changing the locks, Dani couldn't stop Jill from being the first to arrive at the theater and the last to leave.

To grow her business, Dani had to scale up, hiring more help and delegating to others. While the kitchen manager role posted on a job placement site was the top priority, an experienced stage manager could assume many of Jill's tasks. Dani wanted her righthand woman focused on big picture ideas, not worrying over ordering supplies and calling contractors.

She shifted in her seat. Why had the realization to ease Jill's workload only formed after talking to Paul? Why was he so easy to chat with, even when he made her squirm? Half the time she looked for an escape route in case his stormy, steel-colored eyes flashed a warning. The rest of the time she fought a physical pull. If she leaned into him, would his arms wrap around her waist in a tight squeeze?

Over the front door, the bell chimed.

Lifting her gaze, Dani spotted Jill. Dani drained the rest of her coffee, set the mug on the table, and pressed cool hands to hot cheeks. Nothing could happen with her friend's brother.

"You okay? You're scowling." Jill slid across the bench opposite.

I'm better off making faces at you than chasing after your twin. Dani dropped her arms. "I'm fine. I'm arguing with myself."

Jill lifted both eyebrows. "Who's winning?"

"With any luck, the angels of my better nature." Dani drummed her fingers on the smooth tabletop.

Shirley swept past. Sliding a short stack of pancakes onto the table, she filled both mugs and sighed.

Under Shirley's glare, Dani tucked a tendril behind her ear and nibbled her bottom lip. How many cups had she drunk? The scent of butter melting on Jill's breakfast wafted past Dani's nose, and she pressed a shaky hand to her twisted stomach. "After this cup, I'm probably done."

"Mmm." Shirley arched an eyebrow. "You should be." She sashayed toward the next table.

Dani blew across her steaming mug and raised the cup, hiding her grin. No one ever cared about the nutritional deficit in her diet. Shirley's interference officially signaled Dani was a local.

"Are you moving offices?" Jill pointed to the papers fanned on the table, grabbing the napkin-wrapped fork and knife.

"I needed better light. I have good news." Dani rested her chin in a palm. "We have enough money to hire a stage manager."

"We do?" Jill sliced through the pancakes.

"I'd like to fill the role before the Fourth of July show. We have plenty of work for a full-time employee. The sooner I can hand over the minor tasks, the better. You need to focus on big picture stuff."

"You should talk to Paul." Jill poured syrup over the short stack.

Dani nibbled her cheek. Yesterday, she touched his arm and leaned forward. She intended commiseration but stared at his mouth, haywire hormones urging her to make a move. Her hand still burned from his warm skin. She wasn't ready to face him. At her current rate of inappropriate physical proximity, she'd be lucky to avoid litigation for workplace harassment. She shuddered. "Can't you help? You know everyone." Her voice cracked, and she cringed.

"I could, but Paul will be the stage manager's boss. The stage manager really should mesh with him. I'll text him to meet us outside. I think he went to Rob's."

The muscles in Dani's cheeks twitched, and her weak smile slipped. If she had to meet him, she refused an ambush. "Don't bother. I'll find him." Reaching inside the purse, she pulled cash from her wallet, left the money under her mug, and gathered her papers off the table. She slipped from the bench and stuffed the notes into her purse. "Enjoy your breakfast. I'll see you at the theater later."

Lifting her eyebrows, Jill grinned.

Dani blinked and squinted, refocusing on her friend. Had she imagined the sly smile?

Jill stuffed a big bite of pancake in her mouth and flashed a thumbs-up.

Swinging her oversized purse onto her shoulder, Dani strolled through the restaurant. If she persisted in projecting her jumbled emotions onto others, she risked alienating her staff. Pushing out the door, she dropped the handle as the bell jingled and shielded her gaze against the bright glare.

On the street corner, Paul turned.

Her breath hitched. He moved in slow motion, like obeying a director's cues. The sunlight perfectly brightened the angular planes of his face and highlighted his chiseled jaw. She swallowed the lump in her throat and tightened both hands on the purse straps. If she didn't balance correctly, she'd fall from the weight of the heavy bag and his steady gaze. With a town full of people depending on her promises, she was here to improve everyone's life. Her position in the community depended on her earning potential. She had no time for any distraction.

Paul jogged across the sidewalk and held out his phone, the screen flashing with a picture of Jill. "Hey, I got the text from Jill. What's up?"

She rocked back and forth from her heels to the toes of her high-heeled sandals. "Can we walk and talk?" Her limbs pulsed with energy. Her heartbeat thudded in her ears.

With one arm, he gestured to lead the way.

Rolling her foot forward, she caught the toe of her shoe in a sidewalk crack. She wobbled, and her knees buckled.

He extended his arms.

Lurching forward, she locked her legs. She stopped short of his outstretched hands. Her purse collided with his chest. *Maybe I should have fallen.* She curled her toes inside her shoes and straightened. Engineering an excuse for his embrace was pathetic and a little too tempting. Forcing a laugh, she swung the bag to her other shoulder. "I'm fine. I drank all the coffee Shirley had."

"No worries. I've been known to do the same thing, when needed."

She strolled a couple steps.

He caught up and synchronized her pace.

With the added height of her espadrilles, her cheek reached his shoulder. Carrying her purse on the outside, she could reach for his hand. Her arm hung inches away, and her skin tingled. "Do you remember our conversation yesterday?"

"Everything."

His words brushed her cheek in a whisper of a touch. A gasp caught in her throat. Raising a fist to her mouth, she coughed. If she continued their conversation much longer, she'd need medical attention. She narrowed her gaze, ignoring her treacherous body. "Sorry, frog in my throat. I specifically meant about Jill? Not wanting to abuse her good heart?"

"Yes, of course."

"I ran the numbers. We can hire more help. To

start, I want an experienced stage manager. I need her for more important plans and grander things than calling Rob with the order."

"Are you sure she wants someone else to be the liaison with Rob?"

She studied him from the corner of her eye.

He bent his head, clasping hands behind his back.

Tension radiated off the tight lips and stiff posture. Was he upset about Rob and Jill? *Reach for his hand and discover what happens.* She gripped her purse with both hands and kept walking. Comforting an employee definitely crossed a line.

"Do you have anyone in mind for the new job?"

"No, I hoped Jill had a lead. She said you'd need to pick a person since they'll report to you."

"Seems fair, very Jill-like." He nodded, and the corner of his mouth lifted.

"Very." She rubbed her upper arms, smoothing down the tiny hairs. His contagious smile warmed her from the inside out. "I'm still getting used to her deference."

"Me, too." He chuckled.

His low laughter tugged at the tight coil wrapped like a belt around her fluttering stomach. She caught her lower lip with her teeth and stumbled, her shoe catching in a crack on the pavement. Stretching her arms forward, she brushed his bicep with a hand.

Wrapping an arm around her waist, he lifted her against his body.

She focused on his dilated pupils, her chest rapidly rising with shallow breaths. "Sorry," she murmured. "Thank you. I'm tossing these shoes."

He lowered her to the sidewalk. "What a shame."

Staring at the ground, she stepped away from his heat. His actions were merely the polite behavior of a concerned friend and certainly nothing to warrant her jumping pulse. She spotted the square cut in half by a deep, jagged crack. She frowned and craned her neck to study the storefront. The brick building had gaps in the mortar and chipped paint on the window frames. She couldn't march inside and complain to the owner. More than likely, a bank possessed the deed.

On second glance, she studied the detailed masonry. The bricks over the door and front window formed a diamond pattern. At the top, dental molding created a detailed border under the roofline. Once upon a time, someone loved and cared about the building. Warmth flooded her body, and she tapped her tingling fingers against her thighs. With the success of her business, she could spur more businesses to thrive downtown. If she focused, she could do some good. "Back to our conversation. Do you know anyone interested in the job?"

"I do." He stroked his jaw. "Andy Cadman. He was a couple years ahead of me in school. He's a good man, and he's had a hard life. He's been working part-time jobs here and there. With a full-time opportunity, he'll step up."

"What do you mean hard life?" She pressed a hand against the stitch in her side. New Hope wasn't immune to modern troubles. The townsfolk encouraged her to put her trust and faith in community. Fighting against her natural inclination to assume the worst, she didn't want her illusion about the town to shatter.

"After an injury at the factory decades ago, he got hooked on painkillers. He lost his family and stole from the hardware store." Paul ran a hand through his hair. "Rob could have pressed charges. Instead, he saw a guy who could be any of us for a poor twist of fate and helped pay for a stay in rehab. Andy's been clean for a few years now. He'll do a good job."

"Okay, I trust you."

Grabbing her hand, he raised it to his lips and kissed the back of her fingers.

She held her breath. Her skin tingled from the press of his mouth against her knuckles. She didn't pull away from the sudden intimacy.

He squeezed her fingers.

The gentle pressure was friendly, not flirtatious. His cotton and soap scent tickled her nose. For a moment, she was warm and safe. *With him?* She drew in a deep breath.

With a nod, he dropped her hand and jogged across the road, heading down Main Street on his new mission.

Her throat tightened. She was in too deep, and she only had herself to blame.

Chapter Seven

Seated behind the upright piano center stage, Paul hovered fingers above the keys. The spotlight burned his neck. Tilting his head toward the audience, he blinked his watery gaze and squinted. Past the bright light, he couldn't make out anything in the Fourth of July crowd. He swiveled his neck and scanned through the wings backstage. *Where is she?* The youthful cast met his silent plea with blank stares and shrugs.

A cough echoed in the auditorium.

Cold sweat beaded on his forehead. He didn't move. If he lifted an arm and wiped his brow, he might find the courage to hop off the bench and run from the stage. Lady Liberty, aka his boss, should have strutted across the boards five minutes ago to lead the finale. She loved her part during rehearsal. Was Dani intentionally sabotaging his show? Was his onstage abandonment part of some greater test? Shutting his eyes, he breathed in through his nose. With no other choice, he'd have to take charge.

"Good evening, ladies and gentlemen. I'm looking for a friend. Guess I stumbled into your finale. My humblest apologies," a throaty, feminine voice said over the sound system.

Claps, cheers, and whistles boomed through the theater.

Frozen in place, he turned and focused on the

figure strolling across the stage.

Carrying a microphone in one hand, a petite blonde sashayed in sequins.

With her wide grin and shoulders-back stride, she exuded cool confidence and star power. He'd witnessed the same self-possession during his few encounters with major celebrities in LA. He blinked and rubbed his eyes. His Lady Liberty, aka Dani, ghosted him before the rousing finale. In her place, sitcom TV darling, Kara Kensington, appeared. *I'm hallucinating*. He grew up watching her show. The twenty-two-minute, weekly broadcasts revolved around Kara as a pair of twins getting into and out of scrapes. Each episode ended with a feel-good message. As a kid, he was mesmerized and dabbled in fan fiction scriptwriting. In a way, she sparked his career. Why was she here? She couldn't be the real, living-breathing star, could she? Light bounced off Kara's sparkly dress and golden tresses, adding a fuzzy aura to her outline and enhancing the dream-like quality.

"I heard you playing and singing, darling. You're pretty good. What do you think? Can we give these nice people a show?" She widened her blue eyes ever so slightly without dropping her megawatt smile.

The audience roared with laughter.

Her deep voice recalled silver screen sirens of a bygone age. With a nod, he wiped wet palms on his pants. He dashed fingers over the keys and played the next patriotic tune from muscle memory. After the first few bars of "Yankee Doodle Dandy," he spotted her sashaying in his direction and slid down the bench.

She settled on the smooth seat, facing the audience. "Oooh. I know this tune. You probably do, too. I'd love if you helped me sing." Resting her head on his shoulder, she gazed at him.

He stiffened, drawing his arms closer to his body. To the crowd, they might make a pretty pair. Up close, she shot him a hard, no-nonsense stare.

She mouthed *sing.*

Gulping, he joined her in the song and then the next two. As he focused on melding his vocal range to the performance, the rest of the world fell away. Their voices harmonized. She might have been silently commanding him, but he happily followed. He read her cues and sang better than ever. Expensive perfume tickled his nose, and he sniffed. Up close, she was even better looking than on TV, her delicate features exaggerated with makeup. *She kind of looks like Dani.*

With a flourish, he ended the third song.

Kara winked and slid off the piano bench.

He pressed clammy hands against his thighs and studied the keyboard. He didn't want her to leave. Onstage, he discovered something miraculous. He and Kara Kensington had the sort of chemistry for real entertainment success. Why was she here? Was she real? His stomach twisted, and he dragged in a shaky breath.

"Thank you, ladies and gentlemen." Kara sashayed around the piano.

Lifting his chin, he followed her progress as rapt as the audience. He hadn't watched one of her TV shows since childhood. Of course, she'd become more infamous for her life in the age of tabloids and reality series. He hadn't tracked her exploits, but avoiding the occasional tidbit about her was almost impossible.

Under the spotlight, she angled her body into the

light. "You have been a marvelous audience, and I'm having more fun tonight than in the past year. How about one last song? Let's get everyone onstage."

For a petite woman, she commanded attention with charisma and charm. During his years in Hollywood, he hadn't been exposed to star power firsthand. She was mesmerizing. How had she found the theater? Where was Dani?

The cast filed onto the stage, absorbing Kara into the center of the crowd.

He played the national anthem.

The cast sang.

Peeking over the top of the piano, he scanned through the familiar faces of teens but couldn't spot Dani. The stage filled with every member of both cast and crew. In the crush, he lost track of Kara and frowned. Kara Kensington might help him with the big break he needed. He couldn't let his chance disappear.

The song concluded.

Thunderous applause filled the auditorium.

With a glance over his shoulder, he spotted Dani and stood.

Lady Liberty entered from the wings, holding aloft her torch.

Beaming, Dani turned her head and the corner of her smile slipped, her forehead wrinkling.

Lifting one shoulder, he half shrugged and accepted her silent apology. If anything, he owed her thanks because her delay led to his once-in-a-lifetime opportunity. Fighting against the slight twinge in his stomach, he scanned past her, resuming his search for Kara. The star vanished. *If she'd been real.* Was her appearance fate or fantasy? Should he run after her, or would he risk the growing connection with Dani?

Dani stepped forward and bowed.

The cast and crew parted around her.

The crowd quieted.

"Thank you for coming to our town for tonight's show." She raised her chin. "A very special thanks to our genius playwright and lead performer. Ladies and gentlemen, without him we would not be here tonight enjoying a marvelous evening. Please another round of applause for Mr. Paul Howell."

Behind the piano, he hunched and dropped his chin. Her public praise was too over the top. He wanted answers not exaggerated compliments.

Cheers boomed. The crowd jumped to their feet in a standing ovation.

Over her shoulder, she frowned and waved the torch to the spot at her side.

He shook his head. No, she earned the praise.

She rolled her eyes. "Looks like someone has a case of stage fright."

The audience guffawed.

His mouth filled with a sour taste. Clenching his jaw, he swallowed a retort. She might attempt some levity at his expense but a petulant comeback dangled off his tongue. *You abandoned me.*

With one eyebrow arched, she approached, wrapped an arm around his torso, and guided him through a bow.

As he straightened, he moved away, but her grip tightened on his waist. Was she holding onto him in celebration? Or restraining him from escape? He inhaled her light citrusy scent, a refreshing break after Kara's heavy perfume. Sighing, he relaxed into her hold. He had no reason to treat her with suspicion. Grinning for the crowd, he reached for her waist.

She sucked in a breath.

His pulse quickened, a jolt shooting down his spine. He raised his outside arm and waved to the crowd. He liked and trusted her. She must have a good reason for her delay.

Clapping echoed through the cavernous auditorium. The curtain closed.

Dani dropped her grip and stepped away.

At the loss of her warmth in his arms, he shivered. Rubbing both hands, he widened his stance and narrowed his gaze. "What happened? Where were you? Did I just sing with Kara Kensington?"

Dani set the torch and bible on the piano and held up her palms.

Taking a step forward, he crashed into her hands.

She drew in a quick breath.

A buzz of electricity zinged through his body. He stared at her delicate fingers splayed on his chest. He exhaled and forced down his shoulders. "Sorry."

"It's fine." Her chin trembled. "Just give me a minute." She dropped both hands and stepped back. Unpinning the crown from her head, she shook her hair.

He set his jaw and gritted his teeth. Her movements were slow and steady. He imagined her reaction to the accidental touch. She was professional and courteous but not flirty. He had to stop overanalyzing each encounter and fantasizing she shared the same magnetic response to each moment.

"I was caught between the kitchen and the hallway. Dessert en flambé was a near disaster with our old sprinkler system. When we lit the first plate in the hallway, we set off one alarm and almost rained out the theater. Luckily, everyone looks fairly dry in the audience. I haven't heard any complaints about the lack of char on the baked Alaska desserts. Great job on the show. Really, stellar work."

The warmth of her smile cloaked him in a hug. He hadn't worked for anyone's approval for a long time. On a clear path to do his best, he'd sought name recognition alone. Basking in the glow of her approval, he couldn't remember why on earth he'd been so dogged about his pursuit for personal stardom. What could be better than success for the entire community in his hometown? "Thanks. The show came together in the end."

"I loved how you included the town's history. Your show was a hit." She grinned broader, stretching her cheeks and flashing her white teeth. "You deserved every second of the standing ovation."

"Did you watch?"

She nodded. "I snuck into the wings a few times to catch the show. I'm sure I'll watch some videos on the Internet tonight."

"You think so?" He clenched and unclenched tingling hands into fists at his side. He couldn't shake the dream-like quality. If his show resonated with online viewers, he might field calls from Hollywood for his own merits and not depend on Kara Kensington or Dani for a big break.

"Absolutely. It's probably not too early to get started on the Labor Day show. We might run two extra performances." Crossing her arms, she darted her gaze through backstage and leaned close. "Or maybe three."

"Wow." He sucked in a breath and dropped his

chin to his chest. She gave him a chance. "Thank you." Returning home full-time wasn't his plan, but he couldn't rule out the possibility of staying for longer than planned. Every show offered an opportunity to refine his skills. He didn't need to rush. If he had a choice, he had hope. He tightened his chest and deep inside his rib cage his heart squeezed. If his big break happened here, he wouldn't seek success at the expense of family. He could have both.

What about Kara?

Lifting his face, he stared at nothing and frowned. Craning his neck, he scanned the growing crowd. Dani disappeared. He hated the sinking sensation in his stomach. She should be the center of the applause. Instead, she disappeared. He pinched the bridge of his nose. What was real? What had he invented? If he searched for Kara Kensington, he'd shatter the hard-earned good opinion of his neighbors for a mirage. He shook his head and dislodged the image. In no reality would a major star appear on stage at a dinner theater in a one-stoplight town. Someone must have been dressed in costume and—in the terror of the moment being stranded on stage—he hadn't recognized the person.

Chuckling, Paul slipped through the crowd to the stage door, congratulating cast and crew on his way. If the mystery woman was Kara Kensington, Dani would tell him. Dani commiserated over his betrayal from former friends. She wouldn't hold back the truth, especially if she watched the video of his finale. The onstage connection was undeniable and based solely on skills. What he felt for Dani resonated deep in his bones. With so much at stake, he trusted her. She wouldn't keep a secret, and neither would he.

****

The curtains swung shut on the Fourth of July show.

Onstage, the cast cheered and surged inward.

Dani tightened her grip. *Keep him here until she leaves.* She twitched, her fingers digging into his muscles.

Turning, he drew together his brows. "What happened?"

She dropped a hand, still warm from his hot skin, and flexed the fingers against her side. His gray-blue eyes sparkled like polished silver, staring through her. She shivered. When she finished extinguishing the fire in the hallway, she stopped in her tracks at the familiar lilt cooing under the doors. Changing course, she raced behind the curtains, slipped into her costume, and entered stage left. In the second before she crossed to the spotlight, she studied the pair she promised to introduce. Their voices harmonized perfectly. As a couple, they were striking.

Kara sauntered to the center of the stage.

Paul played the national anthem.

With that cue, Dani grabbed the bible, raised the prop torch, and strode across the stage. She intercepted Kara from starting another song and recommended Kara escape to Dani's office before a mob formed. Dani rolled her neck. Appealing to Kara's ego and self-importance was the surest way to manipulate her. Dani hated deploying the tactics but had no other choice.

"Where were you? Was that Kara Kensington?"

Every question hit with the precision of a trained marksman. She pressed her tongue against the roof of her mouth. *Confess now, and he's gone.* She set the props on top of the piano. Turning, she held out her palms.

He stepped forward.

She collided with a wall of muscle, her fingers flattening against his chest. The sizzle started in her palms and crept through her forearms into her ribs and shoulders. Tipping back her chin, she studied him.

His Adam's apple bobbed, and he gulped. "Sorry."

Don't lose him. "It's fine. Just give me a minute." She broke away, pulling the bobby pins from the crown in her hair. Her hands trembled. Between the dual threats of his nearness and the star lurking somewhere in the building, Dani struggled with emulating normalcy. She cleared her throat. "Dessert en flambé was a near disaster with our old sprinkler system. Luckily, everyone looks fairly dry." She forced a laugh. Water pouring from the ceiling's system and drenching the audience wouldn't have been the big finale she wanted. If Kara was caught in the shower, she wouldn't have strolled across the stage like she owned it. Once again, Kara swept in for the accolades of Dani's hard work. Dani gritted her teeth. "Great job on the show. Really, stellar work."

Stuffing both hands in his front pockets, he shrugged and lifted the corner of his mouth.

His bemused smile extended from his upturned lips to his softened gaze, the fine lines crinkling around the eyes. Her congratulations mattered? A wave of happiness warmed her from head to toe.

"Thanks. The show came together in the end."

"I loved how you included the town's history. Your show was a hit." She scrunched her nose, ignoring the tickle in her nostrils. He'd achieved more than she could have imagined. With one show, he proved his skill. If he stayed, he'd make her dreams come true. She owed him the same. *Not with Kara.* "You deserved every second of your standing ovation." Her voice shook.

"Did you watch?"

She nodded. "I snuck into the wings a few times to catch the show. I'm sure I'll watch videos on the Internet tonight."

"You think so?"

"Absolutely. It's probably not too early for you to get started on the Labor Day show. We might have to run two extra performances." Leaning close, she scanned for any eavesdroppers and breathed in his clean scent. After a rousing performance, she sniffed sweat mixed with his typical fresh from the dryer cotton. *And adrenaline?* She gulped. Losing him would be hard from both a professional and personal standpoint. Watching him leave with Kara would crush Dani's ribs. "Or maybe even three."

"Wow." He sucked in a breath. "Thank you." He shut his eyes.

He glowed. With a successful show behind him, he deserved every bit of praise. *Kara will launch him to stardom and ruin.* A flash of sparkle caught in Dani's peripheral vision. Holding her breath, she tightened her smile and turned toward the source. Instead of spotting her sequin-clad frenemy, Dani met the gaze of another cast member holding a gem-encrusted prop. Exhaling a shaky breath, she relaxed her cheeks and rubbed her aching jaw. She grabbed the torch, bible, and crown. Until she determined Kara's motives, Dani couldn't deny her future teetered on the catwalk hanging over the stage.

A crewmember jostled her.

The torch slipped from her grasp. She had enough to worry about without adding broken props to her list. Kneeling on the ground, she snatched the foam and cardboard flame. If she hustled Kara onto the next plane without anyone ever realizing the starlet graced town with her presence, Dani had a chance to save Paul from his ill-advised dream. With her hands on her thighs, she rose and slid through the crowd toward the exit. The excited buzz of conversation increased from murmurs to cheers. At the stage door, she deposited her props on a table and scanned the scene.

In center stage, Paul stood head and shoulders above the crowd. He twisted his neck.

Her chest tightened. She had to leave. If she stayed any longer, she'd be spotted. He might follow her and discover Kara. Under the heavy folds of the sequin toga, she braced both hands against her sides and counted to ten on her next inhalation. Exhaling, she struggled with the tight cramp in her belly. If she didn't address the source of her stress, she wouldn't relax, no matter how much meditation she practiced.

Unsnapping the clasp on her left shoulder, she also unhooked the extra strength safety pin securing the bulky toga in place. The heavy fabric cascaded to the floor, leaving her clad in a black shirt and leggings. Without the added glitz and glimmer, she faded into obscurity. She glanced toward Paul.

In the middle of the group, he grinned and high-fived the cast and crew.

Shutting her eyes, she focused on his deep chuckle mingling with the congratulations. She sighed. Another night, she could join them. Opening her eyes, she grabbed the toga off the ground, draped it over the props, and slipped through the stage door. On the balls of her feet in her character shoes, she tiptoed through the long hall. She didn't have to worry about drawing any attention.

The audience exited at the back of the auditorium. The carpeted stretch between the box office and stage was deserted. She couldn't risk discovery. With a final scan of her surroundings—and reassurance no one lingered nearby—she opened her office door a crack and slid inside.

"Dani, he's perfect. I'm taking him home." Kara stood in front of the cluttered desk, fingers splaying on her tiny waist and one shoulder tilting forward.

"Shhh." Dani shut the door and turned the lock. With years of lessons, Kara trained her voice to carry from stage to the rafters. Dani pressed her ear and cheek against the solid door, straining for any sound. Silence greeted her. Sagging her shoulders, she turned and faced her visitor.

Under the dull fluorescent lighting, she shimmered. *Always a star.* Dani frowned. Did she categorize Kara as a friend, a one-time confidante, or an enemy? Until last autumn, Dani considered Kara a sister. Dani barely repressed her instinct to embrace Kara. With more time, Dani hoped for a reconciliation. Today was too soon.

Scrubbing at her mascara-encrusted lashes, Dani rolled her neck. In a drab office in the middle of nowhere, Kara filled every inch of the space. Dani rubbed a hand over her nose, crossed her arms, and leaned against the door. "What are you doing here?" If her friend noticed the defensive posture, or sensed Dani was, in fact, barricading Kara in the room, the star gave no indication.

Pushing off the cracked veneer edge, Kara walked behind the messy desk and claimed the boss's chair. She rested her feet on top of the papers scattered over the surface, crossing her ankles.

Setting her jaw, Dani waited for a verbal response. Demanding attention, by any means necessary, remained Kara's personality hallmark. As kids, Kara caught Dani's attention with her big smile and over-the-top laugh. While Dani longed for a quiet space to curl up and blend in, Kara performed best in the center.

"Your place is so cute. When you mentioned your idea, I had no clue it would be so…professional." Kara threw back her head and giggled.

At the familiar practiced titter, Dani cringed. If their friendship was an emotional rollercoaster, Kara operated the controls, and Dani clutched the safety straps for self-preservation. *Not again and not today.* Dani popped one hip and leveled her best *get-on-with-it* glare.

"Can't a girl swing by to surprise her best friend?"

Dani scrunched her nose at the sugar-sweet, phony tone. In New Hope, she trusted someone's word. Here, she didn't worry a lifelong best friend would smile while stabbing her through the heart. Her safe refuge, the Kensington home, was the most carefully constructed set of her life. "Maybe if that *girl* wasn't America's sweetheart and didn't appear dressed for an awards show."

Kara turned her palms to the ceiling.

"If we were still friends," Dani murmured, "the surprise would be better." A flicker in the honey blonde's blue eyes almost convinced Dani she'd struck a nerve.

Clasping hands under her chin, Kara tilted her head. "I'm sorry about the whole mess with Zach."

Bracing herself on the doorframe, Dani slipped off her character heels one at a time. "Why now? When you ran off with my boyfriend and pitched a reality show about falling in love on set, neither of you cared about my feelings. What changed?"

"I chose wrong. I should have picked you. Please, believe me." Her voice pitched high.

Dani balanced in a modified yoga tree pose and massaged cramped toes. For a second, Kara wasn't a cultivated character. The squeak in her tone recalled her hushed whispers on the long-running TV sitcom. Kara worried over the end of the show and her next step. At the time, she was too scared to maintain her role playing. Had fear motivated her to track down Dani? "No one picks me. You're not the first." She studied the ground.

"When's the last time you spoke to your mom?"

A chill slithered down Dani's spine. She stopped balancing and set her feet wide on the cold floor. Kara danced between careless and thoughtful with the efficiency of a trained professional. "I sent her an email, but you know how she is." With her toes, Dani traced the cracks in the linoleum floor tiles.

"I know."

Unwilling to meet what she knew would be a solemn expression, Dani dipped her chin. Kara hadn't been told any secrets. She lived them alongside Dani. When Dani discovered the discrepancy in her savings, she sat at Kara's kitchen table and worked through the numbers. Forgiving Mom for pilfering Dani's savings was easy. At one point, Mom was a thorough and capable manager and agent. Her skills rivaled Kara's for creating opportunities and landing roles. Mom earned the money alongside Dani. No longer a dependent, Dani could make a living without the complications of involving Mom. Dani wanted to move forward as a family, but Mom ignored Dani's reconciliation attempts.

At one time, Kara was a welcome sounding board for Dani's ideas, hopes, and fears. Had Kara been a real friend years ago? Or had she performed the role of close companion for two plus decades? Dani fought for a relationship with Mom alone and wouldn't discuss details. Dani needed answers. She jerked her gaze to her former friend. "Why are you here?"

"I owe you an apology." Swinging her legs off the desk, Kara smacked her heels against the ground. "I'm sorrier than you'll ever know about the whole mess."

"Why?" Dani's chin trembled, tears stinging the back of her throat. After the announcement hit the news, the media hounded her for a response. She'd hidden in her apartment, curled into a tight ball, and cried for hours. When her tears dried, she realized she wasn't hurt by her boyfriend's deception. She was better off without him. The betrayal from her best friend scalded.

"You know how it is." Dragging her fingertips along the edge, Kara traced the desk with pink polished nails. "One day, you're turning down work. The next, you can't get an audition. Zach approached me. I didn't want to hurt you, but I also didn't want you committing your life to that kind of guy."

Dani gasped and blinked. "You stole my boyfriend to save me?" Scrubbing her lashes, she dragged in a deep breath. She couldn't piece together the odd rationalization and trusted neither her eyes nor ears. If Kara really believed her actions were justified, why show up at the theater?

On the desk, Kara twisted together both hands into a white-knuckle fisted grip.

Constant cosmetic enhancements restricted Kara's facial expressions, and her brow remained smooth. The blue veins popping to the surface on the back of her hands told the truth.

"I'm sorry. The news hit social media before I had a chance to explain." Kara unlaced her fingers and dropped shaky hands to the desk. "I landed the movie. Zach had a part. I didn't know his role was miniscule. He used me for attention."

Once again, Dani was collateral damage. The words landed like a punch to the chin, and she jerked back and winced. No matter how much time passed or how she willed herself to toughen, Kara would always strike Dani's heart. She sucked in a breath and pressed hands to her hips. "Well, everything worked in the end. I left town to avoid seeing your faces everywhere. Before I boarded the plane, I heard about your movie, your reality contract, and your new scripted TV show. Congrats."

"As it happens," Kara murmured and focused on the ground, her lips pursing.

Here comes the ask... Dani crossed her arms and waited. Kara's next big thing was always a few inches out of reach. Growing up, Dani shared her friend's eager search for a breakout part that would change everything. At some point between childhood and adulthood, she snapped to reality. She refused to chase something elusive and immeasurable. For tangible happiness, she required a steady and secure future.

If she thought Zach, the handsome, up-and-coming actor from a nuclear family in the suburbs, was her chance at typical life, who could blame her? He was different. When she imagined she couldn't fall for anyone else's lies, she'd been his willing and eager victim. Kara grabbed Dani's boyfriend and ran off after the next big maybe. By that point, Dani opened her eyes too wide to shut.

Without worrying over her demise, Dani bought a rundown movie theater in the middle of nowhere and left LA on the first flight. Seven months in, she appreciated how far she'd come. If Mom answered her, she had a chance at contentment. "I don't have time to guess. Tell me what's happening. Why are you here?"

"I'm out." Kara picked at her sequin gown. She raised her chin and shrugged. "Zach and I filmed the reality show. None of the tape was good enough to air. The ratings for the TV movie were so bad the network won't replay it. I've been recast with someone younger and slimmer on my TV show."

"I'm sorry." Nibbling her bottom lip, Dani crossed arms over her belly. Scanning the starlet again, Dani noticed the dark circles under her eyes and the jutting collarbone. Kara was little more than a skeleton. Production found someone smaller? *Someone is always better.* Dani held her breath. If Kara suffered public humiliation over losing her latest roles, she was dangerous and willing to use any means necessary. Dani had been an unwitting pawn once, and she

114

wouldn't repeat the experience.

"Yeah." Kara snorted. "Maybe you are, and maybe I deserve my fate. I came to apologize. In person, avoiding me isn't as easy as silencing my calls."

Dani pressed her tongue to her teeth. Heat crept up her cheeks.

"I couldn't find you. But something miraculous happened." Kara sat taller. "Did you hear us on stage? Did you see us? Who is your piano player? We could have something. If I took him to LA, I bet I could turn around my whole career."

Not on your life. A month ago, Dani promised Paul her show business connections. He overdelivered his side of the bargain. Without question, she would gain positive reviews and word-of-mouth acclaim from his excellent musical. With eight weeks until Labor Day, she had plenty of time to score and compose the next show without his help. She gulped. She didn't want to work by herself anymore. "Hear what?" Dani pitched her voice high and rubbed clammy palms against her black leggings.

When she mentioned her contacts, she ranked Kara number one on the list. Seeing the pair onstage, however, snapped something inside Dani. Could she offer up Paul on a silver platter to someone who would use him? Dani had other people in her network who could help him. After she hustled Kara out of town, she'd call her old manager and email casting agents. In a few more months, he'd be better suited for the fast-paced entertainment business.

In the meantime, she'd pay him and establish her business as a bona fide success. Providing him with a safe environment to rebuild his confidence, she would ease his return to Hollywood. Her help wasn't immediate but promised a better result. Ignoring her knotted stomach and the bitter taste filling her mouth, she cleared her throat. "Sorry, I missed your performance. Management issues. Speaking of, I better lock the building. Let's go." She pushed off the door. She might lie to herself about not caring what happened with their friendship or her estranged Mom, but she couldn't discourage Kara. "Come on, we can have a sleepover." She softened her expression.

Underneath the relentless career drive, Kara possessed a heart. Unfortunately, she focused on herself and ignored the people she hurt along the way. Dani couldn't let Paul be sucked into the Hollywood machine. He was a good guy, and Kara would use him without a second thought. Paul and Kara might argue Dani had no right to interfere. Dani couldn't picture either coming out ahead for Kara's plan. If Dani had to be the voice of reason and stop them, she would. Until she determined the best way to help everyone win, she'd keep them apart.

Chapter Eight

Paul scrubbed a hand over his face, rubbing dry eyes. After exiting the theater, he followed the crowd toward the hill behind the library for the grand finale of a long day. For the better part of thirty minutes, he sat cross-legged on an old picnic blanket in the grass. He should be tired, but he vibrated with unspent energy. Squinting into the dark, he scanned the scene.

Children raced past, their colored glow sticks and light-up necklaces briefly illuminating the crowd. The buzz of laughter and conversation filled the air.

Last week, the town council announced the first fireworks in half a decade. Tonight, everyone showed, eager for a revived municipal traditional. Growing up, he marked his year with the pyrotechnic display. He couldn't fathom how the community celebrated the holiday without the event for five years. From now on, he vowed to appreciate every town gathering.

He was eager for a celebration. Hopefully, his sister and Rob convinced Dani to join them. In the almost pitch-black night, he barely glimpsed the edge of the blanket. If he narrowed his gaze much longer, he'd need to visit the optometrist. After he imagined Kara Kensington on stage, he probably should have his vision checked. He ran a hand through his hair and sighed. He wouldn't need his sight to confirm Dani's presence. When she arrived, her sunshine scent would tickle his nose, and he would relax.

Before meeting Dani, he didn't understand knowing someone so intrinsically. After only weeks of acquaintance, he anticipated her words and actions. If he dropped his guard, he'd be in trouble. Falling in love seemed inevitable. With each moment, he drew closer toward staying in New Hope forever. But he couldn't.

Performing with Kara Kensington would catapult his flagging career out of the atmosphere. Three songs shouldn't be a solid basis for rewriting a future. Within the first few bars, however, he knew with clarity they had something special. He wasn't starstruck and the connection wasn't the emotional bond he shared with Dani. While onstage, he engaged with a sort of detached awareness of the scene. Together, he and Kara projected musical charisma. Was it enough? Did she have that same sort of chemistry with everyone? Kara had the connections Dani hinted she shared. He disliked the idea of skirting Dani to chase a lead. If he didn't grab an opportunity for his dream, he'd always wonder what could have happened. Why on earth would Kara Kensington appear in the middle of nowhere on the Fourth of July?

A flashlight shined on his face, blinding him. He held up both hands, peering through splayed fingers.

"Scoot over, honey." Shirley's deep voice boomed.

On hands and knees, he tugged the blanket over a foot and smoothed down the corners.

Ted opened two folding camp chairs.

"What are you doing here alone?" Shirley sank into a chair.

Blinking, Paul considered a response. She rarely asked questions without already knowing the answer.

As the co-owner of one of the few businesses to weather the economic storm, she earned the trust of her neighbors, and many spoke freely at her diner. He cleared his throat and leaned back, resting on his elbows and extending his legs. "I'm not alone. I'm holding spots for Jill and Rob. They're heading over from the theater."

Ted grunted.

Shirley sniggered.

Paul disliked the implications in his companions' noises. "I left early to grab a good spot. They wanted to ask Dani to join us." Pushing up with both hands, he dragged his legs into a crossed position and rubbed a hand over the back of his burning neck. Under Shirley's steady gaze, he faltered with a continuing explanation. From personal experience, he knew Shirley let people convince themselves of their own lies until she set them straight.

"Huh. 'N so?" Shirley leaned back, the chair groaning.

Exhaling, Paul massaged his temples. The break from her unrelenting scrutiny was like the spotlight shifting to another actor, giving him rest in the wings. After a frustratingly short conversation, he lost track of Lady Liberty. Jill shoved him to the front of the crowd and elbowed him in the ribs. He thanked the cast and crew on behalf of Holidays, Inc. His impromptu speech was met with hearty applause, and he rubbed a hand along his clenched jaw. The triumph was Dani's not his, and she more than earned the right to be heaped with praise. Where was she?

"Well, you put on quite a show tonight," Shirley said. "You should be proud. I knew you had gumption but didn't realize you had talent. I expect you'll want to stay and put on another one."

In her typical, no-nonsense manner, Shirley included an exit clause in her acclaim, suggesting he stage only one more show. Before his impromptu performance with Kara Kensington, he decided on much more. In the aftermath, everything changed. He'd thank Dani for the opportunity, ask her about Kara, and escape before signing a contract to remain in New Hope for the next year. No, he wouldn't slip in a question about Kara in such a glib manner. He'd hold Dani's gaze and discuss the finale. More likely than not, the woman he sang with wasn't the star. Asking directly shouldn't impact anything. *Except what's happening off stage.*

His chest tightened, and he raised a hand to his aching ribs. If he abandoned Dani and New Hope at the first hint of stardom, he was an opportunist chasing after a starlet who—more than likely—wasn't real. Coming home hadn't been appealing. Desperation forced his return, but he was glad to rebuild himself and his battered ego. Would he really risk something positive for an apparition? If he stayed, he might miss his big shot in Hollywood. He was already on the wrong side of thirty with only half of his inheritance remaining. His options dwindled. Fear projected one last chance on a phantom. Rationally, he understood fame relied on a certain combination of hard work, talent, and timing. If he accepted his moment passed, what did he do next? *Stay and build something real.*

"Don't be in such a rush to chase a dream, or you'll miss something more important."

He frowned. "What's more important?"

"Happiness," Shirley said. "A good life. Solid work and a community."

Pressing hands on his thighs, he shifted forward. The conversation veered too close to a lecture. After thirty years of living, he trusted his instincts without outside input. He opened his mouth, ready with the protest tangled on his tongue, and quickly clamped together his lips. Studying her, he no longer flinched under the steady gaze of the older citizen who'd taken him to task as a teenager. The corners of her eyes crinkled in a soft smile. Her words weren't a lecture or condemnation against the punk kid his father swore he was. Shirley offered advice to a friend and a neighbor. If he hadn't spent years avoiding town, he might have realized his neighbors didn't share Dad's opinion. "I appreciate the sentiment."

She nodded.

Ted stood.

"Hey, over there, make room." A deep voice boomed.

Leaning back on his elbows, Paul squinted around the chairs at the approaching figures.

Jill crossed arms low over her body.

Rob stood several feet away, waving a can of bug spray. Reaching the group first, he passed around the defensive measure and joked with Shirley and Ted.

At no point did he touch Jill or vice versa. With Paul's experience in blocking plays, however, he wasn't completely oblivious to tiny physical tells. He utilized body language to enhance an actor's lines. Studying his sister and friend, he glimpsed mirrored postures hinting at secrets and inside jokes. Paul slipped into the background.

Content lying on the blanket, he pillowed his head with both hands and stared at the pitch-black sky. Shirley's talk echoed in his mind. If he could stay and build a life here, maybe he should. After years of chasing fame, he drained his ambition with every dollar pulled from his bank account. Dani gave him a trial run and—after the show's success—would offer him a contract. Through his creativity, he could build something positive for the entire community and leave a lasting legacy. The promise of something tangible was worth far more than his fifteen minutes with a Kara Kensington lookalike.

Breathing through his clenched stomach, he expanded his rib cage and shoved aside the twisty feelings anchoring him in place. Dani wouldn't lie or hide an opportunity. He couldn't project his insecurities onto the specter of a TV star. He must trust he was worthy of a homecoming.

****

The next morning, Dani lowered her shoulders and rolled her neck. Shifting behind the steering wheel, she readjusted her position in the seat. No matter how she moved, she couldn't shake the tension and bone-deep fatigue in her muscles. Driving to the airport was the very last thing she wanted to do hours after a performance. When confronted with Kara, however, Dani had no choice. Her friend always took the lead.

"Of course, I had to say no!" Kara tittered in the shotgun seat.

Tightening her grip on the wheel, Dani darted her gaze sideways. While laughing, Kara coquettishly raised a hand to her throat, tilted up her chin, and leaned one delicate shoulder forward. Dressed in jeans with an old ball cap covering her honey blonde hair, the woman was nondescript. When she opened her mouth to describe scenes from a life far outside the Midwestern norm, she lost her anonymity. For the better part of the past hour, she continued her one-sided conversation.

Dani focused on the road and her plan. Once she dropped off her passenger for a flight headed across the country, Dani intended to lock herself in her little house on the edge of town and forget the intrusion ever happened. Out of sight, out of mind appealed more than she should admit. When she left her old life, she'd emulated the phrase. With enough distance and time, she hoped Kara would follow suit.

Last night, Dani whisked Kara out of the office and bundled her sequin-clad friend into the car parked behind the building. She drove home with no detours and insisted the starlet take the bedroom. Her motives weren't entirely hospitable. She worried Jill might appear to question why Dani disappeared without giving a thank-you speech after the performance. Lying on the couch, she strained for any sound of impending company outside her front door. She wanted Paul to knock on the door and ask where she'd gone. His musical was a smash hit, and she should celebrate his success at his side. They hadn't made specific plans, but she'd been included in the group heading to the library's hill for the grand finale of the Fourth of July celebrations. Her first New Hope Independence Day should have ended with the full patriotic experience of colorful explosions. Instead, she sequestered herself and her uninvited guest in her little house miles from Main Street.

If he knocked on the door last night, he would have drastically changed the course for their respective futures. She would have introduced Paul and Kara and faded into obscurity, hidden by the glare of Kara's razzle-dazzle. Compared to America's sweetheart, Dani was nobody. In LA, she hadn't cared. In New Hope, she wasn't second-best. She promised Paul help with her connections, and Kara cultivated the best network on either coast. With a night's sleep, however, Dani solidified her decision to keep the starlet far away from New Hope. Everything Dani worked for was threatened by Kara's presence. She'd help Paul some other way.

Kara poked Dani in the shoulder. "Can you believe it?"

Straightening, Dani tightened her grip on the steering wheel. With minimal encouragement, Kara could talk for hours. "Hmm? Sorry. I wasn't listening. Lost in thought."

"Thinking about your theater? It really is quite…" Kara stroked her chin. "Quaint."

Her flat delivery defined the word as miniscule. Dani nodded, ignoring the hairs standing on end on her neck. Kara's poor opinion was a positive. If Kara considered Holidays, Inc. unimportant, she wouldn't get involved or otherwise meddle. "Thank you."

"I could help you come back home. If you wanted."

Dani cringed and raised her shoulders to her ears. No, she would never again chase stardom. None of the apartments she lived in over the years qualified as home. "I appreciate the offer. I like my life here."

"Really?"

"Yes, really." Dani pressed together her lips. Every

defense of her adopted hometown involved disparaging Kara and her lifestyle. Dani's search for community ended in the most unlikely of places for a California girl, and she couldn't have dreamt of more.

In New Hope, she found people who cared for one another. She discovered a town eager to rally and rebuild. Her definition and expectations of friendship changed. Jill, Shirley, and Rob supported her. They offered honest advice without any backhanded compliments or schemes designed for their own interests. She dropped a hand to her knotted stomach. By concealing Kara, Dani wasn't extending the same kindness she appreciated to Paul.

"Hungry?"

Dani nodded. The excuse was better than the truth. When she woke that morning, she sent an email to her former manager and was rewarded almost instantaneously with a bounce message. Since announcing her retirement from Hollywood less than a year ago, she was already forgotten and hadn't received an updated email address. *Not by everyone*. For a brief second, she met Kara's gaze. "After I get you to the airport, I can grab something to eat. I'd hate for you to miss your flight. Sounds like you have a lot to do when you get home." The faux cheer in her voice mirrored her brittle smile. With only inches of space between them, Kara remained oblivious to Dani's upset. Should she be relieved or frustrated?

"I wouldn't mind another day to locate the singer." Kara tapped a polished finger against her chin. "But you'll search while I sell my idea to producers."

Glancing in her mirror, Dani signaled a lane change and followed the exit ramp to departures. Her breathy exhale didn't quite exhaust the nervous feelings bubbling inside her chest. As always, she plastered on a tight smile. Covering her trembling chin and glassy stare with a broad grin shielded her from most double looks including Kara's. The idea to help Paul remained a vague plan without any backing or support.

At the moment, Kara couldn't offer him anything concrete, either.

By concealing her former friend's interest, Dani was only stopping Paul from an introduction with disastrous consequences. After the star's string of recent failures, Kara wouldn't likely secure funding for a new project. Holidays, Inc., however, was solvent and real. Dani had no cause for alarm or concern. She sucked in a deep breath and lifted her chin. If she offered him a permanent position and he accepted, she won.

Parking the car at the curb, Dani left the engine running and deployed the hazard lights. She hopped from the driver's side, rounded the bumper, and extricated the rolling carry-on from the backseat.

With a hand shielding her down-turned face, Kara exited the car.

Dani pressed her lips into a flat line and scanned the pavement. The paparazzi weren't on standby at the Milwaukee airport. In fact, she depended on her companion's anonymity. She shook her head and readjusted her grip on the suitcase.

Kara retrieved her bag and pressed a hand to Dani's elbow.

Frozen, Dani lifted her gaze to meet Kara's.

Tiny crinkles marred the outer edges of Kara's eyelids.

Under close scrutiny, Dani flinched. If she hadn't considered Kara family, she wouldn't ache at the betrayal or feel a sting in the back of her throat about keeping Paul a secret. *They'll ruin each other.* She was making the best choice for all parties involved. Lifting her chin, she forced a smile. "Have a safe flight home."

The starlet dropped her grip and nodded. She slipped a pair of oversized sunglasses from her purse and slid them into place. "See you around." Spinning on her heel, she wheeled her suitcase behind her and swept into the airport.

Dani monitored her progress until Kara disappeared from view. Retreating to her car, Dani drew in a shaky breath and sat behind the wheel. She'd find another way to honor her commitment to Paul without throwing him into the lioness's den to be eaten alive. Honoring professional promises was the only lesson Mom taught her. Inside her chest, her heart squeezed, and her thoughts darted again to the open wound of another fraught relationship.

She glanced in the car's mirrors, signaled, and merged into traffic. Despite her protests otherwise, she couldn't help but wonder if growing up in a town like New Hope would have changed her life for the better. Would she have had the family she wanted? For good reason, Mom didn't trust anyone. In LA, Mom had been burned by unscrupulous people. Over the years, she hardened. Dani didn't want a dreamer like Paul to be disillusioned and broken. She'd protect everyone she could.

Chapter Nine

Standing outside the closed office door on Monday morning, Paul rubbed clammy hands against his jeans. A whiff of her citrus scent hung in the air. He breathed deep, filling his lungs with the sunshine smell. If only he could sniff out answers so easily. After his successful Fourth of July show, he spent the weekend celebrating with sizzling meat on the charcoal grill and swimming in the nearby river. When he fell asleep on a towel in the sun to the chatter of his best friend and his sister, he'd relaxed more deeply than he had in years. He'd finally come home. His triumph was all due to Dani. Perhaps she didn't agree?

When she didn't join them on the hill to watch the fireworks, her absence was explained by her professional obligations and logistics of closing the theater. The next day, he wanted to invite her to tube down the river and come to dinner at the house. He hated to think she was alone. She was responsible for sparking the opportunity for everyone else's happiness. Something held him in check. He'd never been eager or unsure about a woman, but he didn't know how to approach her without confusing his feelings. He walked a tightrope between professional and personal feelings. At any moment, he could be jarred off course to disastrous results.

His homecoming hadn't been in pursuit of

redemption. Desperation drove him to town and lack of a plan trapped him here. She offered him a second chance—much more precious than a job. He was no closer to his next big idea than he was two months ago. The tightness of anxiety eased from his chest anyway. With the Holidays, Inc. musicals, he replenished his creativity one project at a time. If he had patience and trust, he knew with bone-deep certainty, the timing would work in his favor. Thanks to Dani, he found hope in an unexpected place. How did he proceed? Did he maintain a professional distance, or could they grow closer under the guise of collaboration?

The doorknob twisted.

He jumped.

Dani poked her head through the slim opening and lifted her gaze.

Her blue eyes sparkled. He ran a hand through his hair. Waiting to enter the office filled him with dread from a childhood of being called to task in the very spot. He couldn't use the same excuse for stalling today.

"Hi, Paul, what's up?"

"I wanted to chat with you." He cleared his throat. "About the other night."

"Great, me too." She pushed open the door and retreated. "Come in."

As he stepped over the threshold, he scanned the room, his nose twitching. A faint hint of drying paint pierced the space. The tiny office was transformed into a light, bright, and airy refuge. The oak paneling and floor-to-ceiling bookshelves behind the desk were painted pale blue. "Wow, the room looks great."

"Thanks, I had time over the weekend and wanted

to make the office mine." She sat behind the desk.

"You certainly have." He settled in the chair opposite. Leaning back, the old wooden seat groaned. Shifting forward, he pressed both hands against his thighs and perched on the edge. He didn't quite fit. For the thousandth time, he reconsidered his plan. Did he need absolute clarification about the Fourth of July? If Kara Kensington had been in town, he would have heard. The Higginbothams, running the only hotel for a hundred miles, would have shared the news. Shirley would have said something. He discovered no proof Kara had been on stage.

His gut, however, insisted on the opposite. He hated to ask, but he had to know for certain. Leaving New Hope wasn't his main concern anymore, but a major opportunity like performing with a TV star wasn't something he could count on happening again. Would he have to relocate to LA? Or could he convince Kara Kensington to stage a one-night-only show here? The publicity would benefit him, Kara, and Dani.

"The show was phenomenal," she said.

"Phenomenal? I don't know about such praise." He rubbed a hand over the back of his neck.

"I do."

"Maybe it was the mystery performer during the grand finale. The crowd loved her." For a moment, her bright blue eyes dulled, losing the sheen. He opened his mouth to apologize, but she shuttered the expression behind a radiant smile.

"I wouldn't call Lady Liberty a mystery. By the time I crossed the stage, the crowd was on their feet."

Her words rolled off her tongue. He believed her. Upon closer study, he realized the physical similarities she shared with Kara Kensington. Had he seen Dani and his weary gaze projected a famous star onto her image? He pressed a hand to his knotted stomach. The woman he sang with was definitely not Dani. She wore heavy perfume and a thick layer of cosmetics. Who was the mystery woman? *The only way to know is to ask.* He opened his mouth.

A small stack of papers hit the desk with a thud. "For you."

He leaned forward and studied the pile. Legal language on the first page blurred into an illegible black and white pattern. Raising his gaze, he arched an eyebrow. "What am I seeing?"

"Our agreement." She tapped her fingers on the top sheet and pushed the stack closer. "You delivered on your end of our bargain, and I'm doing the same. I'd like to offer you a contract for the next year. The terms are renewable annually for as long as you'd like."

Reaching for the document, he crinkled the crisp sheets in his hands then perused the contract. The terms outlined in the first several pages were more than fair. She offered him money, creative freedom, and support. After two months, he couldn't fight his desire to stay home for good. A sour taste filled his mouth. She hadn't answered his question. Or had she? He bit his tongue. If he wanted to be a success and help save the town, he had to trust her and stop worrying over what she wasn't saying. When he accepted her bargain, he'd been determined to put on one show and leave, leveraging her Hollywood connections. He couldn't question her without revealing his own duplicity. He had to sign the contract. "Do you have a pen?"

She handed him a ballpoint.

In the exchange, he brushed her fingers. The touch was fleeting and necessary. The air sizzled. His arm tingled like an electric shock coursed from the pen to his shoulder. Clicking the ballpoint, he snapped the moment in half. He had questions and concerns, but he was certain of one fact. If he wanted to explore what lurked under the shock of awareness, he couldn't chase a phantom. He stayed for someone real. Lowering his gaze, he flipped to the final page of the document, signed and dated, and returned the papers and pen.

She extended a hand.

In exchanging the contract, he skimmed a palm against the back of her fingers. A tremor shook through the brief contact.

In her grip, she creased the legal document. Pulling back, she dropped the papers to the desk and crossed her arms, tucking hands to her sides.

Puffing out his chest, he pushed back the chair and stood. He ran a hand through his hair and breathed easier. He knocked on her door with questions, but he received a different answer. She was affected by their connection, too. "I'll get started on the next show."

"I can't wait to see how you'll top your last musical." She nodded and raised the document, shielding her face.

Why wouldn't she meet his gaze? In the closet-size room, he was too big to avoid. Lifting a hand to his neck, he smoothed down the hairs standing on end. "Okay. Bye." He nodded and backed away. Exiting the office, he headed toward the stage. With his gaze focused on the ground, he collided with a figure.

"Hey, you okay?" Jill asked.

She grabbed his shoulders, steadying him. He met

her gaze and frowned. Glancing over her shoulder, he spotted Rob leaning against the backstage door. "Yeah, yeah, I'm fine." Paul nodded. "Sorry, wasn't looking where I was going."

Jill dropped her hands and stepped back.

"We deduced that much." Rob chuckled.

Paul set his jaw, studying the pair. They weren't touching. His friend was completely at ease, but Jill's cheeks were bright pink. For a fleeting second, Paul caught her gaze.

She dropped her chin to her chest.

"What are you two doing?" In the time since Paul came home, he'd become used to seeing Rob at the theater, the diner, and his house. In their younger years, they weren't a trio. Paul typically spent time with either his sister or his friends without overlap between the groups. In the past few weeks, they'd spent hours hanging out as a group. While he stroked his chin, he connected disparate pieces of information. He never called to invite Rob, but the guy was always around. Jill must be spending time with Rob without Paul. Paul shook his head and stopped projecting.

"I'm going over the maintenance list with Jill," Rob said. "When Dani bought the theater, she had a master plan of what she'd like to repair or replace. We've been slowly tackling everything, and with good ticket sales, we complete another little project after each show."

Scrubbing a hand over his face, Paul wiped away his scowl. Hadn't he dropped his paranoid act? He'd been back too long to assume the worst of everyone. "Oh, yeah? That's great news."

"Too bad you won't be here to see everything

when it's finished."

Paul tilted his head to the side and waited for the rest of Rob's thought. As seconds ticked by, he shrugged and stared. "I don't follow?"

"Sorry, man." Rob shrugged. "I just figured. 'Cause you say, you're not sticking around."

"About my plans." Paul cleared his throat. "I signed a contract with Dani. I'll be staying for a year."

"You will?" Jill clapped both hands over her mouth.

"I will. But, Jill, I was wondering if we could chat, about…" He cleared his throat and glared at Rob. "Dani."

Shaking her head, Jill dropped her hands and pushed against the air. "I refuse to be dragged into the middle of your arrangement."

"Did she ask you about me?" Paul frowned.

"I'm not answering, and I'm definitely not getting involved in whatever is happening. I'm not some unbiased person. I have a very strong opinion on what I'd like to see happen, and I have enough of my own stuff going on." She spun on her heel and stalked away.

"I'm glad you're staying, man." Rob clapped a hand on Paul's shoulder. "That's good, really good."

Was Paul's decision good or inevitable? Slipping a finger under the crew neck collar on his T-shirt, he swallowed the lump clogging his airway. Had he made a choice, or was he serving a sentence? He wanted some semblance of free will.

Rob ambled off.

Paul followed his progress. His friend's pace was normal but determined. If Rob dated Jill… Paul shook his head. They were both adults. Paul couldn't protect his sister anymore, and he couldn't keep discouraging his friend. They both knew who he supported in a worst-case scenario. He couldn't keep looking for relationships around every corner. His work required his full attention. Consequences came later.

****

During the frigid weeks of January, Dani never could have imagined the unrelenting humidity at the end of July. With only a few days until the start of August, she couldn't catch a break from either the thick air or her guilt. In her tiny workspace, she didn't worry about running into Paul. The cost of peace of mind was steep. Her skin beaded with sweat, soaking through the blouse clinging to her back. How many showers could she take before her skin dried completely?

Reluctantly, she carted her notebooks and binders down the hall. At a table in the auditorium, she erected a makeshift office. Overhead, freestanding and box fans circulated warm air from every direction. With a sigh, she arranged the notebooks and binders like fallen dominoes, holding the fluttering papers in place.

"Good news." Jill sank into the seat opposite.

"The air conditioning repair man is on his way in the next five minutes?"

"No, better. Clouds are gathering. We'll have a storm in the next two hours. I guarantee."

Swallowing her groan, Dani reached for a folder. Good news was modern technology blasting the building with arctic air. She would happily don her winter coat indoors. "Isn't the movie theater supposed to be the coldest building in any town?"

"It is. In fact, this building was the first with central air conditioning in New Hope. After a few years

135

without service…" Jill shrugged. "Things happen."

Jill's tone remained bright and cheerful. Dani nodded. Any other response would discourage her friend. No one deserved to suffer Dani's rain-cloud mood. After filing the signed contract in her lock box, she'd been too plagued by conscience for happiness. In the three weeks since the surprise performer, she mastered avoidance. On the off-chance she bumped into him at the theater, she'd half listen to his eager ideas for the next show and agree to anything. She couldn't match his excitement or debate his creative vision. Giving him full control of the production was the least she could do.

With every encounter, she gaped and choked on words she was too cowardly to say. Her efforts to reach her Hollywood contacts backfired in a series of wrong numbers, bounced emails, and unanswered messages. The only person left in her address book was the enthusiastic starlet anxious to fulfill Dani's promise. *Except Kara will destroy him.* If she was asked a pointblank question about Kara, Dani swore to her broken conscience she would reply truthfully. Until then, she maintained her lies by omission.

"How's your day so far?" Jill waved at the collection of paperwork.

"Good. I posted the kitchen manager job online. It's been a pleasant break from marketing. We've already attracted interest from some capable talent outside town."

"Really?" Jill arched an eyebrow.

The subtle gesture was the most incredulity her friend mustered. Dani caught her bottom lip. In the circumstance, Jill's surprise was fair. When Dani arrived in December, she would never have imagined securing sought-after employees for her company from beyond town limits. The idea of competing with major cities was laughable. With the Internet, reviews spread fast and word-of-mouth launched the business out of obscurity. "In fact, I heard from a woman named Nora Thomas with more qualifications than specified. For the past decade, she's opened restaurants with a major Chicago company. I guess she's from town and is eager to return."

"Nora?" Jill scrunched her face, pursing her mouth and wrinkling her nose.

"Do you know her?" Dani leaned close. "I don't have any specifics about her age or marital status."

"I don't recognize the name. Sounds like great news. Her experience is exactly what you need."

Studying the downturn of Jill's mouth, Dani puzzled over the subtle hint of self-deprecation in her friend's voice. Jill was more valuable than a hundred Nora Thomases. If Dani hadn't said the words enough, she'd regret the consequences.

A loud crash boomed through the auditorium.

Dani jumped to her feet, knocking back the chair.

"Sorry, my fault," Paul called from the stage.

"Oh, no problem." Dani pressed a hand against her racing heart and still-damp blouse. Her chest rapidly rose and fell. Considering her options, she bent and righted the chair. She'd have to risk suffocation in her tiny workspace or suffer hyperventilation here. "I'll head to my office."

"No, stay. If you don't mind?" He cleared his throat and ran a hand through his hair. "I'll play you a song from the new show."

"Sure." Dani gulped. Her response was a little too breathy. She gathered the nearest binders to her chest like a shield and resumed her seat.

"I have a meeting," Jill said.

Frowning, Dani bit her lip at the quickly retreating figure. She needed Jill by her side as both assistant and physical deterrent.

"The show is a throw-back," Paul said. "Think a sixties-era beach party. I'll play you the finale song. It's about wanting summer to last forever." He sat at the piano in the center of the stage, racing his fingers along the keyboard. After a few bars, he belted lyrics to an original song.

Exhaling a sigh, she relaxed her shoulders and focused on the figure on stage. Left alone, she still had enough physical distance for her safety. He devoted his energy into the new music. The notes trilled and raced. She tapped her feet and clapped along with the rock-and-roll melody. The song held nostalgia and fun in every bar. The catchy tune lured her to sing along even though she'd never heard it before. The audience would love the show.

If he makes it to Hollywood, America would love him, too.

She stiffened. Her cell vibrated in her pocket. Sliding out the phone, she kept the device under the table and glanced at the screen. "KK" flashed on the display. She winced. Flipping the phone to hide the caller id, she jerked and thumped a hand against the underside of the table.

The music stopped.

"You okay?"

Heat crept up her cheeks and her knuckles ached.

Turning to Paul, she pressed the vibrating phone against her chest, shielding the screen. She couldn't drop her guard for even a second. *Unless I'm ready to pack his bags.* "Your song is great," Dani said, a little too loudly. "I'm sure your show will be great. I've got to take a call." Grabbing the binders off the table, she clutched the paperwork to her chest and strode away at top speed. The phone rang and rang, shaking the bundle in her arms. Outside the auditorium, she ran down the hall to the office. She opened, shut, and locked the door. Panting, she accepted the call. "Hi, K."

"Dani, hi, doll, I'm so glad I caught you. I've got the most amazing news."

"You do?" She cringed. Crossing the room, she dropped paperwork onto the empty chair in front of the desk and sank into her rolling chair. She rested her head in a hand and massaged her temples. In LA, she could stop at her favorite acupuncturist. The woman stuck needles in the pressure points, and Dani's cares floated away in a sharp piercing moment of clarity. Telling everyone the truth was her only method of readily available headache relief.

"Yes, I do," Kara said.

She chirped in her highest pitch of elation. Dani twitched her nose.

"I've been talking to my agent about the guy at your place. Everyone loves the idea of a show about— wait for it—are you ready?" She squealed. "When you hear the angle, you'll scream. It's genius. Hollywood comes to save small-town America. The storyline is perfect, and the script writes itself. Who doesn't adore an underdog?"

Are you stealing my life? Gritting her teeth, Dani

counted to ten and breathed through her nose. She definitely wanted to scream. Over the past three weeks, she hadn't heard a peep from Kara and assumed the plans stalled. Dani hoped her oldest friend found another idea for her latest comeback pitch. Dani pinched the bridge of her nose. The idea of the two united as a pair twisted her heart more than Kara running off with her ex-boyfriend. "I... I... I really don't know what to say."

"Don't say anything. I'll come back for your next big show, and I'll spring it on him then. When is your next production?"

Opening and closing her mouth, Dani couldn't form a response. She should have choked on all the lies she told. Unwilling to add one more to her guilt, she sighed. "Labor Day."

"Great, Labor Day. I can't wait. Bye, doll."

"Yeah, bye." Dani ended the call and dropped the phone to the desk. Tugging the blouse off her back, she fanned herself. She had until Labor Day to tell him the truth, convince him to stay anyway, and oppose the friend who'd been as close as a sister. Each line item on the checklist was more insurmountable than the last.

As kids, she and Kara were delighted by their similarities. In recent years, however, Dani couldn't ignore their differences. Dani wanted an honest, hard-working life and had to explain the situation to Paul before Kara stole her chance. He deserved the truth and the choice. While she couldn't make his decisions, she could decide when and how to approach him. With every ounce inside her, she would hold on to what control remained.

Chapter Ten

A week later, Paul stood on stage. Unlike most days, he wasn't seated at his piano but faced backstage and surveyed the crowd in the wings. Holding open auditions for the Labor Day show, he was impressed and heartened by the turnout. His hard work wouldn't be in vain. Once he composed the finale song, he breezed through the rest of the show. Sleepless nights returned. Fueled by a relentless creative energy, he didn't mind. From dawn 'til dusk and back again, snippets of dialogue and catchy chords flooded him. The only niggling doubt was Dani. Had he upset her? Lately, she was hard to read and acted almost skittish, her gaze never meeting his. Since he signed the contract, he couldn't deny the shift in their dynamic. Was she losing confidence in his abilities? He'd prove his worth with the show.

Holding a megaphone, he lifted his chin. The piece of equipment, even if not terribly advanced, unequivocally declared him the boss.

Andy stood at his side, the corners of his mouth tilting up.

Rob's talk about Dani's business transforming the town and inspiring hope was only abstract words. Paul needed concrete action. Standing shoulder to shoulder with his employee before a crowd of eager faces, Paul witnessed the changes. In the month since becoming stage manager, Andy eased the workload for both Jill and Paul considerably. When he strolled past the building thirty minutes earlier, he'd been humbled and pleased with the line wrapping around the corner. The impact of Dani's vision slammed into him full force. Holidays, Inc. galvanized a community. He wanted a chance to explain his vision of the future to his boss and reassure her. He wouldn't risk the potential for something great happening to the town because of his feelings.

Andy cleared his throat.

Running a hand through his hair, Paul focused on the crowd of hopefuls ready to audition for the Beach Blanket Summer Farewell and raised the megaphone. "Thank you for coming." His voice boomed.

The buzz of conversations hushed.

"Our stage manager, Andy, has already given everyone a number and had you sign in with your contact information."

Andy lifted a clipboard and waved it.

"If you haven't seen him yet, please step forward. If you have, please form a line in numerical order by the stage door." Paul pointed toward the door propped open. Light from the hallway spilled inside.

Several heads bobbed and slipped through the crowd.

Maybe I should use this thing all the time. "In a minute, I'll join Ms. Winter in the audience. You will wait backstage until your number is called. Andy will cue you. After your performance, you'll be free to leave. If you've been cast, you'll receive a call over the next few days. Break a leg." He handed the megaphone to Andy and jogged across the stage to the stairs.

Applause erupted.

Catching his next breath, he turned. He hadn't heard adulation since his patriotic tribute on the Fourth. The sound warmed him. With a wave to the group, he strode across the carpet and settled at the table in the very center of the room. From his vantage point, he studied the entire stage from wing to wing.

Andy hustled the prospective cast off the boards and into a single file queue.

Paul reached for the legal pad he'd left on the table and uncapped a pen.

"You were right. He's a great hire," Dani said.

Jumping to his feet, he dropped his paper and pen onto the table.

Her arms were laden with stacks of paperwork. She readjusted her grip.

He moved forward. For a second, he met her gaze. She widened her blue eyes, and her pupils contracted. He frowned and reached for her heavy bundle.

She jerked and dropped her arms. Notebooks and manila folders fell from her grasp, sliding in every direction onto the table and floor.

Dropping to the ground, he knelt and retrieved the pages nearby. What had he glimpsed in her larger-than-normal blue eyes? Had she been afraid? With a sigh, he reached for the nearest folders. "Sorry, I wanted to help."

"It's all right." She bent to gather the scattered sheets and folders on the other side of the table.

Her voice was steady. He shook his head. At some point, he scared her off. Grabbing the last few notebooks, he got to his feet and set the stack on the table. How could he apologize when he didn't know what he'd done wrong?

She finished clearing her side.

Bending, he offered her a hand.

She didn't raise her head. Instead, she braced hands on her thighs and stood.

Nibbling the inside of his cheek, he frowned and pressed both hands against the ground. As he stood, he dragged a chair, scraping against the linoleum floor.

Her brow wrinkled, and her nose twitched.

Was she readying an explanation or censure about his treatment of the building?

Sinking into her chair, she sat with ramrod-straight posture and a blank expression.

He lounged on his seat, leaning back, stretching his legs, and crossing his ankles.

She flipped through the papers and sorted the documents into piles. After covering the table in neat stacks, she pulled a notebook and hovered her pen over the blank page.

"Andy is a great hire," Paul said.

Cocking her head to one side, she frowned.

He coughed. "To answer your earlier question, I'm pleased. He really helped smooth over everything with the Fourth of July show."

She nodded and reached into her purse for a water bottle.

In the second before she uncapped the drink, she flashed a pained smile. As she sipped, she rested her arms at very precise angles on the table and held herself erect. He scrubbed a hand over his face. When they'd dropped off tickets and strolled down the street, he assumed her natural smile indicated ease in his company. He didn't recognize her now. What changed in the past month? Hadn't she shared the electric charge in the moment he nearly kissed her? He remembered her quivering chin. He folded his arms over his chest. His instincts steered him wrong in LA and New York. Maybe he'd been mistaken again.

She finished her drink. "I'm glad. Andy is a great addition."

"Hey, is everything ok? Do you need help?" He gestured toward the stacks.

"How much do you know about ordering supplies for a kitchen?" She rolled her neck and shoulders.

He curled his upper lip. "Nothing at all. But if I can ease the workload, I will."

She touched his arm.

Raising his gaze, he spotted the flutter at the base of her throat. He covered her hand and held her fingers in place on his arm. The chemistry wasn't imagined, but the confusion was real and ever present.

"Thank you," she murmured.

"Any time."

Andy whistled. "We're ready, boss."

She withdrew her hand and straightened.

Paul's throat was too tight to offer a verbal reply. Turning, he flashed Andy a thumbs-up.

Andy led an elderly couple to the microphone.

The man wore a seersucker suit and held the hand of a woman dressed in a floor-length, pastel gown. Under the stage lights, the couple's white hair and pale skin glimmered. "Hello." The man bobbed his head. "Thank you for having us. We are Margaret and Sherman. We will sing a duet." Sherman waved to Andy and held out the other hand.

Margaret stepped forward and stood on the

opposite side, interlacing her fingers with her partner.

Focused on each other, Sherman and Margaret belted a pitch-perfect standard.

Paul straightened. The performers commanded attention, and the sweetness of their interaction enraptured him. *I'd like to have that someday.* He slipped a finger under his crew neck collar. With only inches of separation, he heightened his awareness of her so close to his right side. He hadn't felt anything either professionally or personally for a long time. At the theater, he couldn't deny the rush of excitement for both. If he made a move, he risked his career. Would holding back shutter his heart?

Dani leaned toward him. "Now, they have a spark," she murmured. "I can't believe your family isn't the most talented in town."

Breathing in her citrus scent, he tilted his head and studied her. He wanted to tip up her chin, kiss off her smirk, and soak in her effervescence. She was a bright burst of sunshine, bringing light to a dark town and his black heart. Instead, he flexed and crossed his arms, fighting the ache to touch her. "Wasn't I the one to suggest holding auditions?" He arched an eyebrow.

"Touché."

Up close, her blue eyes were glossy, sparkling in the dim house lights, and her breaths were shallow. Her playful words teased him, lifting the hair on the back of his arms. How close could he get without spooking her? "They are great." He tilted his head toward the stage. "How would you feel if I cast them in the lead roles?"

"I would love it." She covered her mouth with a hand and leaned close. "If you can get a good enough supporting cast…"

Margaret and Sherman finished their song.

Dani jerked away. She pushed back her chair, stood, and clapped.

Turning toward the stage, he watched Sherman kiss Margaret's cheek. Had Paul misread Dani's cues? His throat closed, and he shook his head. He couldn't make a move on her here or anywhere. She was his boss. Scrambling to his feet, he joined her in the standing ovation.

"If the other auditions are half as engaging, you might have your show cast before noon."

Her warm breath tickled his neck. He should step back and put distance between them. Or maybe he should push the limits. He closed the gap and lowered his mouth to her ear. "They are the exception, not the rule."

She stopped clapping and sat. Dropping her chin to her chest, she jotted notes, scratching the notepad with her pen.

Biting the inside of his cheek, he turned toward the stage and cupped both hands around his mouth. "Thank you. We'll be in touch."

Margaret and Sherman waved.

Andy crossed the stage and helped the older couple exit. He queued the next performer and shot Paul a thumbs-up.

With a nod, Paul sat and reached for his legal pad. Staring at the sheet, he couldn't focus on the words, his vision blurry. He didn't want to work. He wanted to leave his notes on the table and rediscover the seconds-long moment of comfortable companionship.

From the corner of his gaze, he spotted the tremor rattling her dominant hand as she wrote. Maybe he was a fool to pursue more, but he didn't want to regret not taking a chance with someone who sparked something deep inside. In her company, he tapped into emotions he ignored for the better part of the past decade and existed in a heightened state. Without her, the world was black and white. After experiencing full color, he couldn't return to shades of gray. "Did you hear about the buildings near the post office?" Cringing, he pressed his lips flat. His dull brain circled around the world's worst conversation topics.

She wrinkled her brow and tapped the pen against her chin. "You've been to the diner today?"

"No, I talked to Rob." He shook his head and dropped his shoulders. His conversation wasn't heading in the direction he wanted. "Which is just about the same thing, being across the street. The minute something is announced at the diner, patrons cross over Main to tell Rob everything. It's rather scary how much he knows."

"I'll be sure to watch what I say around him." She shifted in her chair. "I heard the buildings were under contract, two of them side by side."

Turning, he scanned the stage, spotting Andy in discussion with several people in the queue. He relaxed. He didn't want the friendly moment with Dani to end but hated to delay the auditions. Shifting closer, he met her gaze. "Yeah, a microbrewery is going in. We got a lot of attention from the Fourth of July show. Apparently, our part-time realtor left her day job as a bank teller to facilitate showings."

She froze.

Her brittle smile and blank gaze transformed her into hard stone. He hadn't meant the comment to be a dig. He wanted to compliment her on the success. Since the last show, he struggled for the right words. Every time he attempted a conversation, he barely managed hello before she excused herself. Talking to a wall proved more successful.

She stared at the papers on the table.

"The next performers…" Andy called from the stage.

Paul cleared his throat and focused on the next audition. As he fought to keep from wincing during the following performances, he had cover for his swirling thoughts. If he hurt her feelings, Paul would apologize. Something in her reaction unsettled him. If she had life-altering information, she would tell him. Hadn't they agreed to help each other succeed?

****

After enduring several hours of auditions, Dani excused herself from the auditorium for lunch. Hidden in her office, she ate her sandwich and remained in the room for the rest of the afternoon. She sought refuge from a problem of her own making. With the air conditioning repaired, she could spend all day in the quiet space, mentally twisting herself to justify her actions. Exhausted from her subterfuge, she was no closer to a solution. Beyond professional connections, she cared about Paul and couldn't hide the ill-timed deepening of her feelings. The longer she knew him, the more she liked him, and the harder rationalizing her deception became. Was she worried about his best interests, hers, or the potential of *them?*

A knock pounded on the doorframe.

"Come in." She studied the door, pressing a hand to her tight stomach.

The heavy oak panel opened.

When her gaze connected with Jill, Dani exhaled a shaky whoosh. She both dodged another potentially disastrous confrontation and missed her chance to have something good happen today. Every time she was within a few yards of Paul, her senses sharpened. She longed to approach him but needed more distance. Each encounter tempted her to blurt the truth and release the burden from her lie by omission. A little over a month remained.

If I tell him, I wouldn't be lying in wait for him to discover the truth.

She rubbed her eyes and waved Jill into the room. The door shut in its frame, and she relaxed. She drummed her fingers against the desk. "Jill, hi, what can I do for you?"

"I'm asking you the same thing. You okay? You seemed a little distracted earlier when we were talking to the kitchen supplier."

"Sorry." Dani shook her head. "I'm fine." Distracted was the nice way of describing Dani's behavior. Over the past month, she hadn't done much beyond stress over the calamity of Paul learning the truth. As her workload lightened with new hires, she drowned herself in extraneous paperwork instead of collaborating on the new musicals. Kara would be here again on Labor Day and—short of an epic comedic switch requiring elaborate misdirection—she'd be discovered.

"I wanted to discuss something."

"Of course," Dani replied without hesitation. "Anything you need."

Jill sat straight and stared through the wall.

The stoic figure was so unlike the woman Dani knew. She relied on Jill for help and advice. Jill gave Dani fresh hope and convinced her the theater dream was attainable. With Jill's support, Dani found success. One day, she might be worthy of her friend's kindness. *You could be now if you'd just talk to her brother.* Dani tightened her grip on the pen.

"You've said you'll still need me here after you onboard Nora Thomas. Please be honest. Are you sure? I don't need pity. I want a solid career." Jill crossed her arms and leaned back.

"Trust me. Benevolence doesn't factor into my business." Dani cleared her throat. "I value your level-headed advice, energy, and dedication. You far exceed your salary. I don't know how the new hire will fare in her role." Dani tapped her right toe against the ground and drummed her fingers on the desk in the same rhythm. "On paper, the woman is capable and qualified. But I need more than lines on a resume. We're still a small group, and we need synergy. I hope her personality fits our organization. Andy is great, and I can't remember how we managed without him. If we don't mesh with Nora, we'll resume the kitchen work in addition to other responsibilities. Truthfully, I want to hire staff for the day-to-day. You and I should focus on bigger projects. I want you running this whole place by my side."

Jill sucked in a sharp breath. Her face scrunched.

Unless you don't want the role. Jill drew in almost all the oxygen in the tight room, and her pinched look hit Dani with the force of one of the diner's pies to the face. She hadn't stopped to consider what Jill wanted. Dani included Jill in plans without consultation. *Like*

Mom and Kara did to me. Like I'm doing to Paul. Dani curled hands around her forearms. "If you don't want the role, you can tell me."

"I love working here, and I am so happy for your success. I've had a dream my whole life." She lifted her chin. "I've always wanted to open an inn. Watching you do so well and seeing the town bounce back is inspiring. Everything is falling into place. Maybe now is my chance, too."

Jill shone brighter than the stage lights. Dani's chest tightened. She was happy for Jill to reach for her dreams. What would happen without her friend around? Swallowing, Dani lifted the corners of her mouth in an approximation of a smile. "Wonderful news. You're opening an inn. Where? Can I get a stack of brochures for my customers?"

Jill chuckled. "Whoa, whoa, hold up. I haven't bought anything, yet. I have the opportunity to purchase the Higginbothams' motel on the edge of town. They're ready to retire. The motel is the only lodging for fifty miles around and is already operational. With the money I have from my Dad's estate, I should be set. Eventually, I'd like to modernize."

She's already gone. Dani pressed her tongue to the roof of her mouth, halting an immediate response. She owed Jill so much more than a smile and nod. For months, Jill gave her time and energy, investing in a crazy idea. Dani owed her friend no less than absolute support and encouragement. "Do you need help? Did you already buy the motel?"

"At the moment, I'm drafting my proposal. I need a strong presentation. Their son, who you don't know…" She shuddered. "He is helping. I'm banking on hometown spirit to sway the decision. I have a fair offer. But I wouldn't be surprised if the son pushes for more money."

Dani flattened both hands on the table and leaned forward. "Okay, great. Can I help you with your proposal? Want to talk business plans and strategy?"

Jill fluffed her bangs. "Thanks, but I've got some expert help already." She nudged up her glasses on her nose.

If Dani wagered, she'd bet everything left in her meager savings account a certain local store owner provided professional advice. Rob's attentiveness to deliveries continued after Andy began the supply runs. She'd never seen Jill and Rob nearer than three feet, but they were in constant close proximity. "When does everything happen? When are you talking to the Higginbothams about the sale?"

"Not until after the Labor Day shows. Their son is coming to visit, and they'll decide as a family."

So soon? Dani stretched her cheeks taut. "With our new hire coming on board, I can't fault your timing."

"Thanks, Dani. I'll get back to work." Jill stood and exited the tight office. In the hallway, she paused and leaned inside. "Do you think you could stop by and give Paul a pep talk?"

Dani frowned and tilted her head to the side. "What do you mean?"

"He seems off." Jill shook her head. "He's on stage struggling with a song."

The show wasn't scored yet? Dani pursed her lips. After listening to the rousing finale song last week, she assumed he'd finished the score. She should be aware of her employees' needs. During auditions, he seemed relaxed and happy. When she leaned close, she noticed the hairs standing on end on the back of his neck. She'd assumed the reaction resulted from close proximity. What if he worried over replicating his success? Sagging her shoulders, she nodded. "Of course. I'll be by in a minute."

With a thumbs-up, Jill left.

The door shut.

Dani sighed and cradled her head in both hands. Replacing Jill daunted Dani. Where would she be without her indispensable go-to gal? How could someone else fill the role? The answer was simple. No one could. Her friend deserved a life lived to the fullest potential and shouldn't be held back. *Doesn't Paul have the same rights?* If Dani spoke honestly with Paul, she wouldn't be fighting near constant heartburn.

When she arrived in New Hope, she sought escape from other people's plans but found herself controlling Paul's. Had she missed the chance to discuss Kara's offer? If Paul knew about Kara now, would he be angry?

She hated to witness Paul—a good man—sucked into a life he didn't understand. Pushing back her chair, she dusted both hands on her dress and rounded the desk. She couldn't keep avoiding him, and he deserved to make his own choice. When the time came, she would muster every acting skill she possessed and convince him she had no idea about Kara's interest in his career. Her jaw ached. Unclenching her bite, she consciously stopped grinding her molars. If she accepted each added deception as necessary, she might regain her equilibrium and save herself a trip to the dentist.

Chapter Eleven

After a morning of auditions, Paul cast the show
and called each member of the new company. With
each elated response, Paul's confidence soared. His
hard work was valued. *I wish Dani agreed.* When he
ended the last call, he wheeled the piano into the center
of the stage. Dashing fingers over the keys, he trilled a
tune from the instrument. He should record the notes on
the writing pad on the stand. The music wasn't terrible
and could be a launching off point for the Halloween
show, but he needed something bigger for the Labor
Day finale.

The Fourth of July musical's success complicated
his too-good-to-be-true job. If he couldn't replicate the
smash hit, would he lose his job? Did Dani question
whether he was a one-hit wonder? He understood his
mystery singing partner wasn't Kara Kensington. After
the Independence Day weekend, he searched the
Internet for videos of the performance. Devoting an
afternoon to the hunt, he located only one out-of-focus
recording. The show wasn't a viral hit, and he
uncovered no mention of the star.

Readjusting the hood on his old collegiate
sweatshirt, he shivered under the blast of chilly air on
the stage. He hadn't wanted to come home and never
spared New Hope a second thought. He owed his sister
for never pressuring him to return. With his career

aspirations and family obligations suddenly aligned in the most positive outcome possible, he couldn't rest until he earned the job. He wanted to stay here and succeed.

"Still here?" Dani said.

Her melodic voice carried over the mechanical hum of the AC. He glanced over the top of the piano. *Where else?* "Yeah, still here."

She approached from the wings in a sleeveless summer dress. Frowning, she crossed her arms and rubbed her bare skin.

After the repairs, the old AC blasted air icier than a glacier. What happened to her bulky sweater? He pressed his tongue to the roof of his mouth. Asking a personal question might scare her off. He should be grateful for her attention. Instead, he worried what she wasn't saying. He cleared his throat. "I'm working on the final song."

"You have to mean practicing." She stopped a few feet away. "You already played it for me, and I can't imagine how you'd improve."

He cocked his head to the side. "You think so?"

She blushed. "Slide over."

Her soft command tingled along his spine. He wasn't the kind of guy to let someone else call the shots or make demands. Apparently, he made an exception. He offered her half the bench. The tight confines pushed her against the side of his body. Raising hands to the keys, he brushed her ribcage with his forearm.

She sucked in a breath.

Ignoring the jolt shooting down his arms, he filled the silence with the score composed for the show. Catchy melodies harkened to a bygone cinematic vision of the sixties. Lifting his chin, he sang the lyrics and relaxed. While crooning about the summer sun, he couldn't remain stiff as a statue. With a flourish, he ended the tune.

"You really have a talent for showmanship," she murmured.

If he lowered his shoulder a few inches, would her breath tickle his neck? He held his torso rigid. Was she inviting a return to the easy camaraderie? Once again, he dashed his hands over the keys, playing the chords of the love ballad at the end of Act One. "Thanks. Making up songs has always come easy."

Crinkling her nose, she tilted her head. "But you wanted to be a writer? I'm guessing screen plays and TV scripts?"

"I wanted to write something capturing..." He'd been so ready to leave New Hope, but he never considered why. Like so many others, he chased fame. Unfortunately, with such a vague goal, he never met the target. In New York, he was obsessed with the idea of being the next great American playwright. His attempts at dramatic plays floundered with flat characters. He wanted to capture an elusive feeling he couldn't quite verbalize. Selling his shows required explaining a premise he couldn't narrow down to investors and collaborators. "When I got to Hollywood, I wanted to write musicals. Despite everyone saying they're eager to revitalize the genre, no one is ready to risk the money on a new screenwriter. I worked on TV pilots and kept missing the mark. My heart wasn't in my scripts."

Under the bench, she tapped her toes. "This job landed perfectly in your lap."

"Sort of. Coming back to New Hope, I'm grasping

what had been slipping through my fingers for so long."

Her feet hit the ground with a thud. She scrunched her face. "What?"

From his peripheral gaze, he studied her but continued playing. If his hands weren't occupied, he'd do something crazy. He'd tilt her face and kiss her senseless. He wanted to do good work, get attention for his merits, and strike his own path without any hint of impropriety. "I wanted to capture the spirit of New Hope with a musical about dreamers never giving up. No one was interested in my point of view. I sold out and took any job I could."

The corner of her mouth lifted and the opposite shoulder shrugged. "I thought you hated living here?"

"No, I hated not having any choices. Until you settled here and changed everything, this town didn't support new ideas."

"Am I a force for good or bad?"

He bumped his shoulder against hers. After a little over two months, he recognized her self-deprecating tone. If he glanced, he'd spot her nibbling the corner of her bottom lip and wrinkling her brow. He gulped. He knew her well enough to anticipate her body language? *So much for professionalism.*

"I don't want the job to restrict you."

He stopped playing and turned his head.

She dropped trembling hands to her lap.

Without a second thought, he pulled a hand from the keyboard and traced her jawline with the pads of his fingers, caressing her cheek with a palm.

She sighed.

His inner caveman triumphed in her breathless response to his touch and urged him forward. "This job has offered more in the last few months than I've had in the past few years. You've given me a chance. I don't take any second for granted."

With a nod, she darted her tongue along her lower lip.

The slight shake knocked his hand away from her face. He rested the hand on the bench behind her, pressing closer.

"I'd love to see what you develop next."

Is the offer still on the table for your LA contacts? The words tickled his tongue. He folded his investigation into her background and credentials. Like the rest of town, he was satisfied with what she told him. He didn't want to break the spell of the moment with more questions. In LA, he wasn't likely to spark anyone's professional interest. In New Hope, he had complete creative control. She gave him independence. "You've sparked something in this town. You're making me chase dreams I'd forgotten. I focused on other projects and lost what mattered. You helped me rediscover my passion."

For a second, her gaze lost its usual luster, the sapphire blue eyes fading. She deserved praise. What wasn't she telling him? Didn't she want her playwright and director happy?

She parted her lips and leaned forward, shutting her eyelids.

He closed the distance and pressed his mouth against hers. He had a flash second of understanding. While he'd been angling for a romantic moment, he only had to trust in the universe's timing.

Her arms wrapped around his neck. A soft sigh escaped her lips.

Dani wasn't hiding something. She fought the growing closeness between them. What he interpreted as guilt was desire. He relaxed, deepening the kiss. In light of her enthusiastic response, he cleared her of presumed culpability.

****

Why had Dani agreed to an after-hours, off-site meeting?

Standing against the street lamp in front of her theater the next week, she braced a foot against the old cast iron and dragged in a deep breath. He wasn't taking her on a date. She wore her favorite sleeveless dress, the amethyst color contrasting with her blue eyes, by accident. The last shred of her conscience refused to enjoy a romantic night. She crossed her arms and leaned back, scanning the block.

After humming with activity all day, Main Street was deserted. Construction continued at a fast pace at the microbrewery. Banks sent in crews to refurbish the other foreclosures in downtown. The scent of wet paint permeated town like the best perfume she'd ever sniffed. Repaired windows sparkled in the late afternoon sunlight. She pulled back her shoulders and stood taller. When challenged, she vowed to spark change within four months but hadn't pictured such a remarkable transformation. In a week, for better or worse, the Kara situation would be over. With Labor Day behind her, she would relax.

"Hi, sorry."

A deep voice called. Dani raised her gaze and furrowed her brow.

Paul strolled down the sidewalk, carrying something.

160

"What do you have?"

"You agreed to help with town research." He grinned and raised a large to-go bag. "The least I could do was provide sustenance."

If we eat together, our acceptable work meeting becomes a date. The crazy logic flared in her chest. She pressed hands to her sides, breathing through the scalding pain in her ribs. Somehow kissing him onstage was acceptable behavior? "I have heartburn. I better not eat anymore."

"According to Shirley, you don't eat anything but pie. Real food is exactly what you need."

She bristled. As her torso tightened, she brushed her right foot in a slow shuffle. Honesty was the only medicine she required. Lifting her chin, she arched an eyebrow. "Maybe I'm a talented at-home chef but can't quite replicate dessert."

"Oh?" He widened his gray eyes. "My apologies. Frank told me he'd never seen you."

"Frank?" She frowned.

The corner of his mouth lifted. "He runs the grocery store."

Busted. She giggled, and Paul joined her. Finding any excuse to put distance between herself and Paul became an even more overwhelming task than her round-the-clock job. Finally, she relinquished the fight. She didn't want to waste any second of time. If he left with Kara, he might never return. "Fine. I haven't been inside the grocery store."

"How? You've lived here for nearly a year."

"I can't cook. At all. Jill stocks the staff fridge at the theater, and Shirley feeds me at the diner." Growing up on set, Dani ate most meals off the table from food service. At home, she grabbed a quick bite to-go or stopped at a favorite restaurant. Mom wasn't a chef. "Besides the occasional run for junk food at the gas station, I don't need groceries."

"Really?" He nudged her with his shoulder. "I could teach you a few basics."

If she said yes, she agreed to more after-hours meetings. Could she handle a knife in her kitchen without spontaneously combusting from his nearness? How different would be a private setting from their current public display? They strolled side by side. If anyone saw them right now, they'd think the two were on a date. Heat swept over her. She braced the arm nearest him, gripping her bare elbow. If she held tight, she could almost ignore the ridiculous urge to hold his hand. One kiss onstage was an accident. Two would start a pattern she wasn't ready for…yet. She cleared her throat. "You can cook?"

"Normally, I'd say no. But by your standards, I'm almost Michelin star rated." Leaning close, he lowered his mouth near her ear. "I've never burned toast, and my buttering rivals the pros."

His warm breath tickled her collarbone. Reaching a hand to her neck, she smoothed the hairs standing on end and put more space between them. His movie star looks hadn't faded. As she'd gotten to know him better, she'd come to appreciate the depths of feeling his steel eyes expressed. In the early evening light, his gaze was warm and welcoming.

"Have you been to the library yet?"

"No." She shook her head. "I've been busy."

"The building is New Hope's most impressive and oldest structure."

She arched an eyebrow. Paul spoke about landmarks and commenting positively? The attitude change heartened her. Maybe she had more reasons than she realized to entice him to stay. *Kara wants him to throw away community for stardom.* She shook her head. "I'm sorry I've overlooked a special part of town."

"You definitely don't want to miss next year's celebration." He pointed toward the sky. "The fireworks launch behind the building. The best view is either on the hill or in the middle of the street. Standing in the center of a deserted road is a tiny thrill."

"Sounds great." Her chest constricted. Any mention of the Fourth hit Play on her inner dialogue. She pressed both hands against her rib cage and breathed through her nose, gritting her teeth as she held a smile. "Is this spot where the Christmas tree will go? In front of the library?"

They'd reached the end of Main Street. Elevated by a natural hill, they climbed the steps in front of the nineteenth-century brownstone building. On the first landing, the town erected an obelisk monument to soldiers sent to the World Wars.

"They decorate a tree in front of the library." Paul brushed her upper back.

The gesture was brief. Fingertips flicked over her dress and bare upper arm in a whisper of contact. The fleeting warmth absorbed through into her bones.

He stepped away.

Come back. She crossed her arms. Her conscience was supposed to be in control. Her pesky sense of justice had permission to resume the reins from her hormones. She longed to lean into each and every accidental touch.

He cleared his throat. "At least they used to, and they would shine lights here on the memorial." He paused by the stone structure.

She stopped a few feet away and studied the view of town. Dusk quickly darkened to night and—without competition from skyscrapers and illuminated signs— the streetlamps cast a warm glow. New Hope was her home. She couldn't let anything—or anyone—ruin her town.

"Shall we?" With a palm, he grazed her shoulder.

She jumped and stared at the spot he brushed. Her skin tingled. Shouldn't the tiny patch be brightly illuminated, radiating with his warmth? She raised her chin, but he vanished. Turning in a circle, she spun until she spotted him.

He stood at the last step of the final stretch of stairs and glanced over his shoulder.

Something flickered in his gaze. Excitement? A dare? Clasping her hands, she followed him. The building loomed large.

He reached the door first.

Quick on his heels, she crossed to a window. Cupping both hands around her narrowed gaze, she assessed the darkened interior. "Closed?" Her voice was sharp. She raced to the other side and repeated the action. Scanning through another window, she craned her neck. *No, please, no.* Slowly, she accepted what she saw. The building was shut for the evening. Without the pretense of business, they really were on a date. In other circumstances, she'd be pleased. She covered her mouth, hiding the automatic smile plastered on her features. With years of experience grinning through an uncomfortable moment, she couldn't unlearn the defense mechanism.

"I'm sorry." He shook his head and ran a hand through his hair. "I should have known."

"No, no, it's okay. The sky stays bright until almost eight. I have a hard time wrapping my head around what the clock says." She forced a laugh and cringed. The too-bright titter was brittle.

"Come on, we're here. Let's eat and enjoy the view." He sat on the steps and began pulling containers from the bag.

She dropped her gaze. Her feet rooted to the ground. Had her body finally started responding to her brain? Her stomach growled.

A broad grin stretched across his face. "Shirley put a slice of apple pie in here for you." He wiggled his eyebrows and patted the vacant spot at his side. "Against her better judgment."

With those words, Dani was lost. Powerless to resist sweets, she crossed the pavement and sat. The bag between them provided a poor barrier from his radiating body heat.

He opened a container and extended it with a fork.

She shut her eyes and sniffed, inhaling the scent of roasted veggies and seasoned beef. She speared a sizeable chunk of meat and brought it to her mouth. Pot roast wasn't summer food, but the first bite comforted her. For several minutes, they both dug into their food. Working long hours and late nights meant she wasn't the only one without proper nutrition. After she was a bona fide success, she would do a better job. She snorted.

He arched an eyebrow. "Penny for your thoughts?"

Chewing, she swallowed her bite. "I don't think they're worth half a cent. If I take your offer, you can bankroll next year's productions." Dropping the fork, she lowered her container to her lap. "I don't understand how you could leave." She gestured down the street. As if she waved a magic wand, she pointed and lamps flickered on, and business signs illuminated.

"It's nice to see the town coming back to life." He nodded and put the empty containers in the bag. "When I left, I had no reason to stay. The town was on its way to rock bottom. I had no idea one person could turn around everything. Definitely couldn't have been me."

She flushed. Secular savior wasn't her ultimate goal. When she first dreamt about leaving LA, she only had an inkling of how beat down and broken she was. She arrived in a worst state than New Hope with a plan to take control of her life and stop being hurt by her supposed loved ones. If she put on a show every holiday, she had the perfect excuse to avoid celebrating the special day alone.

He ran a hand through his hair and leaned closer. "Dad held onto the theater with a tight grip. In his desperate attempts to keep a family business going, he didn't invite innovation and couldn't cope with changing demands. You used the same building and sparked change. He wasn't a dreamer. Our town deserved one." Tilting his face, he smiled. "We needed you."

Shaking off his praise, she tapped her toes on the step. "I needed stability. Guess I have a lot in common with your dad."

"You didn't have stability?" He frowned. "I thought you had a lot of acting credits."

A career isn't family. She arched an eyebrow. "Always in minor roles and my residual checks are gone. My resume is very full. I've been luckier than a lot of aspiring actresses, but I never had a home. My mom is who she is." She sighed. If she received an email or call from Mom, Dani would gladly be fooled again. New Hope wasn't glamorous, but she was building something here she'd like to share. She never forgot her childhood fantasies about the family she could create. Convincing Mom, however, proved impossible. "Mom was determined to be rich and famous. She used me for her purposes." She shrugged. "I never blamed her, but I don't understand her choices."

"Your dad?"

"I have no idea." Talking about her unconventional childhood never got easier. Longing for something she never had and—couldn't fix—shouldn't sting. She sniffed. "I was a commodity to one parent. I didn't have any desire to be used by the other. I was lucky. I found a friend as close as a sister. Her family took me in and welcomed me."

"Wow." He widened his gaze and drew back his chin.

She nodded but didn't reply. How much could she share without him scouring Internet search results and filling in the blanks? The last time she typed her stage name into a search engine, she'd been relieved the salacious articles about Kara and Dani's ex bumped down the list of results. No doubt, Kara and her team buried the stories.

Until Paul, Dani hadn't cared about the not-so-blind items. If he explored gossip sites, he'd discover her previously close friendship with Kara. Would he determine Dani pretended to misunderstand him? By sharing her past, she waded into dangerous waters. But her soul lifted. When she should be wracked with guilt, she had no right to feeling easy. If she gave herself permission for one night off from self-flagellation, what would happen? "I still have contacts. I can put you in touch with people."

With a lopsided grin, he grabbed her hand.

The unexpected touch curled her toes. *Tell him now.*

He entwined their fingers, dropping his lips to her knuckles.

She stared at his bent head. He kissed her with tenderness. Words caught in her swollen throat. She'd fallen in love. The thought hit her with a crashing force. She wanted him to choose her and create an unexpected show business life here. If he was given the option, he'd pick Kara and leave. No one ever selected Dani. Could her heart stand another break? Or would losing Paul shatter her for good?

His thumb traced the back of her hand. "Thank you for coming with me tonight."

"Oh, sure, yeah, I mean, of course." She pulled the hand from his grasp and reached for the rest of Shirley's to-go meal. The bag crinkled, and she retrieved her forgotten pot roast and speared another bite. She focused on the task.

"After the shows next weekend, would you want to go on a date?"

She swallowed. He studied her with a clear, intent gaze. Her heart soared with hope. Maybe for once she'd win. After next weekend, she was clear. "I'd love to go on a date.'"

A grin stretched across his entire face.

She stretched her lips in an approximation of a smile and stuffed another bite in her mouth. He could never learn what she'd done. She didn't deserve his trust, but she couldn't handle his rejection. Without support, she'd be on her own for good.

Chapter Twelve

From the wings of the stage, Dani observed both the cast and the delighted audience. Adding shows to each night of Labor Day weekend—for four performances instead of one—was the right call. Holidays, Inc. sold out every performance. *For Halloween, I'll add matinees.* She wanted to believe the miracle was due to word of mouth. Pressing a hand to her jaw, she breathed through the tight smile she couldn't release. If she relaxed her face, she'd display her nagging worries for public view. She didn't want a ripple effect inciting fear and panic. The well-rehearsed company performed better than expected and deserved assurances and accolades from the producer. The pain passed, leaving behind the dull ache and ever-present worry Kara somehow orchestrated the massive crowds.

Laughter filtered backstage. Sherman challenged the rival of the opposing clique, a pimpled sixteen-year-old and the only other performer capable of matching Sherman's imposing stage presence.

She giggled with the crowd. In less than thirty minutes, she would shut the curtain on the final performance, congratulate the cast, and start preparations for the next show. *Almost in the clear.* She raised a hand to the back of her knotted neck. If she thought making it through the weekend was her biggest hurdle, she hadn't factored in her conscience. Kara had betrayed her first. In-kind behavior wasn't Dani's style but hadn't stopped her from withholding an opportunity for both her former best friend and her love interest. With a sigh, she rolled her neck, dropping the hand to her side. She still couldn't bring herself to be honest. Guilt would lessen in time. By Christmas, she might almost celebrate. "Just a few more songs."

"You're telling me," Paul murmured.

The soft words tickled her neck. She jumped and covered her mouth, masking her gasp at his nearness. Slowing her breathing, she crossed her arms, but the tightness in her cheeks remained. "The crowd loves your show."

"I can't believe you found this many people to come for four nights."

She shrugged, her shoulders barely lifting. Her marketing plan hadn't changed. The website gained a few more positive reviews. Fear kept her from digging too deeply to discover any concrete reason for her sudden success. Dani avoided scouring the media for any interviews and mentions by a certain starlet, clinging to the thin protection of deniability. She cleared her throat. "Maybe I can help you with the upcoming shows."

"What do you mean?" He focused his gaze on the stage, crinkling the corners of his eyes.

Turning her head, she followed his gaze. Onstage, the teen fought Sherman in song for Margaret's affection. The three talented leads kept the scene from descending into complete farce. *Only a few more minutes.* Once the danger of discovery passed, she could look forward to an official first date.

"Sorry, you were saying?" He tilted his head.

"I think I can hire a few more managers. I can help with the fall schedule. If you want…"

He brushed a hand against her shoulder.

When she met his gaze, she caught her breath at the promise in his steel eyes. In minutes, the ghosts of her former life would be fully exorcised. She could dream, write, and love. "Are we still on for toni—" The words died on her tongue. Her mouth tasted metallic, and her tongue swelled. She couldn't move. Glancing past his shoulder, Dani spotted a honey blonde near the stage door.

Kara arrived. With gloved hands on her hips and a narrowed gaze, she crossed the boards toward them.

Dani sucked in a sharp breath. Had Kara sensed Dani's less-than-enthusiastic response to facilitating a meeting between Kara and Paul? Kara was much cleverer than anyone credited. Once again, Dani was outplayed.

"Of course, we are." He swiveled his head.

As her heart dropped to her stomach, Dani locked her wobbly knees. She was powerless to stop his collision with the truth.

Kara stood feet away. Dressed in a slinky floor length gown skimming her curves and shimmering in the dim light, she commanded attention.

"Aha, now I see where you've been hiding him. My, my, my." Kara sashayed, swinging her hips and pressing a hand to her throat.

Paul dropped his jaw and wrinkled his forehead. He ran a hand through his hair and met Dani's gaze for half a second.

From the corner of her gaze, Dani glimpsed his lopsided frown. Her upper lip curled and her breath rattled. Clapping a hand over her face, she covered her sneer. Her disgust aimed solely at herself.

"Hiding?" Paul tilted his head. "I don't understand."

Kara approached and extended a hand.

Like a golden age movie star on the red carpet. Kara never did anything by half measures, including destroying Dani's dream. Dani breathed through her nose and rubbed a hand over her flaring nostrils. The star's expensive perfume irritated Dani's senses.

Following the unspoken request, he raised her hand and kissed her knuckles.

Kara kept her fingers in his and leaned close, resting her other hand on his chest.

Pushed aside, Dani stepped back, scanning the ground, the stage door, and the curtain for escape. She wanted to be anywhere else. Pressing an icy hand to her burning cheek, she breathed deep. Hadn't she mentally played a scenario of Kara unmasking Dani's deception? She expected a weight to lift from her tensed shoulders. Instead, she was unable to leave, her heart snapping in half.

"Darling, I've been searching for you since our rousing performance on the Fourth of July. I'm Kara Kensington."

At Kara's low purr, Dani rolled her eyes but didn't dare lift her chin. If she glanced up, she'd burn under his hot-eyed stare. The low fire smoldering in her gut for two months burst into flames. Once the truth was shared, no one in town would forgive her. She scrunched her nose and rubbed the bridge. With the sudden knowledge deep in her bones, she understood what eluded her in every worst-case option she played.

Worse than betraying Paul, she deceived everyone in New Hope. She wanted to pry up a loose floorboard, curl up into a tight ball beneath the stage, and be forgotten.

"I don't understand." He cleared his throat. "I've been working here since early June."

Dani lifted her gaze.

Kara pressed a hand to her chest and stared from one to the other. "Dani told me she didn't know when you'd return." She tsked and waggled a finger at Dani. "I have a marvelous idea. I've been pitching every production company in Hollywood. She didn't say anything about your big break?"

Paul drew his eyebrows into a solid line.

His gray eyes hardened to freshly forged steel. "I...I..." Dani stammered and shuffled backward, blood draining for her limp limbs. "We worked together. You and me." She pointed a finger back and forth. "I discovered you, and your shows have helped the town. New Hope is a destination because of your work. I gave you the chance." Her voice cracked. Her subterfuge hadn't protected him. She'd restrained him. The lies and manipulations she railed against were the same tricks she utilized. His pained expression finally made clear what she ignored. While focusing on her best interest, she'd hurt the one person who saw her. Drawing in a shaky breath, she pulled back her quaking shoulders and lifted her chin. As the executive producer of the mess, she couldn't escape her credit in her demise. Better to face the truth than run and hide.

"You knew Kara was here?" Paul pressed his mouth into a straight line and ran a hand through his hair. "After the Fourth of July show, you knew? I asked. You ignored the question and handed me a contract." He curled his upper lip. "I was the fool, right? I imagined a partnership, but I was never an equal. You lied to my face."

His words were lethal. Tears stung Dani's watery eyes, and she rubbed the back of a hand over her runny nose. She darted a gaze at the actors several yards away. In seconds, the cast would bow and swarm backstage. If she wanted to talk, in private, she was losing valuable time. "Paul, let's go somewhere else and discuss everything." She extended a hand. "Please."

With Kara at his side, he recoiled from Dani. "I'd like to go talk to Kara about the opportunity. Sounds a lot like something you promised me a long time ago. Only, this woman doesn't know me and has no reason to lie." He scanned her from head to toe. "Unlike you."

"No, Paul, please." Her voice cracked, and Dani winced.

Shaking his head, he crossed to the stage door with Kara on his arm.

Snippets of Kara's excited conversation filtered past Dani. Words like magazines, TV, movies, and big deal chirped in her ears. Her heart shattered. By concealing the truth, she stole his decision and questioned his worth. Her paper-thin excuses disintegrated in clammy hands, and she tightened her grip on little more than confetti.

He pushed the door and held it open.

Kara glanced over her shoulder. With a wave and a wink, she exited.

For a moment, Paul stood in profile, illuminated by the hallway lights.

Stiff as a statue, he held himself erect and clenched

his jaw. He was pure stone. Pulse pounding at the base of her dry throat, she clenched and unclenched fists at her sides. She wanted to run into his arms, to explain everything, and be instantly forgiven. She wasn't acting in a movie. She was living unscripted. With one careless act, she ruined her life and changed his.

The door slammed shut.

Frozen in place, Dani listened to the last bars of the finale. Applause erupted. Hoots and hollers echoed throughout the space.

If she didn't move, she'd be surrounded by cast and crew. Within sixty seconds, she'd be dragged through the curtains to take a bow. Everyone expected her cheek-to-cheek grin and a rousing speech. For once in her life, she couldn't smile through the pain. She sucked in a sharp breath and strode toward the door, exiting her stage.

Never had she been good enough as is. Trapping him had been her only chance at love. He left for forever, and she only had herself to blame.

****

If Paul thought the white-hot anger burning through him would disappear the next morning, he'd been wrong. As he paced outside Dani's office, he clenched and unclenched his fists. He wanted to bloody his knuckles against the door and demand answers. He dragged a hand through his hair. Once he confronted her, he wouldn't turn back. Less than twelve hours ago, he believed in her grand plan. He'd imagined himself a partner in leading the whole community to a bright future.

The familiar smells of lingering paint and lemony cleaner tickled his nostrils and tugged at his heart.

When he opened the office door, he'd sniff her citrus shampoo. With every sense, he'd identified her but his heart no longer recognized the woman in charge. Scrunching his nose, he cleared his nostrils of the piercing scents. In his shock at Kara's revelations, he'd turned to Dani. No way could any of the nonsense the star claimed be true. Dani couldn't possibly conceal so much after they'd grown close and shared their hopes and fears.

Without asking, he read the answers. Inches away, she couldn't meet his gaze, stop the flutters at the base of her throat, or breathe without a hitch. Everything Kara said was true. Every terrible accusation landed at Dani's feet, and she didn't sidestep or pick up her feet.

While the final performance happened mere feet away, he couldn't react. Creating a scene would distract from his hard work. He couldn't toss aside his and the casts' laborious efforts in rage. He wouldn't invalidate himself. As he faced the stage, he superimposed a memory over the ensemble. Instead of the beach set, he projected the memory of sitting at the upright piano with Dani pressed against his side. Their first kiss overwhelmed him with a rush of warmth, comfort, and peace. When he held her in his arms, he finally came home. But the entire time, she lied.

Last night, she offered no explanation and didn't intervene when he left with Kara. *I didn't give her a chance.* He shook his head. She offered a few lame excuses. When Kara draped herself on his arm and led him away, he hadn't encouraged or discouraged the contact. Kara's presence, her body pressing into him, was inconsequential. He only saw Dani. Through a restless night's sleep, he couldn't calm his electrified nervous system, radiating with frustration and anger. She didn't fight.

Taking a step back, he stared at Dani's office door under the harsh glare of the fluorescent lights. Had her assumption of his father's business destined her to control Paul's life like the old man? Shutting his eyes, he could almost trick himself into rewinding last night before the interruption. He'd been elated. The show was a success. Ideas for Halloween flooded him. Dani relaxed. They had the promise of plenty more tomorrows and productions. Holding up his palm, he slapped the office door, the hand vibrating with memory of the shivers and shudders wracking her body at his touch.

His hand numbed. He clenched his fingers and rotated the wrist. With the side of his fist, he knocked on the door. Without pausing, he pounded. The dull wood against muscle and bone released the tension from overnight. After he listened to Kara's ideas for the better part of an hour, most of them focused on her, he'd tuned out the conversation. He knew the most pertinent fact. Kara promised an immediate escape. His dry throat constricted, cutting off his airway. He came home out of desperation, discovered so much more, and was happy in his hometown. How much had been a lie? Cradling the throbbing hand against his heart, he dragged in a deep breath and slowly exhaled. The dull ache in his soul mirrored his bruised fist. With only one choice available, he'd make the decision and leave.

The doorknob twisted, and the panel door opened.

Half hidden behind the solid oak, Dani glanced up and then backed away, disappearing from view.

He pushed the door and entered, rubbing a hand

over his curled upper lip. Had he snarled? Shutting the door, he crossed his arms and leaned back. He dragged in a full breath. His behavior was better suited to a bear than a person. Was he a wild animal she'd caged and domesticated?

She skirted the room and sat behind the mountains of paperwork on her desk.

He couldn't make heads or tails of the piles. Incoming, outgoing, or urgent, the scattered sheets formed one giant sloppy stack. With his non-aching arm, he could shove the pages onto the floor and demand her undivided attention. His mind raced with possibilities. If he kissed her, could he erase the last eighteen hours? Did he want to pretend she hadn't lied? Setting his jaw, he growled. He wasn't here to talk about them. With her choice, she'd killed the potential. "Why?" His voice cracked. Reaching up to his clenched jaw, he massaged the spot below his ears.

She took in a deep breath and studied both clasped hands on the desk. Her thumbs circled one another.

Was she pretending not to have heard him or understand his question? How far would she continue the act of feigning ignorance? How specific did he need to get with a woman he'd thought understood him on a soul-deep level? His chest tightened. Even his instincts had been way off base.

"Because I was scared."

"Scared?" Repeating the word, he moved his lips independently of his brain. What was she scared of? He was frightened to death. Her job and encouragement spurred his creativity in a way he hadn't experienced since graduating college. In her company, he broke into song, swept her into his arms, and dreamt for more. He imagined a future in his hometown and the rush of lightheadedness at her nearness terrified him. A bark of laughter tore from his throat and saved him a better response. Where did the lies end, and the truth begin? Had she deceived him about everything? His reactions and responses hadn't been studied.

"I didn't want you to leave," she murmured.

He shook his head, but the confession was closer to something he understood. Trapping him here, with a job he loved and an attraction simmering between them, would not have been such a miserable fate. If he'd never learned the truth, he would have had a successful career surrounded by family and lifelong friends. After a couple decades working together, he wouldn't have cared about the revelation beyond a nostalgic *what if*. *Stop rationalizing her behavior*. He couldn't draw in a full breath through his constricted airway. Spots clouded his vision, and he scrubbed a hand over his face. "You stole my chance."

"I never meant to stifle you." She lifted her gaze. "I didn't know how to explain."

Her words were halting and her blue eyes sparkled like water. Turning, he gripped the doorknob. He had to escape, before she cried crocodile tears, spouted more lies, and he believed her. Because he desperately wanted what he felt between them to be real.

"Stop."

With the cool metal in his tight grip, he paused. He needed something true in his life. Not so long ago, he found purpose in his community with her, but he had been so wrong. Glancing over his shoulder, he watched her round her desk.

"Listen, please," she said. "If you think you will

get to write what you say you want, you need to reconsider. She might have said you'll be allowed creative freedom, but you won't." She dragged in a shaky breath.

Without turning, he held up a hand at shoulder height. He didn't want any other explanations, pleas, or tears. She still wasn't offering him what he needed. Last night, as he tuned out Kara's endless monologue, he understood accepting the starlet's offer meant gladly flying into a gilded cage. Dani forced his choice. He wanted to pound on her door some more until his hand broke and the heaviness on his chest eased. "I'm here to shred the contract. We can both agree any document between us is void."

No comment to deny his ability to retract his signature? He revoked his word. Unlike her, he broke his promise in person. She wasn't baited into a discussion? Her acquiescence burned. He would never have wanted her cut so deep. After he commiserated with her over their respective betrayals, he thought she was trustworthy and incapable of duplicity. She couldn't even give him a response? Against his instincts for self-preservation, he faced her.

She didn't move.

If he didn't notice the flutter at the base of her throat, he would be concerned she wasn't alive. While he didn't want her melodrama, he needed better answers with different words forming a believable argument. He'd fallen for her before he'd even had the sense to realize a relationship with his boss wasn't just complicated but an impending disaster. He hadn't cared. He wanted to laugh and lighten the tension she wore on a daily basis.

In retrospect, he understood what he perceived as work-related stress was actually guilt. Had she used his feelings against him to ensure he wouldn't pursue any other option? "Kara and I are flying to Los Angeles today. I won't see you again." His words ended in a sharp bark. He winced but wouldn't rescind the sentiment. She'd given him no reason to return.

****

Paul accepted the glass of champagne from the flight attendant and set the glass on the tray table extending from his seat. In the dusky light of sunset, the bubbles in the pale golden liquid sparkled. He settled deeper into the plush leather seat and studied his surroundings. Sitting in first class between the plane's window and America's sweetheart, he hadn't recovered from the surreal sensations plaguing him for the past twenty-four hours. Was he in a dream or a nightmare? Last night, he stood on stage celebrating a successful show and plotting the next. Today, he floated through the motions of living without any clear heading.

After a summer of atoning for his mistakes, he reappeared on the other side with purpose. He'd been excited for his future in his hometown. Relinquishing the idea of Los Angeles, he decided to remain in New Hope for a chance at something real and lasting. Alongside someone with dreams to rival his, he wanted hard work to improve the lives of an entire community. Dani's enthusiastic vision was unrelenting in its ambition like the woman at the heart of the business. She strove toward her goal with single-minded focus. If he hadn't been such a fool and imagined an unspoken bond of mutual respect and admiration, he'd have understood earlier he was only part of the business model. He shut his eyes and rubbed the bridge of his nose. He hadn't been good enough for anyone else. Why was she any different?

"You okay?" Kara murmured.

He cleared his throat and met her gaze. "Yeah, fine."

"Should we toast?" She raised her glass and stared at the glass near the window.

Following her gaze, he lifted the drink. "You lead the cheers."

She grinned and nodded. "To a successful, multi-layer partnership." In one motion, she clinked together the glasses and brought the flute to her lips, draining it in a single gulp.

He sipped. The dry wine tickled his nose and burned his tongue. Returning the nearly full glass to the tray table, he considered her words. "What do you mean by *multi-layer*?"

"I have big plans. In addition to the stage act, I've approached producers about a behind-the-scenes reality show. We have a lot of interest. With any luck, we could land a holiday special, too." She tapped a finger against her chin. "Although we are too late for something on screens this year. But it's never too early to start preparing for next December."

Her sparkling, bright blue eyes flashed a warning. She'd steer him in a direction of her choosing. He didn't remember discussing any plans outside the stage show. Scrubbing a hand over his face, he wiped away his frown. They must have discussed more specifics than he realized the night she told him the truth. She didn't hide her goals. He was definitely better off than if he stayed with someone who didn't show him such basic respect.

If he was his Dad's worst investment, he transformed into a penny stock at some point, his value skyrocketing. Between Kara's schemes and Dani's subterfuge, he almost believed he was a commodity. He sniggered and shook his head.

Kara smiled and rested a hand on the center armrest, inching over the line between the seats. "You excited for your Hollywood comeback? I'm sure you have a lot of friends to call."

He shrugged. After leaving with a failed project, he should have some emotion about heading to LA in triumph with a star on his arm. With a sigh, he rolled his neck and rubbed his blurry eyes. At the moment, he was emptier than Kara's champagne flute. "I can't really think of anyone off the top of my head."

"Really?"

He waited for more protestation. Her brow remained wrinkle free. He shifted in his seat. Was her reaction obliviousness? He wanted empathy. With a shaky breath, he sagged his shoulders. A professional arrangement was exactly what he needed. After Dani's lies cut him deep, he focused on self-preservation and separated emotions from business. Of course, he could misinterpret her smooth face. She could have undergone too many plastic surgery procedures for normal facial movement.

"I'm glad you'll be staying in the guest room at my beach house. We can maximize our time. I don't have to tell you how many hours are wasted commuting in Southern California traffic." She laughed and shook her honey blonde hair.

The delicate lift of her chin exposed her neck and

lured him to drop his gaze lower. The move was smoothly performed like she rehearsed the gesture. He ran a hand through his hair. She was an actress, and he should probably accept a certain level of practiced behavior in her everyday life. After the betrayal cut him sharper than a blade, he couldn't expect the worst from everyone. If he did, he'd lose the parts of his soul rooted in New Hope. Somehow, he had to move forward without hardening his heart. "If it's not a burden."

She inched her fingertips closer. "Not at all. Of course, you are welcome to invite friends to visit. We'll be working long hours. I believe in playing hard, too."

His skin prickled where she rested her hand. He fought the urge to recoil from her touch and lifted his lips in a tight smile. Silently, he counted to five and extracted his arm under guise of lowering the window shade. He clenched his jaw and constricted every muscle in his torso. Her innocuous gesture was too familiar for his comfort. He entered into a mutually beneficial business arrangement with Kara but refused her admittance into his personal life. After his entanglement with Dani, he promised his weary heart a permanent break.

Chapter Thirteen

A thick layer of frost on the diner's window obscured the predawn landscape outside. Dani shivered and reached for the hot mug of coffee on the booth's table. She'd arrived in New Hope nearly a year ago and already experienced the bone deep chill of a Wisconsin winter. She hadn't anticipated how quickly autumn left the upper Midwest. Sitting in the diner on a cold October morning, she could hardly believe the calendar hadn't flipped to January.

The nutty smell of cinnamon and spice from pumpkin bread in the kitchen, the carved jack-o'-lanterns near the cash register, and the bright orange decorations on the end of every booth reminded her one more week remained until Halloween. Could she fast-forward through the end of the year? With enough time, would she sleep again? Filling every minute of her schedule couldn't completely distract her from her poor treatment of Paul or the dull ache from her still-absent parent. Both were gone.

"Just one more second." Shirley poked her head through the swinging kitchen door.

Dani drummed her fingers against the table and tapped her toes. She wasn't going anywhere even if, according to her schedule, she was already a month late. She couldn't alienate one more person.

With her feathered hair sprayed into place, Shirley

hustled from behind the counter, carrying a coffee pot. She flipped and filled two mugs and refilled Dani's.

Ted slid into the booth and reached for his coffee.

Dani stopped fidgeting. Her interactions with the stoic man were limited. He'd never spoken in her presence. Would today be the day? Jill assured her the man once yelled at Jill's brother and Rob behind the diner. According to Jill, the stunned silent pair were terrified to show their faces around town for a good six months.

The corners of her mouth lifted. Imagining teenage Paul goofing around with Rob was easy. If he'd been around while Jill told the story, he'd contradict his twin. His gray eyes would glimmer with a smirk, and he'd wiggle his eyebrows, including Dani in the joke. She massaged the heel of a hand over her heart. Six weeks ago, she hadn't included him. His distance was her punishment.

Shirley slid into the booth, patted her hair, and cleared her throat. "Thanks for coming by so early."

"Of course." Dani flattened both hands on the table. "Thank you for meeting me."

Shirley waved a hand. "Honey, how else are we supposed to plan the menu for the holiday shows?"

"I appreciate your support." Dani's voice pitched high, and she swallowed. "Without you, I would have been run out of town months ago." *Maybe I should have been. If I left, I wouldn't have interfered with other people's lives.*

"I don't think so." Shirley lifted one shoulder. "You've brought optimism to town. We're happy to do our part and help a neighbor."

"Still." Dani dropped her gaze to her coffee and

interlaced her icy fingers around the warm mug. "You couldn't have anticipated running my kitchen most of the year. My top candidate promises to start before Christmas."

"I've never been one for sweet words." Shirley slapped the table.

Utensils clinked against each other. Dani dragged her gaze to Shirley.

"I prefer action. We'll help your new manager. If the person doesn't work out…" Shirley patted her hair again. "We won't abandon you."

It's okay if you want to. The words clogged in Dani's throat. She was scared her remaining allies would abandon her at the first opportunity. Everyone took the better option. No one chose her.

"Honey, no one blames you for anything. Least of all us. We support you. We're here for you. No matter what and no questions asked."

Ted nodded and sipped his coffee.

She never considered such a small movement important. The tiny motion was the most dramatic response she'd ever witnessed from Ted.

"See?" Shirley straightened. "Enough chatting about feelings. Let's talk business. The supplier wants the order for the theater and the diner. I'm guessing you want turkey for Thanksgiving. What about Christmas?"

"Could we serve ham?" Dani sipped her coffee.

Ted scowled.

"No." Shirley crossed her arms on the table. "Ted only cooks ham for Easter."

"Okay. I guess turkey for both?" Dani dragged the last word.

Shirley and Ted shook their heads.

Dani stared straight ahead, willing a neutral expression. At any moment, she might crack. *Please, do not snap here.* She dropped her gaze to the table and the half-empty mug in her grip. If she didn't have to plan the menu, she'd be more than fine with the arrangement. She might start dancing in the diner. For once, she'd love a break from decision making.

Her choices led on a lonely path of solitary confinement. She couldn't let anyone notice her devastation. Since Labor Day, she'd been waiting for notice of her exile from the community. Expecting her theater egged the morning after Paul left, she mentally prepared herself for a lifetime in town as persona non grata. After what she did, she didn't deserve kindness. New Hope's benevolence extended even to the unworthy. When she opened the doors, she discovered a line for auditions wrapping around the block. Her employees worked hard, hopeful cast members auditioned, and everyone tried their best. If only she could somehow manage the whole operation without crumbling, she might be okay. *At least, I still have Jill.*

Shirley tapped a finger on the table top. "You don't want customers getting bored with Ted's cooking."

"I'm not sure we have to worry. I doubt we'll get repeat guests for Thanksgiving and Christmas," Dani murmured, raising her gaze.

"Are you kidding?" Shirley drew back her chin. "Our town and your theater are hot tickets. Didn't you see the big article in the Milwaukee paper? Oh wait." She pressed a hand to her cheek. "Of course, you did. You couldn't miss it. I stuck the clipping on the theater door."

Dani winced. She hadn't read much beyond the

headline *TV Darling Kara Kensington Brings Mega Watt Star Power To Struggling Town.*

Kara hadn't sold the angle to the paper. In every conversation, she was impressed by Paul and hadn't spared a thought to the rest of New Hope. She had connections in media but not at a regional newspaper.

After a lifetime in the entertainment industry, however, she was savvy. Without question, she'd build off the idea and use her new role to best position herself for whatever big project was on her radar. Dani couldn't be angry. Once upon a time, Kara's ability to create an opportunity from an awkward pause in a conversation landed Dani a job. With a resume full of commercials and countless walk-on roles, she had her big break as Kara's body double.

Kara starred as a pair of identical twins in a role spanning eight seasons and building her status as America's sweetheart. *Without her, I wouldn't have had the opportunity to dream.* Dani sighed. In the wake of Paul's departure, she was only mad at herself. Studying her companions, a couple who still believed in her, she fought for a conversational tone. "I would like to serve whatever Ted wants to cook. We probably don't need to worry about ordering extra for an after-party. I'm sure the cast will want to get home to their families."

Shirley nodded and stretched both hands, reaching across the table.

Her warm fingers rested on Dani's cold hands. The soft touch was motherly, comforting, and unlike anything she'd ever experienced. Mom never held her. Dani filled her lungs completely and shut her eyes against the unshed tears blurring her vision. She was safe here because she was home. She needed the support of community desperately. Paul did, too.

"New Hope is behind you, Dani." Shirley squeezed both hands. "Being an outsider here has never been easy."

"What do you mean?" Dani sniffed and tilted her head to study Shirley and Ted.

"We moved here from up north in the seventies and opened our business. People in town weren't so welcoming." Shirley drew back her hands, reached for a mug, and drank deep.

Ted nodded, dropping the corners of his mouth into a frown.

Dani bit the inside of her cheek. She didn't know what to say. Everyone in town knew she forced Paul's departure. She deserved the town's censure. Apparently, at one time, she would have been the recipient of their collective enmity.

"New Hope has changed a lot." Shirley shuddered. "Thanks to you. We've never been busier."

"If it's ever too much… If you don't want to—"

"Shhh." Shirley held up a finger. "Don't you worry about us. We're glad for the business. Don't concern yourself about him either. He'll come back."

Sucking in a quick breath, Dani flared her nostrils.

Shirley slid from the booth and grabbed her coffee pot. "I've got to put on another pot, and Ted's firing the cooktop. We'll take care of the menu and let you know when we've finalized the details."

Dani nodded.

Ted offered her a smile and followed Shirley to the kitchen.

Dropping her mouth, Dani gaped. She couldn't have been more floored if he'd actually spoken. The kitchen door swung behind them, shutting her on the other side. She sipped her coffee and stared once more at Main Street. While she talked, she missed the sun rise. Thin rays of sunlight cast a blue tinge on the frost-covered ground and remaining leaves. In an hour, the construction crews would be busy at the opposite end of Main and mechanical whirring would fill the air.

The world kept spinning, and life kept moving ahead, regardless of her inner turmoil. She didn't know how to apologize for the deep hurt she caused Paul. She did know she owed the town more. Her debts couldn't be paid by sitting still.

****

Strolling through the open doorway, Paul squinted and raised a hand to shade his gaze. Bursts of light assaulted him the moment he entered the restaurant's outdoor dining section. He scanned the nearby tables. The other diners didn't notice the constant flashes or were much better actors, ignoring the bright pops from cameras. Clearing his vision, he focused on Kara.

A few steps ahead, she threw back her head and laughed, strolling through the maze of white linen-topped tables.

Her honey blonde hair shimmered in the sunlight, and she shook the locks over her bare shoulders. Draped on the arm of a tall, good-looking man, she was a woman to be envied and ogled. To an outsider, Paul probably appeared like a scowling lover. Nothing could be further from reality. After only a few weeks under Kara's tutelage, however, Paul learned how fickle and bendable truth was for public consumption.

The man leading Kara stopped at a table on the perimeter. Dressed in a starched white shirt and pressed black pants, the server was one of the many aspiring actors and models eager for a big break. He pulled out a chair.

Kara sat and thanked the man.

Paul sank into the opposite seat and accepted the menu offered by the server. Raising the leather portfolio slightly, Paul studied his surroundings. Their table overlooked a busy sidewalk. Across the street, photographers roamed the pavement. Without any cover, they were on full display for the row of eight paparazzi snapping pictures.

A perfectly manicured hand blocked the top line of his menu. He frowned.

She lowered the menu. Reaching across the table, she rested her hands in his.

Sucking in a sharp breath, he stilled, ignoring the urge to cringe. Every time he was grabbed, he shuddered, his blood running cold. She clutched him, overlooking the conventional three feet of personal space, like he was a possession. Maybe he was. When he signed the contract six weeks ago, he hadn't perused every clause. With his history of work associates using him, he should have learned his lesson long before the starlet crossed his path. After he understood the depth and breadth of Dani's lies, he accepted Kara's offer without question. He swore he had no other option. Was he wrong?

"Paul, what's the matter? You're scowling." Kara leaned closer. "If you're not smiling, please wear your sunglasses."

She delivered her command without a flicker of emotion on her placid face. He withdrew his hands, retrieved his sunglasses from the front of his shirt, and covered his eyes. He hated to give in to her directions and hand her more power. But he couldn't ignore an excuse to free himself from her bony grip.

"Better?" She chuckled and pressed a hand delicately against her collarbone.

"Sure, fine." He reached for his water.

She wasn't wrong. If he was on display, he shouldn't frown. Unfortunately, the constant cameras gave him no break to relax off the record. He hadn't smiled in a long time. *Since the minute before Kara arrived in New Hope*. He shook off the thought. "You said we were here to work. Are we meeting someone? Did you want to discuss the score?"

Throwing back her head, she laughed. "All in due time."

Which is when exactly? He wasn't sure what he pictured for his return to Los Angeles but he definitely included hours of meetings in his daydreams. So far, he had been introduced to a manager, a nutritionist, and a personal trainer. Kara ushered him to various, well-publicized red-carpet events. He suspected she valued his appearance more than his talent. *She's giving me a chance.* "Shouldn't we be somewhere we won't be overheard?"

"Oh, darling." She leaned forward and reached across a hand. "You have so much to learn."

Whatever he needed to study by her standards, he'd rather not. He hated the calculated glint in her gaze. Withdrawing his hand from her icy palm, he again reached for his glass. Grateful for the prop, he sipped his water. Los Angeles wasn't what he expected the second time around. When he'd left months earlier, he was the person on the sidewalk staring at the important people and longing to belong with the beautiful faces showered with attention. Until he joined the glittering throng, he'd never considered what those same people relinquished for their positions. "If it's easier, I can record the songs I have so far, and you can listen at your leisure. I had a few ideas for the story, too."

"Don't worry." She flicked a wrist. "I have a team working on scripts and music. We need to talk about the reality show. We start filming after Thanksgiving."

Didn't you want to work together? He frowned and studied the melting ice in the glass. Was he being pushed aside? "Isn't the reality show about the act?"

"It is, but more importantly, it's about us. You need to call Dani. She's being completely ridiculous."

Setting the glass on the table, he wiped both hands on his napkin. He didn't want to talk about Dani with Kara and especially not in a very public space. If possible, he'd rather stop thinking about Dani, too. "Why?" he asked through gritted teeth.

"Because she won't take my calls."

Her exasperated tone caught his attention. Despite the smile plastered on her face, or the flirty gestures she directed his way, her gaze was hard and distant. He staved off a shudder. Blinded by anger, he signed a contract, legally obligating himself to a stranger. "Why do you need her?"

"I want to shoot at the theater. Re-enact how we met for the reality show. I also thought why go to the trouble of scouting other locations for the TV movie?" She propped an elbow on the table and circled a wrist. "Why don't we film there? Everyone loves a feel-good story. What's better than Hollywood saves small-town America?"

A frigid tremor shook his spine. He glanced at the nearest palm tree to assure himself he was still on the west coast. The icy sensation was too reminiscent of a cold October morning in Wisconsin. He expected leaves rustling in the cool wind and wood smoke curling in the air. Instead, he listened to honking car horns and sniffed enough exhaust to snap back to the present. She wanted to save faltering Midwest communities? If he wasn't concerned for the implications of her plan on the folks at home, he'd laugh out loud. She wasn't an angel of mercy but a harbinger of death. She'd use anyone to further her aims. Why hadn't he stopped to listen to Dani before he'd left? Without any consideration for others, he evacuated, anger propelling him. "No."

"Oh, please." She shook her head. "You've been mad since we left. And you have every right to be angry. You're the injured party. If she recognizes your number, she'll answer. What's the problem?"

"What's the harm in using her?" He raised his eyebrows. "Aren't you her friend?"

"We are friends," she murmured, staring past him.

The protestation in her statement tightened his jaw. He rubbed a hand against the clenched muscles but couldn't ease away the niggling doubts. When he left Hollywood, he'd been pushed to the side by a friend seizing an opportunity. In his limited experience, the act had been a one-off, a rare occurrence not likely to be repeated. As he listened to what Kara said—and didn't—about Dani, her supposed lifelong confidante, foreboding seized his tongue. Spite pushed him into a contract without reading the fine details, but he wouldn't compound the pain by contacting Dani. She was in his past. Now, his future was Kara.

The server returned.

"We'll both have the salmon and undressed salad, thank you," she told the server.

"Very good." The man retrieved the menus from Kara's outstretched hand, nodded, and retreated.

Paul's stomach growled. He longed for the three b's of a good lunch cooked by Ted: butter, bacon, and beef. A warm breeze tickled the back of his neck. If he shut his eyes, he could easily picture Dani here. He imagined the light tropical scent of her citrus shampoo. The very perfume he'd thought encapsulated her so well. She should be on the beach in the bright sun so her dazzling smile and golden hair could sparkle in the light.

He nearly smiled through the ache in his ribs. She hurt him too badly to forget. One day, when he thought of time spent together, he wouldn't feel so raw and exposed. Today, however, memories held more pain than nostalgia. He wouldn't do Kara's bidding and use Dani in some twisted eye-for-an-eye campaign. Reaching for his water, he sipped the cool drink. He missed the contentment he'd taken for granted. Without knowing if or when he'd return home, however, he couldn't relax or drop his guard. He made his choice, and he had to accept the consequences.

Chapter Fourteen

In her warmest boots, Dani trudged along Main Street the day after Thanksgiving and sipped from the large to-go cup. Shirley didn't skimp on the whipped cream topping the hot cocoa. Dani relished her indulgence and the first mid-morning break in weeks, crunching road salt on the neatly shoveled pavement with each step. Raising her gaze to the overcast sky, she squinted and spotted a rogue flurry. When she wasn't packing the town with tourists, she didn't mind snow. With the Halloween and Thanksgiving shows under her belt, she had a few weeks' respite from worrying over traffic. In a bout of insomnia two nights ago, she scripted the entire Christmas musical. Rehearsals started tomorrow afternoon. Professionally, she had never been better prepared.

Emotionally, she was a mess. When she closed her eyes, she was haunted by the memory of Paul's icy and hot stare. Her reasons for lying lost the thin thread of logic. She hadn't protected him but preserved her self-interests. Her actions forced his exile. She wanted his help to realize both the town's and her business's full potential. *But not his?* She sucked in a breath.

Without a doubt, he was Hollywood's latest darling. She avoided the Internet, but a stray splashy magazine left in the theater supplied all the juicy details. Destined to become America's sweethearts,

Kara and Paul appeared at glamorous events arm in arm, snuggled at the beach, and holding hands at cozy dinners for two. Dani should have called Kara in July, pushed Paul into her friend's arms then, and saved herself the raw ache of what followed.

Raising the paper cup, she sipped her drink. The whipped cream melted, leaving a flavor rich as melted chocolate bars on her tongue. The sweet drink couldn't rinse away the bitter taste of her regrets. At the alley between the kitchen and Holidays, Inc., she walked, hurried along by the howling wind forced through the tight space. She continued past her theater, heading toward the end of the street. Construction crews halted their progress for the holiday weekend, but New Hope buzzed with Christmas preparations. In every corner, she spotted shoppers with arms full of brightly colored bags, businesses hanging decorations, and families selecting pine trees from the sale in the parking lot at the post office.

Tipping back her head, she stuck out her tongue. A snowflake dropped into her mouth and melted. *It's almost perfect.*

"We'll get more tonight," Jill said.

Dani froze. Slowly, she shut her mouth and raised her scarf over her nose and cheeks. With the toe of her boot, she traced lazy circles on the sidewalk in front of the grocery store.

Jill crossed the pavement. "Snow, I mean."

Frowning, Dani pieced together Jill's greeting. "You think so? My phone didn't say anything."

"You trust a phone designed in California over a born-and-bred Wisconsin girl about snow?" Jill shook her head and chuckled.

"Good point." Lifting the corner of her mouth, Dani smiled as much as she could. Since Paul's departure, Jill had shown her more grace than anyone should. Following Jill's lead, New Hope forgave and accepted her. If Dani stopped berating herself for her dealings with Paul, she'd almost be happy. Her throat swelled shut.

Jill bumped her shoulder. "Where are you headed?"

"Nowhere." Scrubbing a hand over her face, Dani scanned the street. "I'm looking for a little more inspiration for the Christmas show. Thought wandering through town would supercharge my muse."

"Mind if I join you?"

"Not at all, but don't you have groceries to take home?"

Unfurling the paper bag, Jill tilted it with a broad grin.

Peeking inside, Dani glimpsed sprinkle cookies and candy canes. Jill shopped for Santa's workshop and not a person's pantry.

"Candy cane?" Jill reached inside the bag and retrieved a wrapped candy. Waving the red-and-white striped stick in the air, she wiggled her eyebrows.

Shaking her head, Dani sipped her cocoa. The peppermint stick might be a sweet diversion for a few minutes, but the Christmas treat mocked her. With a to-do list long enough to paper the theater, she needed no reminder of the quickly approaching holiday. Or the wish destined to remain unfulfilled this year. She scrunched her nose. "I'm good."

"I'm heading in the same direction. Nowhere." Jill unwrapped the peppermint treat and sucked on the hook end.

"Are you still thinking about the motel?"

Jill nodded.

Strolling past the grocery store, Dani ambled toward the library. With Jill at her side, she slowed in front of the microbrewery next to the post office. Observing the progress on the new businesses had become the town's favorite pastime. Today, a rip in the paper covering the plate glass exposed an enticing glimpse of tool kits, drop cloths, and extra lighting inside.

"You could run a B&B five times more successful," Dani said, slicing the silence in half. Her heartbeat pounded in her ears. Should she have forced her help on Jill? Would her backing have made any difference? *Why can I respect one person's boundaries but not another?*

On the heels of Paul's departure came Jill's disappointing news. The owners of the motel decided against selling to Jill in favor of a major corporation.

Dani studied her friend. With her thick pea coat, colorful scarf, and wrinkle-free profile, she looked too young to be peering inside a brewery. *A clear conscience does wonders for the skin.* Pushing down Mom's old words, Dani sucked in a breath. "Don't be a copy. You're an original. Open your own place."

"I've been thinking." Jill tilted her head. "I've decided the motel wasn't the problem." She shrugged. "I wasn't dreaming big enough."

"Really? What did you have in mind?"

Jill pulled back her shoulders, readjusted the glasses on her nose, and removed her candy cane. "I think I'm running for mayor."

"Fantastic news." Dani grinned her best camera-ready smile, pretending she didn't know. Shortly after Labor Day, Shirley told Dani about the political conversation. Dani hadn't pressed Jill. She wouldn't push away another Howell.

"You think so?" Jill frowned and fluffed her bangs. "Rob and I are forming an exploratory committee. I'm not sure I'm the right candidate. I want to understand what issues are most pressing for the community and determine if I could tackle those problems."

Dani leaned back against the brick wall, crossing one leg over the other. "Are you kidding? If I polled everyone in town, I'm certain you would have an overwhelming majority."

Jill shrugged and rounded her back. "What would my platform be?"

"Your platform? How about putting the town on the map? I'm not speaking figuratively. Finally, Internet searches display our actual location on the first page of results with images."

"I did nothing." Jill crossed her arms and gripped her elbows. "You started the resurgence. You deserve the praise and credit."

"No way." Dani drained her cocoa, stepped away from the wall, threw the paper cup in the trash, and grabbed Jill's shoulders. Was Jill's lowered self-esteem another unforeseen consequence of Paul's departure? "You have initiated a lot of positive change entirely on your own." She met her friend's gaze. Jill's frown reached her blue-gray eyes. Dani wanted to shake the truth into her friend but stopped, balancing between what she wanted to say and overstepping. "Who organized our trick-or-treat event? Who petitioned the banks to clean the foreclosed properties before the first show? Who talked the town into a Christmas caroling event after the show next month?"

"Me," Jill murmured.

"You underestimate your importance. You are the glue in our town. You have more heart for the people living here than most have for themselves. You've made me believe my dream was possible, and look at our accomplishments." The words scraped Dani's constricting throat. She dropped her hands.

Jill stepped forward and extended her arms. "Thanks, Dani."

Standing still, Dani didn't shake off Jill's hug. But she couldn't reciprocate. After her deception, she didn't deserve Jill's friendship or her business's success, but she found both. If she lived the rest of her life doing right by the people of New Hope, she might erase the big wrong off her conscience. "Of course." Her phone vibrated in her pocket. She stepped out of the hug, retrieved the cell, and frowned at the name on the screen.

"Everything okay?" Jill tilted her head.

Dani jerked, shoving the phone deep in her coat. "I… umm…" She plastered on a smile, and her left eye twitched. Squinting, she rubbed her lashes. Chilled to the bone and losing control of her nervous system, she didn't know whether to laugh or cry. Why was Mom calling? "I'm fine, but I need to take this call. I'll catch you at the theater tomorrow."

With a frown, Jill nodded.

Tucking her chin into her scarf, Dani retraced her steps, searching for space from her friend and any curious onlookers. At the next block, she scanned her surroundings. No one stood near the library steps. With clammy hands, she fumbled for the device. Her fingers slipped over the smooth case. Could Mom sense Dani's vulnerability? Was her call an effort at reconciliation or an emotional kick to the ribs? Dragging in a deep breath, Dani grabbed the phone, tapped the screen, and pressed the cell to her ear. "Mom?"

"Hi, honey, how are you?"

"Umm…" Her chin quivered. After receiving no response to her emails, Dani struggled with the demise of the relationship. She conducted imaginary conversations and rehearsed in case Mom called. Presented with an opportunity to chat, however, Dani couldn't force words through her clogged throat. Was something horribly wrong? "What's going on? Why are you calling?"

"I guess I deserve the accusatory tone," Mom muttered.

In her shaking hands, Dani lost her grip. The phone clattered to the ground. Kneeling, she retrieved the device and darted her gaze. A crowd gathered outside the grocery store on the next block. If she didn't control her nerves, she'd provide entertainment. She rose and climbed the steps to the memorial, sinking onto an icy bench. Pressing against the cold slats, she sagged her shoulders and recalibrated her conversational goals. If she wanted a relationship, she'd ignore her grievances and listen. "Mom, I'm sorry, I—"

"No, honey, I'm sorry. When I heard your plan, I didn't take you seriously. I read your emails and never responded. I'm sorry."

The clear and steady tone reverberated over the line. Rubbing a hand over her burning nose, Dani sniffed and leaned back, glad for the firm bench under her wobbly limbs.

"Dani, you there?"

"I am." Her voice cracked. "I hate our situation, but I can't endure any more emotional torture. We deserve better."

"I didn't call to fight. I'm apologizing."

Pressing her phone against her ear with her shoulder, she tugged off a glove with her teeth and pressed fingers against her throbbing temple. "If you can't admit we have problems and get to the root of the argument, we can't move forward. I want us to have a real relationship. I want us to be a family."

"I thought you preferred the Kensingtons." Mom sniffed. "You featured prominently on their picture-perfect social media accounts."

Wincing, Dani shut her eyes. For decades, she considered herself a Kensington. No matter what happened with Kara, Dani refused to rewrite the good years. Without their kindness, she would be a different person. "You can't blame me or anyone else for our struggles. Mom, you weren't around when I needed you. They were. They took care of me and loved me."

"Until Kara ran off with your guy."

Dani disliked the hint of a sneer in Mom's self-congratulatory tone.

"You were always the more talented actress," Mom said. "All those dance lessons and hours of voice training wasted. You threatened her chances, and she sidelined you into being her extra."

"I made money. Wasn't I doing enough?" Dani swiped at her lashes.

"Oh, honey. I wanted so much more for you."

"I didn't. I wasn't interested in fame. I liked being behind the scenes. I still do. I'm happy here." She shut her mouth. The conversation shifted offtrack and veered toward blame. She yearned for peace and not an ongoing war. "Let's focus on our relationship. Don't worry about other people. Do you want us to be a family? Or do you want to make sure I'm not part of someone else's?"

"I want to be a family." Mom's voice hitched.

Shifting forward on the bench, Dani tapped her toes on the sidewalk. "Good. I do, too."

"When are you coming home?"

Lifting her gaze, she smiled.

Cars and trucks drove along Main Street. Shop lights spilled onto the sidewalk. A couple strolled past and smiled.

A year ago, the same stretch of road was deserted. What more could happen by next Thanksgiving? Warmth spread from her broad grin to her toes. She sighed. "I'm already here. I'd love for you to visit."

"You're really never leaving?"

Not if I can help it. Dani filled her lungs with brittle air. Winter loomed, promising dark and chilly nights. She welcomed the change and the opportunity for quiet self-reflection. "I'm sticking around for good."

"Okay. I'll check my schedule and let you know. I'll call again soon."

Dani held her breath, but the curt rejection slapped her cheek. Years of disappointment hadn't hardened her against the pain of spending Thanksgiving and Christmas alone. As an adult, however, she understood Mom's limitations without comprehending her motivations. "I'll look forward to hearing from you soon. Bye."

Dani dropped the phone into her pocket. She nearly said, *please come, I love you.* The words implied reciprocation. She wasn't sure she could handle the rejection of not hearing the sentiment. Clasping her hands, she shut her eyes. If she needed to manage expectations, she would.

As solemnly as an oath, she meant her words about New Hope. She wasn't leaving but wanted to open the border for more new arrivals and homecomings. If given a second chance, she would make so many different choices. With one holiday miracle achieved, was asking for another tempting fate?

****

No one killed the calorie-laden joy of Thanksgiving weekend as effectively as Paul's newly acquired personal trainer. Followed, in close second, by the nutritionist hired to rework Paul's diet. Jogging along the ocean, he wiped his sweaty brow and squinted in the bright sunshine. He pushed against the sand, welcoming the unrelenting resistance burning his muscles. After he tortured himself on Thanksgiving Day, picturing the spread—and pies—at Holidays, Inc., he dove into his workout with more vigor than he'd mustered in weeks. Two days later, he finally stopped salivating at the memory of butter-encrusted leftovers.

In his first two months in LA, he worked long hours without creative fulfillment. Composing songs for an act that might never materialize, he drew inspiration from what should have been his Christmas and New Year's shows. When he found rest from the lyrics trilling through his mind, he was assaulted by flashes of blue light in a barrage of constant texts and alerts on his phone from Kara and team. The information involved but never included him. Over many sleepless nights, he stared through the break in the curtains at a sky that never darkened. Outside, the crashing waves boomed like constant construction. He missed the pitch-black nights and absolute silence of his one-stoplight town. No one needed or expected an immediate answer. Such behavior was considered impulsive.

Moving into Kara's house was one of the non-negotiable line items in the contract he'd signed before checking the fine print. Under her roof and laser-sharp gaze, she outlined his days stretching into the future. He had to stop trusting everyone he met, but he didn't want to relinquish hope in his fellow man. He wanted to believe community could still be found, and people could lift each other without personal motivations.

Sounds like New Hope.

Jogging the stairs from the beach to the house, he glanced at his watch. Boot camp and missing home soured his holiday spirit but didn't dampen his mood. Kara should still be at an appointment. He could steal a few minutes of unstructured free time and call his sister. Whistling, he entered the glass house. He slipped out of his trainers and crossed the main room to the fridge. The impeccably decorated, open-plan modern home chilled him worse than a Wisconsin January. He opened the fridge and shivered. Sweat plastered the wet shirt to his torso. He grabbed a water bottle and drained the entire thing.

"Don't leave the door open, please," Kara said, her voice deep.

He stilled and clenched his jaw, grinding his

molars. He'd missed his chance. Shutting the door behind him, he took his time before facing her. After his anger at Dani cooled, he understood her warning and rationalized why she'd lied. In a twisted and overreaching way, she sought to protect him. Without guidance, he navigated the twists and turns of dealing with Kara alone to the best of his ability. Separated by the large marble island, he held Kara's gaze and didn't glance any lower.

She spent most of the last ten weeks dressed in scraps of fabric, ignoring personal boundary space, and speaking in low, husky tones. Any of his guy friends, except Rob, would trade places in a flash. Every encounter with Kara was another attempt at seduction. He wanted to be far away. "Aren't you supposed to be somewhere?"

"I'm showering before I leave. Looks like you are getting cleaned up, too. Maybe I should join you." She leaned across the island.

Gritting his teeth, he shook his head. "Stop, Kara, please? Just…" He turned his head to the side. "Stop."

"Stop what?"

Wincing, he scrunched his face and waved a hand in her general direction. Without lifting his gaze, he knew what he would find. She'd position herself on the stone counter in some contortion to highlight her cleavage and tiny waist. Serving herself like the main course at a feast transformed her into a caricature siren from a bygone age. Over the past several weeks, she ramped up her attempts at seduction. With each encounter, he scanned the vicinity for the nearest exit. He could only pretend not to notice for so long. They both deserved better. "When we're performing, we have great rapport. We don't have chemistry off stage. Don't force a romance."

Straightening, she crossed her arms and narrowed her gaze. "Maybe we could if you'd try. How can I sell a show about a non-existent relationship?"

Unlike her usual husky tones, she spoke with a shrill voice. He wouldn't be tangled in anything hinting at love. After surviving heartbreak in New Hope, he wouldn't feign interest. He agreed to a professional connection and nothing else. He shrugged. "Why are we filming a reality show? Why can't the act be enough?"

"Because of turnaround." She raised a hand and snapped. "We need to make a splash before the story of my discovery is archived. An act isn't quick, and neither is a movie. Reality TV is lightning fast."

I'm a supporting player in her story. Scrubbing a hand over his face, he rubbed his heavy lids. He must have signed away more rights to his likeness than he realized. He owed himself a thorough reading of the fine print. "I'm taking a shower. Alone."

She shrugged. "Suit yourself. You signed a contract. The crew starts filming tomorrow."

Her words were like ice water poured down his spine. He walked through the kitchen to the front hall, climbing the steps two at a time. At the second floor, he power walked to the guest suite and locked the door. Until filming began, he had some semblance of privacy within the space. Would she insist on cameras in his room? He glanced in the bare corners of the ceiling. She hadn't installed surveillance, yet.

Retrieving his phone from the nightstand, he dialed his sister's number and retreated to the en-suite bathroom. With his shoulder holding the phone in place, he opened the glass shower door and spun the knob. High pressure water poured from the rain shower head and drowned ambient sounds like a white noise machine. He needed cover from any curious ears on his end of the call. Crossing to the sink, he dried his hands on a towel and leaned against the vanity. The call connected. "Hello? Jill?"

"Hey, how are you?" Jill asked.

Her disembodied voice was an instant balm to the stressors of his seemingly glamorous life. He sagged his shoulders and swallowed the sigh building in his throat. "Happy very belated Thanksgiving."

"Oh, right. I'm sorry." She dropped her voice. "I didn't forget. I called before the show but got your voicemail. I didn't leave a message, because I was planning on calling you back. Afterward, I was so wiped I don't remember coming home. I'm sure I would have been too late."

I was probably alone and awake. Pressing a free hand to his ribs, he breathed through the stitch in his side. "I get it. I'm just giving you a hard time. How are things?"

"Here? In New Hope? I'm sure not nearly as exciting as your life. How about your show? How's everything going with Kara Kensington?" She pitched her voice higher.

For a second, he couldn't read her tone. Without seeing her face, he wasn't sure whether she was mocking him or not. If he wasn't worried about eavesdropping, he would have video called. He glanced over his shoulder, his skin tingling. In Kara's house, he was never alone.

"Paul? You okay?"

"Oh, sorry." He cleared his throat and tugged at the crew neck collar on his sweat soaked T-shirt. Steam fogged the mirror. He accidentally turned on the hot water. The rising humidity soothed his lungs, but the damp shirt tightened into a clammy straitjacket. *Good and bad in equal measure.* He shook his head. In the last six months, he found his creative streak. With his new Hollywood contract, he stalled. "Checking my schedule…" He paused. "We start filming with the reality crew tomorrow."

"Dad must be rolling in his grave." She chuckled.

Paul grinned. Their father had been a deeply private person. The siblings joked they still didn't know his favorite food or color. Of course, Paul knew Dad's number one twin. If Paul earned approval for his career, he would have lost the praise at the first hint of a reality show. As network television was overrun by the programming, Dad grumbled about the concept of oversharing personal information. *That's my only remaining career option.* Dad disapproved of the show business dream, stressing the importance of hard work over instant celebrity. Paul cleared his throat. "What's going on in town?"

"You know New Hope," she said.

He slumped. No, he didn't. When he boarded the plane, he left a town on the cusp of a renaissance. What happened with Holidays, Inc's autumn shows? How were plans for the Christmas musical coming? Did Dani ever mention him?

"If you want to ask about her…"

"I agreed not to bother you."

"Right now, I'm on the phone with you in the

middle of Frank's grocery store talking about feelings. I'd rather finish the conversation quickly before I become tomorrow's gossip."

"Fair enough." He pictured her in the bread aisle. She slowed her pace near the boxed cupcakes and hand-pies. His heart tugged. He wanted a view into New Hope through her eyes. How much snow had fallen? Had anyone hung their holiday decorations yet? He couldn't ask without her challenging him to come home. "How's the business?"

"Good. The last couple shows were big hits. We hired help so Dani could take over productions without any problems. She seems happy. Staging musicals is the reason she opened in the first place. We all miss you. The cast asks if you're coming back."

He squeezed shut his eyes. "I can't." His voice cracked.

"Can't?" She paused. "Or won't?"

"Can't. At least not yet."

"Is there a possibility? Maybe I'm hoping for a Christmas miracle."

The smile in her voice was contagious. Lifting the corner of his mouth, he enjoyed the bittersweet moment. He had to believe at some point he could return. He missed town, his sister, and Dani. She was right. Kara wasn't interested in his ideas and projects. His days were spent being told what to do, what to wear, what to eat, where to go, and where to stand for the paparazzi photos. Kara had him chasing fame so doggedly he couldn't imagine why anyone willingly sought notoriety. Dani offered freedom, but she'd trapped him, too.

If he didn't love her, he'd have accepted her

machinations and pursued a successful—strictly professional—partnership. Her deception ripped him into shreds. His aching heart forced his departure. He couldn't stop wanting to kiss her and dream about a shared future. With her lies, she shut the door. He couldn't unlock it. "I'm not coming home. Ever."

Jill gasped. "You want to make that official? Should I buy your half of the house?"

He pinched the bridge of his nose, his forehead pounding. Unloading the property simplified his financial portfolio and concluded his remaining business in New Hope. "Didn't you have plans for your inheritance?"

"I did." She cleared her throat. "I'd be happy to assume sole ownership of the house. Maybe I'll remodel."

A lump of emotion lodged against his Adam's apple. If he pushed too hard, raw feelings he'd successfully buried might resurface. "Tell me about what's been going on. Do I need to speak with Rob?"

On the other end of the call, she drew in a sharp breath.

"I'm kidding." He sighed.

"I have some news, but I'm not quite sure how to share."

"What's going on? Is something wrong? Are you in..." He gulped and fisted a hand, his stomach twisting. How far had her relationship with Rob progressed? Paul's sandpaper tongue scraped the roof of his mouth. "Are you pregnant?"

"What?" She gasped. "Not in the slightest. Please, let's never talk about *that* again."

Until he blurted the thought, he hadn't ever

considered being an uncle. Jill had a house and a love interest. She wasn't waiting for her brother's return to live her life. He unclenched his jaw. At some point, everyone would forget him. "Okay. Sorry. Go on."

"Rob and a few neighbors are encouraging me to run for mayor. Am I making a fool of myself? Is it a ridiculous idea and a huge mistake?"

"Mayor?" He tilted his head and grinned. "No one loves our town more than you. No one would be better suited to the job."

"I'm not sure… I have to get a bunch of signatures and submit a petition to be added to the ballot for the March election." She sighed. "Who would support me? I'm not someone who… I've never been very… No one thinks…"

Swallowing a groan, he half listened to the self-deprecating ramble he knew too well. He hated her pattern of doubting herself. If he was home, he'd put his arms on her shoulders and refuse to let her confidence slip. From his location in a California bathroom, he relied on tone. "You'd be great. Wish I could see you in office."

"Oh, okay. Right."

He ran a hand through his hair. Her disappointment shot through the phone. Hurting her never got easier, but he couldn't let Jill hope he'd somehow reappear. Dani made a choice, and he dealt with the repercussions. If he could retract his reaction and give himself time to consider every option, he would. Without a miracle or legal loophole, he couldn't find his way home. *I can visit.* He coughed, forcing down the hope bubbling in his throat. Visiting for the occasional long weekend, he'd only torture himself with what could have been. "I'll call you in a few days. I have to run to a meeting. I'm proud of you."

"Thanks, Paul. Talk to you later." She ended the call first.

He set his cell phone on the counter, turned on the sink faucet, and splashed water onto his face. The cold droplets didn't jolt him to a moment of clarity. If he had a solution, he wouldn't be hiding from his troubles in a locked bathroom on the west coast. Months ago, he stumbled home and never imagined his wants coinciding with his needs. For a short time, he found something too good to be true. Returning to Los Angeles, he finally achieved the big break he swore he wanted. In the process, he couldn't stop his heart from shattering.

Chapter Fifteen

Giant snowflakes spiraled through the air in front of the theater and landed in the thick white blanket on the ground. If the snow continued through the night, New Hope would wake to a white Christmas Eve. Dani bundled deeper into her puffy coat, the knitted scarf tickling her nose and cheeks. The air wasn't chilly enough to force her inside, and she wanted to absorb the moment. As a kid, she'd participated in enough shows to know the production value of a snowy holiday. Until she'd come to New Hope, however, she'd never appreciated the quiet of the snow or how the tiny flakes shimmered under streetlights.

Since Thanksgiving, she rushed through her days without a chance for quiet contemplation. Nora Thomas couldn't arrive any earlier than December twenty-fourth. Dani understood contractual obligations but couldn't quite shake foreboding at the continued delay.

In the fading afternoon light, she stomped her boots on the steps of the library. Three months after she forced Paul's departure, she finally slept through the night, thanks to bone-deep exhaustion. She was here, on the night before Christmas Eve, exactly where she wanted to be a year earlier. She'd been right in her initial assessment. Working on holidays occupied her thoughts from missing the family she never had. How could she be sad over an idea? She hoped next year

Mom would join her, but she didn't yearn for Mom's attention like she had during childhood. With her business and her adopted hometown, she built something better. The dull ache in her chest centered on Paul. She breathed deep and inhaled the smell of damp yarn from the scarf wrapped around her face.

A sharp elbow to the ribs poked her side through her pale blue pea coat. She snapped open her gaze.

Jill extended a to-go cup.

Dani pushed down her scarf and grabbed the cup. The steaming beverage filled her senses with the smell of chocolate. "Thanks." She savored a long sip. The almost-bitter taste finished with spicy cinnamon. She drank again. The second mouthful coated her taste buds with richer flavor. "Is this hot cocoa from the diner?"

"No." Jill shook her head and raised her own cup. "It's Mexican hot chocolate. A sample from the new chocolate store opening next to Frank's grocery."

"A chocolate shoppe?" Dani widened her gaze. "I don't know if I should be thrilled or start exercising now."

Jill chuckled.

Scanning the packed crowd, Dani smiled at the familiar faces of her neighbors. When Paul told her about the holiday celebrations of his childhood, he inspired her to revive the lost traditions. With the support of the other business owners, the town council approved her petition and resurrected the tree-lighting ceremony. Tourists nearly outnumbered the locals on the library steps.

The Higginbothams' motel sold to a major chain. With no time to renovate before the rush, they'd left the property untouched. The big company had flown in a team to operate the building. More vacant lots and formerly dilapidated and bank-owned properties found second life in town.

If only Paul could notice the progress.

She sipped her hot chocolate and blinked. Atoning for her lie would take more than one special event. She'd told Mom the same. Asking for a fresh start with her family and forgiveness from Paul was too much for one Christmas. If she was a very good girl next year, she'd ask Santa for help.

"Did I miss it?" Rob jogged up the steps, stopping at Jill's side. Leaning close, he rested his hand against her back.

Dani sighed. At least she was the only fool in town who ruined a chance at love. "Miss what?"

Nibbling her bottom lip, Jill gazed at the newcomer under her lashes. "No, you're right on time." She nudged him with a shoulder. "You'd better go."

He dropped a kiss on her cheek. With a nod to Dani, he spun toward the platform and headed for the interim mayor at the podium, the crowd parting.

Curiosity electrified Dani, prickling her skin. She had more questions than time for answers. She'd save her interest in the burgeoning relationship for a less public place. Leaning close, she ignored her friend's flushed complexion. "What's he doing?"

"He fixed the light strands for the tree and crisscrossed the strings between the lamps on Main Street." Jill swept a mitten over town.

Narrowing her gaze, Dani spotted the tiny bulbs. "I hadn't even noticed."

"You will." Jill grinned. "Once the switch flips, those bulbs will be hard to miss."

"I know something else hard to miss," Dani muttered under her breath.

Jill drew back her chin, her pupils dilating.

For a fleeting moment, Jill's blue eyes turned gray. Dani coughed and cleared her throat. She had to stop seeing Paul everywhere. "Oh, come on. How's it going between you two?"

"It's…" Jill dropped her gaze and fluffed her bangs. "I don't know. We spend a lot of time together. I don't think we're dating."

"What do you mean?"

"We're working on the petition for my mayoral run. If we get hungry, we grab food. He hasn't specifically asked me out. Maybe he's just a good friend." Jill rounded her back and hunched forward.

"Of course he's interested." Dani shook her head. "He just kissed you."

Jill blushed and turned toward the tree.

Dani followed her friend's gaze.

Rob lifted a hand and waved.

Only a fool could miss how Rob brightened when he spotted Jill. "Why not ask him? You're a modern woman. Take charge." Dani nudged Jill with her shoulder. "Maybe he's as unsure as you."

"Maybe." Jill tilted her head. "How about we strike a deal? You call my brother, and I'll ask Rob to dinner."

Dani lowered the scarf. Frigid air burned her cheeks. With her heartbeat thundering in her ears, she focused on the scary question exposing her fears. "Does he want to talk?"

Lifting one shoulder, Jill shrugged.

Her friend's response wasn't any sort of answer.

Exhaling a heavy sigh, Dani dropped her chin into the warm knit cocoon loosely hanging from her neck. With her flight instincts on hiatus, she studied her battle plans. Ultimately, she was responsible for losing the war. She would acknowledge surrender. "I can't compete with Los Angeles. Kara updates me almost weekly on the status of their reality show and the buzz from their interviews. She never misses a chance to send me a new picture of them wrapped in each other's arms."

"Are you sure?" Jill scrunched her nose. "Every time he calls, he sounds lonely and tired. He's always in the bathroom, like it's the only place he can talk."

Dani cocked her head to the side. If Paul came home, he'd need a job. She would no longer be solely in charge of her productions. *How much better could these shows be if we were working together?* She longed for collaboration. His return depended on his ability to forgive her. She rubbed a hand over her aching heart. She was unworthy. "He'll be a huge star. He doesn't want my phone call. I'd be a distraction. His life is in LA, like he wanted."

"Maybe his wants have changed." Jill dipped her chin and fiddled with her coat buttons.

What aren't you telling me? Dani wrinkled her brow. They'd agreed to avoid discussing each other with Jill. His absence hadn't changed the terms, and she honored the request. *I kept one promise.* She tightened her scarf, cutting off a response.

"As a kid, Paul wasn't desperate to leave." Jill fluffed her bangs. "He didn't want to be forced to stay. He needed options to choose his path. After our mom died, our dad threw himself into the business.

Manufacturing jobs evaporated one by one until the near collapse of the local economy during our high school years. Dad was scared and kept his world small. My brother hated restrictions." Jill chuckled.

The laugh wasn't mirthful. Dani wanted to hide from the regretful sound.

Jill shook her head. "Paul was already gone when the town hit rock bottom a few years ago. Dad doubled down and refused to listen to any new ideas. After years of a relentless pace, he collapsed and his body quickly succumbed to illness."

What Dani long suspected from their conversations was confirmed. Paul was a dreamer born and raised in a town without any use for creativity. She was welcomed because the town didn't have another choice. "Why didn't you ask Paul to come home when your dad got sick?" The answer was suddenly very important and the final piece she hadn't realized was missing.

Jill drew back her chin and sucked in a sharp breath. "He told you?" She shook her head. "Of course he did. He never had the freedom to choose being here. I didn't want to add to his burdens by demanding he come home."

"Do you think..." Dani coughed, loosening her tight throat. "Did I?"

"Unintentionally..." Jill shrugged. "You revoked Paul's choices. Once he understood an opportunity was hidden, he left. I think he wants to come home, but he has to make the decision."

He can't. An icy gust swept over her flushed cheeks and chilled her to her bones. Dani raised the collar on her coat. She rescinded Paul's independence. In her desperate fight for control over her life, she'd stripped his authority. Kara would leave no loopholes in any of her written agreements. Buying his way out of Kara's clutches would be at a steep cost. Dani wouldn't share her worries about an iron-clad contract. If he could buy his future, he'd face Dani and the lies she'd told him. A tremor rattled her body. Jill hoped for an impossible homecoming.

Wrapping her arms around herself, Dani wanted to slink off and hide. No one in town would let her. They'd formed the community she imagined during her lonely childhood. The townsfolk cared for her best interests and worked toward a solution. If something upset her, they'd call her to task for her choices. Jill, in the nicest way possible, had already done so. Dani owed Paul a call. Pouring her heart to his voicemail wasn't ideal, but she had no other choice. When confronted the morning after Labor Day, she harbored enough guilt to negate any defense of her actions. At the time, she thought she was giving him a clean break, but what if she hadn't?

The interim mayor counted down from ten.

The crowd echoed the numbers.

When she hadn't told him everything, she'd been protecting herself. She was in love with him. She wanted him to stay and give them a chance. Most importantly, she wanted him here because he belonged in his hometown.

Without a goodbye, she slipped from the crowd and walked Main Street alone. When she reached the front door of the theater, she tilted her chin to the sky. Overhead, strands of white lights illuminated, casting a soft glow. She spun in a circle. The tiny bulbs added to the bewitching spell. She needed magic, fairy dust, or a miracle. She'd go home and practice exactly what she'd tell him. After another night's sleep, she'd call and apologize. A shudder wracked her body. Finally, she understood the terrible debt she owed. She never much liked the cliché that a town couldn't be shared. Now, she accepted the truth. She didn't deserve his forgiveness. He belonged here, even if she didn't.

****

Dani shot out of bed the next morning with a start. Was Santa filled with the same anxious energy? Christmas Eve dawned, marking the start of the biggest productions and busiest week of her calendar year. With any luck, she'd arrive at the theater to meet her newest, and longest awaited, employee. After scraping the ice off her car, she drove to town, grabbed a to-go coffee at the diner, and settled behind her computer.

Within a minute of her arrival, a soft knock sounded on her office door.

Glancing at the time on the corner of her monitor, Dani froze. She expected the new hire in five minutes. After months of delays, had the woman arrived on time? "Come in."

The visitor complied, opening the door.

A brunette with a chic, styled bob, plum sweater dress, and knee-high suede boots entered the room.

The woman dressed for a big city and not rural New Hope. Hadn't she said she grew up here? Dani frowned and studied the ground, catching her bottom lip with her teeth. The soft suede on the newcomer's boots would rot from the slush and salt on the sidewalk in downtown. If the woman walked around the residential streets, she'd trudge through deep snow and destroy the finish. She was beautifully out of place. *Just like me.* Dani glanced at her own feet, half expecting to glimpse the platform sandals that caused her so much trouble over the summer. Her throat clogged and her waist tingled from the memory of Paul's hands wrapped around her. Dusting hands on her jeans, she stood and hovered a hand in mid-air. "Nora Thomas, I presume?"

"Guilty." Nora shook the outstretched hand.

"Please, sit." Dani gestured toward the chair in front of the desk and shook her aching fingers. The firm, almost crushing, grip was probably intended to convey strength.

Nora sank into the chair, crossing her legs at the ankles and smoothing her skirt over her knees.

The woman carried herself with an air of quiet confidence and sophistication. Dani dropped her shoulders. At first glance, Nora might not be Dani's first choice in a companion, but Nora fit the take-charge persona required for overseeing the kitchen. She didn't need another friend. Her heart tugged at the dull ache. In New Hope, she counted everyone integral to the community. She hated the sense she wouldn't have another instant connection, especially with another fish out of water. "Better late than never."

"Thank you for holding the position." Nora tucked a tendril behind her ear and glanced away. "I didn't expect the delay to be so lengthy."

Dani nodded. From firsthand experience, she understood too well how quickly a life could change. She wouldn't torture the woman by dredging the past. "You're here now and none too soon. For the next seven days, we will be running around the clock. Would you like a quick tour, and I can show you to the kitchen?"

Nora sat straighter. "Yes, please."

Pressing flat both palms, Dani pushed to standing. She rounded the desk and crossed the space, holding open the door for Nora. Leading the way through the carpeted hallway, she motioned to the side entrance. "The kitchen is located in the building next door. It used to be a p—"

"The pizzeria?" Nora widened her gaze.

"Long gone before I arrived." Dani shrugged and continued to the employee entrance to the auditorium. With a hand on the knob, she swung open the door. "And this is the theater."

Nora stepped through and gasped. "Wow." She turned in a slow circle. "I never imagined Howell Cinemas could be transformed into something so grand. What you've done here is miraculous."

Entering, Dani lifted her chin and studied the room like it was her first time. She swept her gaze over the neatly arranged tables, sloping toward the stage. The closed, red velvet curtains shone under the house lights. She clasped hands behind her back and stood tall. "Thank you. I couldn't do any of the work alone. New Hope has supported me every step along the way, as I'm sure you can appreciate."

Nora nibbled her bottom lip and smiled.

The expression was tight and uninviting. Dani drew in a deep breath. After she learned her lesson with Paul, she wouldn't again interfere or overstep in someone's personal business. Crossing toward the exit leading to the main entrance, Dani unlocked the door and glanced over her shoulder. "If you want to stop in at the diner, you can chat with the owners about their schedule for tonight's show. You know Shirley and

Ted?"

"Of course." Nora chuckled and followed. "Everyone for a thirty-mile radius knows them."

Entering the lobby, Dani laughed alongside the newcomer, and a weight lifted off her shoulders. Nora wasn't exactly the Christmas miracle Dani wanted, but she was glad to have the kitchen under control. She shut the door to the theater and turned to her statue-still companion. Following Nora's gaze, she jumped.

Across the room, Jill and Rob stood near the front doors.

Their wide-eyed expressions mirrored Nora's.

"Ellie?" Rob asked, a muscle twitching in his jaw.

"Ellie?" Dani frowned at the woman at her shoulder.

"Yes, or at least I used to be." Nora pressed together her lips, flashing a dimple in her cheek. She tilted her head to the side. "Jilly? Is that you?"

Darting her gaze between the group, Jill raised a hand to her collar and nodded.

"I guess I'm the odd man out." Dani chuckled, forcing joviality into her tone. Jill was whiter than the snow outside. Rob scowled with a dark expression, twisting his typically pleasant face into carved stone. Should Dani run for help or stay and smooth over reintroductions? "I'm sorry. I thought you said your name was Nora?"

"Eleanor. When I was a kid, I went by Ellie. I haven't used the nickname in a long time." She arched an eyebrow and stepped closer to Rob and Jill, flashing a smile. "But, maybe it fits."

"I don't agree, Nora." Rob crossed his arms and scowled.

Nora took another step toward Rob.

"Are you in town long?" Jill gripped the coat, hiding the bottom half of her face with a knit mitten.

"Sorry, Jill, I should explain." Dani stepped forward. "Nora is the kitchen manager we've been so eagerly awaiting."

"I'm surprised. When we were growing up, you said nothing and no one could keep you here." Rob widened his stance and tipped his chin, narrowing his gaze.

"Things change." Nora shuddered, her chin trembling.

"Like names." Rob stroked his jaw.

Nora winced.

Dani cringed at Rob's callous tone. While she didn't know the history between the trio, was airing the woman's dirty laundry to her new boss on the first day of her job really Rob's angle?

"Yes, I was married." Nora pulled back her shoulders and raised her chin. "Divorced now. I worked with every major restaurant group in Chicago. My last job gave me a major opportunity in London."

"Why are you back?" Rob pinched the bridge of his nose.

Jill darted a look toward Dani. "Maybe we should get—"

"I made my choices." Stepping forward, Nora neared Rob and lifted her chin. She smoothed her chocolate brown hair behind her ears and placed a hand on Rob's elbow. "You should know I have regrets."

He nodded and didn't shake off her touch. With ramrod stiff posture, he clenched his fists at his side.

Dani crossed her arms over her belly. Something

like pain flickered in Rob's green eyes. She turned to Jill. Her friend shuddered and stared at the floor. The moment was too intimate for Dani's intrusion, but how could she resolve the meeting if no one would make eye contact?

"I could have moved overseas. I wanted to come home." Nora lifted a shoulder.

"And we're delighted to have her," Dani said with a bright smile and chipper tone. She wanted to hurry up and resolve the awkward pause. With only hours until the biggest show of her year, she had too much on her list to add a highly charged reunion demanding privacy.

"If you'll excuse me." With his gaze on the ground, Rob nodded.

Jill extended a hand in his direction.

He turned and retreated. Crossing the lobby, he reached the door without another glance.

Nora pushed past Jill.

Flexing her fingers, Jill drew the hand to her side, stepped back, and shut her eyes.

As the door opened, Nora caught Rob's arm at the elbow and exited at his side.

A gust of cold wind snaked through the lobby, and the door slammed shut.

Jill took in a deep, shaky breath. Fluffing her bangs, she pushed her glasses into position on her nose and faced Dani.

"What am I missing?" Dani shivered and folded her arms over her chest.

Heaving a sigh, Jill shuddered. "Nothing. Just history repeating itself."

Dani widened her gaze. "Them?"

Jill nodded and hair fell over her face.

In a single second, Jill reverted to hiding behind her hair. Dani bit her tongue, hating to witness her friend shut down. *I ruined everyone's future.* She swallowed the sour taste in her mouth. "Go after him. Stop them." She pitched her voice.

"Why? What's the purpose?"

Her soft words tugged at Dani's heart. "To stop something, anything, from happening. He cares about you, not her. How can you sit by and watch their reunion happen?"

"I should probably ask you the same thing," Jill muttered under her breath.

Dani recoiled, stepped to the side, and drew back her chin.

Jill sucked in a breath. "Dani, I didn't mean... I'm sorry... I wasn't think—" She stepped closer.

"Stop." The word scratched her dry throat. After causing so much pain, Dani wouldn't play the victim. She held up both hands and rounded her back. "It's fine. I've got a lot to do today. It's Christmas Eve." Without another word, Dani spun on her heel and retreated to the theater.

She had done a lot wrong. When she lied to Paul, she destroyed her chance at happiness. To fulfill her Christmas wish, she'd dig deep for the courage to call him. If she exposed her heart during a conversation, she might be crushed forever. Could she take the chance?

Chapter Sixteen

Parking at the curb in front of Rob's store, Paul raised the collar on his coat and hopped out of the rental SUV. Frothy snowflakes, reminiscent of the foam on top of the coffee house drinks he'd been force fed to keep working round the clock, floated in lazy circles. Reenacting staged drama with Kara for inane filmed storylines taxed his brain and drained his energy.

Last week, the camera crews captured their fake Christmas. When he didn't react to Kara's manufactured plot of burning the holiday dinner, he'd endured hours of re-shoots. Today, he hadn't needed any extra boost to his system. The crew was on vacation, and Kara left for a few days with her family. He jumped into action. Taking control provided the necessary adrenaline boost and energized him for the eight hours starting with packing in Los Angeles until driving from Milwaukee to home. He rounded the car and stopped in the center of the road.

Lights strung between fully illuminated streetlamps cast a multi-color glow along the entire street, leading toward the tree towering in front of the library. Every storefront displayed either a welcome sign or a notice promising to open soon. Parked cars lined the curb, leaving no free space. A hush fell over town.

Wood smoke perfumed the frigid night. In a few steps, he reached the sidewalk outside the diner and followed the handful of nattily dressed couples. Excited murmurs and bright smiles filled him with even more anticipation.

Hours earlier, before the sun rose over California, he jolted awake. Realization slammed into his chest, and he couldn't shut his eyes. He was waiting on Dani's explanation. If he wanted control of his destiny, he couldn't passively hope for change. Over the pain of the past year, he reached one stark conclusion. He commanded his decisions. Maybe she'd taken away his ability to choose, but she hadn't been wrong in her assessment. He'd relinquished his freedom by moving to the coast with Kara. New Hope and Dani were his choice.

"Paul?" Rob called from the sidewalk.

Paul jerked his head to the side. He'd made his way to the theater and joined the line waiting for the box office. Meeting his friend's gaze, he stepped out of line and grinned.

Rob swiped at his eyes before grabbing Paul for a one-armed hug. "You're here?" Rob pulled away but kept a hand between Paul's shoulder blades.

"I'm home, for good."

With a pat, Rob dropped his grip and tipped his head. "Hey, follow me. If you don't have a ticket, you're not getting in. The new box office manager is a stickler, and tonight's show is sold out." He strolled toward the alley between the theater and kitchen.

After a few beats, Paul fell into step beside his friend. "New manager?"

"She's hired all the managerial jobs and focuses on the productions. You're in luck." Rob nodded toward the buildings. "We can still sneak in through the alley.

The two buildings aren't connected yet. Too many construction jobs around town."

"A lot of changes since I've been gone, huh?" Paul tugged the scarf knotted at his neck. In control of her vision and the shows again, Dani was probably better off without him.

"You have no idea," Rob replied under his breath. Wrenching open the side door, he craned his neck and stepped inside, stopping near the wall. "Ellie's back."

Paul gaped and crossed the threshold, the door swinging shut behind him. On graduation night, he had consoled Rob after Ellie announced she was leaving for good. *Why didn't Jill tell me?* How far out of the loop was he? If everyone else had already moved on, he should, too. *I have no place here.*

"Yeah, I had the same reaction." Rob shrugged and exhaled a heavy breath. "She showed up this morning. She's the new kitchen manager."

"Wow, yikes," Paul murmured. Unclenching his jaw, he rubbed a hand over the tense muscles and relaxed. He missed one surprise homecoming. Maybe he wasn't too late.

"It's been a long day. Come on." Rob clapped a hand on his shoulder. "We have enough time to grant someone's Christmas wish."

Inside Paul's coat pocket, his cell vibrated. Unbuttoning the coat, he slipped a hand inside and retrieved the phone. When he pulled the device free, he stared at the number flashing on the screen. *Now or never.* Extending the device for his friend's perusal, he slowly lifted his gaze and met blank air. Rob disappeared. Swiping a thumb over the home-screen, Paul answered the call. "Hello?"

"Hi, Paul," Dani said.

Her voice was slightly breathless. Hidden in the shadows, he leaned against the wall in the theater's hallway. She finally wanted to talk? He shook his head at his impeccable timing. Maybe he was a natural for the theater. "Dani, hi."

"Merry Christmas, by the way."

He chuckled. "How's the show going?"

"It's okay."

The crowd's loud applause interrupted them, reverberating through both ends of the line. Wincing, he pulled the phone off his ear and covered the microphone. He didn't want to be found yet. The clapping quieted, and he returned the cell to his ear. "Sounds like the audience would rate your musical ten out of ten."

"You know, always room for improvement." She paused. "I heard about the new TV show. How's filming?"

He cringed. "It's… going."

"Paul, I'm…" her voice hitched. She dragged in a gulping breath. "I'm so sorry for everything."

With a nod, he ambled through the employees' only hallway toward the stage. The thick carpet muffled his heavy booted steps. "I am, too."

"You have nothing to be sorry about. I screwed up. I didn't want you to leave, but I forced you. I didn't tell you the truth, and I didn't give you any reason to stay."

Dragging in a breath, he exhaled, feeling light for the first time in months. "Do you have a reason for me to come home?" At the end of the hall, he pushed open the door. Rising on the balls of his feet, he climbed the steps to backstage and picked his way through discarded props. He walked by Andy and Sherman. Paul pressed a finger to his lips, silencing the pair before either issued a verbal greeting. Continuing, he passed several of the high school cast he'd worked with and nodded at the curious faces he didn't know.

"Nothing I have to offer can compare with Kara's plans," she murmured.

At that moment, he saw her.

With the headset in one hand, she pressed the phone in the other against her ear. At the curtain, she gazed at the performers with one arm slung over her chest and her torso rounded.

She looked small and fragile. He fisted both hands, hating that he was the cause. She should never give any impression of weakness. He stopped several feet away and lifted a hand like he'd pull her into his embrace. *Not here*. He didn't want her reaction to interrupt the show. If he judged by the cheers and claps, he'd rate the performance as another well-deserved success. He wouldn't ruin her work. "Turn around," he murmured. The thick lines of her furrowed brow greeted him first.

Rubbing her eyes, she blinked several times and dropped the phone into her pocket. With a few steps forward, she extended a hand and paused.

Was she worried he was a mirage? For a moment, he stared at her hand.

She dropped the limb to her side.

Dragging in a sharp breath, he focused on her and ignored his heartbeat pounding at triple speed. She'd been his tall glass of water in the middle of a desert. He took a tiny step forward and then another. Inches away, he brushed a thumb against her hand.

A tremor shook her.

He interlaced their hands and raised the grip, kissing her knuckles. "Can we go somewhere and talk?"

Wide-eyed, she froze.

The tiny flutter at the base of her neck was barely perceptible. He couldn't look away from the rise and fall of her shallow breaths. Loud footsteps approached. When he heard a throat clear, he broke from the spell.

Andy stood nearby. With a grin at Paul, he extended his hands toward his boss.

Pulling free her hand, she stepped away. Handing over her headset, she crossed her arms and turned back, arching an eyebrow.

His fingers itched to touch her. He should mimic her stance. Maintaining physical distance kept his thoughts—and emotions—in check. If he was lucky, he'd get forever to hold her. He stuffed hands in his pockets and dipped his head.

Picking her way through backstage, she tiptoed across the boards and out the door. In the hallway, she pulled back her shoulders and strolled forward.

Her movements were stiff and silent. He ground together his molars. Why the sudden awkwardness when she'd been so relaxed on the phone?

At her office door, she stopped.

"No." He rested a hand on the door.

With a shudder, she turned her head over her shoulder.

In her blue eyes, he saw confusion and something else. He swallowed. Hope flickered inside his chest and warmed him from the inside out. Whatever happened, he didn't want any interruptions. "Let's talk outside."

With a nod, she turned the knob and reached inside

the room. A pale blue coat swept through the opening. She slipped into the wool outerwear and shut the door behind her.

The color matched the office walls. He opened his mouth to comment on her favorite hue and stopped, pressing his tongue against his teeth. Could he ever tease her again?

She strode down the hall.

Falling into place at her side, he released the tight grip squeezing his heart. Finally at either the end or the beginning, he'd have to accept the outcome. At the side door leading to the alley, he remembered his chivalry, stepping in front and holding open the door. The blast of chilly air reinvigorated him. None of the punishing workouts or long runs on the beach could offer quite the clarity of Wisconsin winter air. The scent of fresh pine hung heavy, and he glimpsed the boughs strung over the entrance. Her tropical scent mingled with the seasonal smells and created something better. *Mele Kalikimaka.*

In silence, he strolled at her side to the front of the theater. With the show in full swing, the box office was shuttered, and the block in front of the theater silent. He leaned his back against the nearest street lamp and waited.

She took in a deep breath and looked down. "I screwed up." Her chin quivered. "The longer I hid the truth the worse I felt. I was terrified. I didn't want you to leave, but I forced your decision. You left hating me. I caused your pain."

At his side, he tapped his fingers against his thighs, fighting the instinct to grab her. Her blue eyes shimmered with unshed tears. He wanted his kiss to erase the mistakes, but he couldn't rush her confession. "Why?"

"Because we have something special at the theater."

He shook his head, his chest squeezing tight. "We owe each other the truth."

"Because I fell in love with you. No one has ever chosen me." She sniffed and shifted. "Everyone picks Kara."

Under the street light, her cheeks glistened. He caught his next breath, holding the air in his lungs. She believed what she said. How could she convince herself of such a damaging lie? In two steps, he reached forward and wiped the tear with the tip of his index finger. He longed to reach forward, his hands shaking. Instead, he forced himself back into position against the lamp post and crossed his arms.

Dragging in a breath, she lifted her chin. "I am happy Kara is helping you achieve so much. Your dreams are coming true without me. After the confrontation, I owed you a clean break. I worried telling you what I felt would anger you even more. I doubted you'd believe me." Frowning, she dropped her gaze to the ground.

Deep in his soul, her words reverberated. He'd never been chosen either. When he left home after high school, no one stopped him. Years of dodging his responsibilities to the town and his family, no one called him to task. Until Dani, he never met anyone who wanted him to stay, and he ran before the pain of apathy could take hold. "I believe you," he murmured. He stepped forward, inching closer. "I forgive you."

"You do?" She tilted back her face.

He nodded. "I had to leave because I loved you. When I heard what you'd kept from me, I doubted us. I assumed I didn't know you. Fear and pride forced my decision. I don't want any more misconceptions. I love you, Dani. I want to come back." Turning his head, he studied the ground and frowned, his torso slumping. He didn't want to witness her disappointment. "I can't."

"Why?"

"Kara won't void the contract. I read the fine print on the flight. I can't buy my freedom."

"I might have an idea," she replied, dropping her voice. "But only on one condition. The money is an advance of your salary for the next few years."

Exhaling a heavy sigh, he dropped his shoulders, free of the weight of his mistakes. "I'll give you forever." He lifted his chin, extended a hand, and pulled her into his arms.

She stretched on tiptoe, wrapped her hands around his neck, and leaned forward.

He'd gladly strain his neck to kiss the petite powerhouse. He meant what he said. He wanted forever, stretching to eternity and beyond.

"Come on, we have to put on a show," she whispered.

"In a minute," he murmured. Lowering his lips, he tightened his grip on her before kissing her with every last ounce of benediction in his soul. He wasn't ever letting go. Her crazy idea sparked an entire town's renaissance. More than the town's salvation, she saved him, too. She'd vanquished her past and disheartened his ghosts. He'd spend the rest of his life thanking her.

Epilogue

Dani gripped the heavy velvet curtains and peered through the thin gap. In the six months since Labor Day, she hadn't stood on stage to glimpse the audience before the performance. With another nine holiday shows under her belt, she expanded the theater's reputation to constant sell-out success. Tonight, however, she needed a sneak peek at the crowd.

Beyond the stage, she couldn't discern individual identities. If she wanted to learn who was in her audience, she needed another tactic. Walking across the stage under the guise of fixing something was her best option to casually observe the tables. The odd sensation of simultaneously flying and falling, however, tossed the idea—and her dinner—in a fitful surge of stage fright.

Dropping the fabric, she pressed hands against her rolling stomach. Under the guise of smoothing the wrinkles from her sleeveless black sheath dress, she recollected the time and place. Tonight wasn't about her. Despite her nerves on her friend's behalf, she could breathe evenly. The results of the special election would change the future of New Hope. Her hometown deserved nothing less than the best, and she hoped her neighbors agreed.

Lifting one corner of her mouth, she relaxed. In a little more than a year, despite hiccups and setbacks, the tiny Wisconsin town became her home. If Jill succeeded and won the mayoral vote, the community officially entered a new era.

The mixed smells of cotton, soap, and sweat wafted in the air. Dani scrunched her nose against the familiar tickle, her skin prickling. Crossing her arms, she rubbed the goose bumps through the sleeve of her emerald cardigan. With only a curtain separating her from the audience, she couldn't succumb to one of her boyfriend's knee-bending kisses. She spun on her heel, planted hands on her hips, and tilted her chin in preparation for a teasing reminder not to surprise her. Instead, she stared at nothing. With a frown, she dropped her gaze.

Paul knelt on the floor.

His movie-star grin stretched from ear to ear in a blinding display of gleaming white teeth. With one leg bent and the other flat on the ground, his pose looked uncomfortable. Dressed in nice slacks and a sweater, he'd rub a hole into the dressiest pants she'd seen him wear.

He held something in his palm, his fingers closed tight over the object.

If she didn't know any better, she'd think he was proposing. She rolled her eyes and snorted. Why would he? *Why not?* Her heart leapt into her throat. She gasped and clapped both hands over her gaping mouth.

He narrowed his gaze.

Her skin prickled with awareness of his rapt attention, and the surroundings faded into the hazy periphery of her vision. With a smile brightening his entire face, he shone like a spotlight trained on his handsome features. Her heart swelled with excitement, love, and a sense of right. Her senses heightened, and she breathed in deep the backstage smells of the heavy curtains, sawdust from the under-construction sets, and him. Her fingers ached to graze his five o'clock shadow and wrap herself in his arms. He was about to propose and the word *yes* tickled the end of her tongue. Since the Christmas kiss, three months of couple-dom might be too short a time for some people to know their hearts but not her. The stars aligned in a way she'd felt at first sight and only now understood.

He frowned.

The fragile web of hope and elation snapped. She lowered hands to her sides and took in a shaky breath to slow her racing heart.

Dusting both hands on his slacks, he stood. "I didn't mean to startle you." He extended the closed palm and uncurled his fingers, displaying a rusty nail. "I saw this nail and thought I'd save you from a tetanus shot."

With a nod, she furrowed her brow and tugged the hem of her cardigan. "Oh, right, yes." She pulled back her shoulders and raised her chin. If she could steel herself against the sudden and desperate urge to run, she could accomplish anything.

He pocketed the nail and ran a hand through his hair. "You didn't think I was ready to…" He cleared his throat and frowned. "I mean. I've thought about it, but you know… We've only been…"

In two steps, she closed the gap between them. She brushed her fingers along his wrinkled forehead and cheek. "We're fine." With the truth, she sagged her shoulders. She worked hard for the good things—and people—in her life. She refused to scare away her future. If she could muster the courage to chase a dream to the middle of nowhere, she could dig deep and muster patience for the right time. For him, she could wait forever.

Smiling, he drew her into his arms and tightened his grip.

In his embrace, she was safe and loved. She wouldn't rush. She rested her face against his chest, but the rapid beat of his heart didn't soothe. Leaning back, she glanced at his stony features. "What's wrong?"

He gulped, his Adam's apple bobbing. "What would you have said?"

The question was an urgent croak. She stiffened but didn't pull away. Since Christmas Eve, she stopped hiding from the truth. "I would have said yes."

He nodded and tucked her head under his chin. "What do you suppose I would say if you asked me?"

She scoffed and pulled back to study him, narrowing her gaze. His jest matched the playful dimple peeking in his cheek. She swatted at his chest lightly and stepped from the circle of his arms. "I know what you'd say. You think it's a typical occurrence for a woman to grant the rights to fictionalize her life story to a Hollywood starlet to free a guy from a contract without certain assurances?"

Extricating Paul from the legal tangle proved more complicated than either imagined. With years in the business, Kara and her legal team produced a nearly airtight document. Dani had one trick. She utilized Kara's mantra "*everyone has a price*." Dani wouldn't relinquish Paul or the future, but she sacrificed something else almost as dear. Granting the rights to tell the story of Dani's dinner theater in whatever manner the starlet saw fit eliminated the original contract.

With a shrug, he crossed his arms. "How do you know you want to spend your life with me?"

"You want the whole story?" Lifting a shoulder, she clasped her hands behind her back. "It starts like a bad joke. A guy walks into a dinner theater."

The corner of his mouth tilted up. "But he's in the wrong place?"

Shaking her head, she didn't break away. His gray eyes flashed platinum and mirrored the hope, worry, and promise vibrating through their every conversation. When she first locked her gaze on the stranger looking for someone else, she was powerless against the surge of destiny coursing through her veins. Every twist and turn in the path only solidified the truth. She was meant to know him forever. "No, he's in the right place at exactly the right time. He just doesn't know it yet."

He lowered his mouth to her ear. "I'm sorry you sold your rights for my freedom."

His hot breath tickled her neck, and she shivered. "A small price to pay." She buried her face against his chest and breathed deep his smell.

The role of town savior hadn't been Dani's aim. While she welcomed the community's support, she didn't want the title. Kara, however, relished the portrayal. The unexpected compromise achieved more than cleaning up a messy legal problem. By extending an opportunity, Dani opened communication with her oldest friend. Kara's scouting trips to town over the past several months further stimulated New Hope's economy. Each meeting became marginally less awkward. With production on the made-for-TV movie scheduled in nine months, Dani had enough time to adjust to Kara's continued role in Paul's and Dani's life. Mom expressed interest in visiting, too. Although a date hadn't been finalized, Dani refused to live in a world without hoping for the best, no matter how much she might be hurt.

His arms remained steely strong, but his heartbeat slowed. Honesty was a character trait she struggled with every day. Every raw moment of expressing a hidden vulnerability, however, paid many times and chipped away at the trust issues surrounding her heart.

"Ahem." A stern voice loudly interrupted.

Paul relaxed his arms.

Reluctantly, Dani stepped away to face the intruder. When she spun, however, she connected her gaze with two people.

Shoulder to shoulder, Rob and Jill stood nearby.

Dressed in a navy pinstripe suit, Jill looked every inch the mayoral candidate. On closer inspection, Dani noted the tight smile and hunched shoulders.

Rob scowled and offered an arm to support Jill. In a pressed shirt and tie, the hardware store owner and handyman extraordinaire was almost unrecognizable in his campaign manager garb. His role was an unexpected choice for a man known for his love of manual labor. Of course, the incentive of spending time with his candidate one-on-one must have been a draw.

Dani caught her lower lip with her teeth and tapped a finger against her chin. She couldn't determine if the political duo were more than friends or if their burgeoning romance fizzled for the sake of professionalism. Her ribcage tightened like someone squeezed her heart. When no one supported her, she relied on Jill. Jill's friendship had become a cherished bond. If luck served, one day Dani would call her sister. She refused to pry about Rob. She'd encourage Jill's confidence in whatever means possible without overbearing remarks. "All set?" Dani stepped away from Paul and rubbed her hands. Her too-eager tone clashed with the sour stomach expressions of her companions. "The crowd is seated. Any results yet?"

On cue, a cell phone chirped.

Holding up a finger, Rob fished his cell from his back pocket. He focused on the screen.

Dani caught her breath in her chest and pressed a hand against her churning stomach. She darted her gaze between Paul and Jill. The stony-faced twins gave no hint of their inner thoughts.

Paul locked on Jill's gaze and vice versa.

If Dani hadn't monitored the pair with an unblinking intensity, she would have missed the barely perceptible head nod.

Jill dropped her shoulders.

Paul scrubbed a hand over his knitted brow, erasing the wrinkles.

Twin talk. Dani shivered and folded her arms over her chest. She'd always clearly understood Paul's and Jill's body language. In the moment, however, she couldn't read either.

"You won," Rob said.

Dani chirped, covering her mouth with both hands. Stepping forward, she wrapped her arms around Jill and hugged her friend. "Congratulations, Madame Mayor." Jill stood as still as a mannequin from the costume department. A frantic laugh bubbled up in Dani's throat. Swallowing the start of a giggle, she swiped her lashes and rubbed her nose with the free hand. Over the past few months, she practiced for Jill's inevitable departure. Instead of calling Jill with a question or asking for her advice, Dani attempted to first reach a solution without help. She hadn't prepared well enough for the reality of losing her right hand.

A tap on her shoulder jerked her out of the awkward hug. Dani connected her gaze with Paul.

He arched an eyebrow.

Clearing her throat, she dropped her hold on Jill.

"Congrats." Paul brushed past her shoulder. He lifted the still-silent mayor-elect a few inches off the ground. "Couldn't have happened to a better sister."

Jill gasped and laughed, hitting her twin on the shoulder.

With a broad grin stretching from ear to ear, Paul swung her in a circle. Returning Jill to her feet, he strolled toward Dani and wrapped an arm around her waist.

Anchored next to the love of her life in her successful business, Dani couldn't imagine a better outcome. She had every reason to plant her roots in New Hope for the rest of her life. "You ready to greet your adoring crowd?"

Jill nodded and tucked her chin against her chest. She fluffed her bangs and fidgeted with her suit coat.

Rob stepped closer and lowered his head to her ear.

Leaning forward, Dani strained to decipher the words in Rob's hushed tones.

Paul tightened his grip on Dani's waist.

Turning her head to meet his gaze, she caught her bottom lip with her teeth.

Frowning, he pursed his lips.

Heat crept up her neck at his silent admonishment. Not commenting about Rob and his apparent interest in her friend was a difficult task. She wanted everyone to be as happy as she was with Paul. Getting out of her own way had been the key to her relationship success, and she wanted the same for her friend. Jill must abandon the self-sabotage and fight for the man who made her face light brighter than a Christmas tree.

Jill cleared her throat. Raising her chin, she lifted the corner of her mouth in a half-smile. "Okay. I'm ready."

Dani nodded and jogged to the side of the stage.

Paul mirrored her and power walked to the opposite side.

Tugging on the cord, she opened the curtain.

Thunderous applause filled the auditorium. A whistle trilled over the clapping.

Jill stepped to the microphone in center stage.

Dani hung in the shadows, backing away from the edge of the stage. On tiptoes, she picked her way through the rows of past set pieces toward the backstage door. Emerging from behind the plywood beach shack used over Labor Day weekend, she spotted him.

Leaning against the wall near the exit, Paul arched an eyebrow.

His expression hovered between predatory and proprietary. Her heartbeat pounded in her eardrums, drowning the new mayor's victory speech. Dani neither slowed nor evaded. He was the perfect mix of danger and dependability, and he was hers. She strolled toward him and stopped at his side, resting against the backstage door. The cool metal soothed her tingling bare arms.

Inching close, he lowered his head. "About what you said earlier." He pressed a soft kiss below her ear. "Glad we're on the same page."

Her knees wobbled, and she rested her head against his shoulder. "You believe in happily ever after?"

With the tips of his fingers, he brushed a stray strand of hair off her face and tucked the lock behind her ear. "Only if I have you." He stroked her jaw and lifted her chin, staring deep into her gaze.

Past the job titles and flashy reputation, he looked into her soul. Honesty wasn't easy, but he rewarded her vulnerability with a trust she'd never dreamt existed. With her pulse pounding, she stepped forward. She stretched on tiptoe, interlacing her hands behind his head.

He lowered his lips.

She melted into his arms, her body relaxing completely. New Hope gave her so much more than a theater to stage her over-the-top musicals. She discovered a strength she didn't know she had thanks to a resilient community. If she wrote the script of her life, she ended her fairy tale here at the beginning. Her best days remained in her future.

A word about the author...

Rachelle Paige Campbell writes contemporary romance filled with heart and hope. No matter the location—big city, small town, or European kingdom—her feel-good stories always end with a happily ever after.

She's grateful for the support of her family, her robot floor cleaner, and her reluctant writing partner (her dog).

http://rachellepaigecampbell.com

Another Title by this author
Love Overboard

Thank you for purchasing
this publication of The Wild Rose Press, Inc.

For questions or more information
contact us at
info@thewildrosepress.com.

The Wild Rose Press, Inc.
www.thewildrosepress.com